Raise Your Glass! Bartending in English

# BARTENDER 的
# 英文手札

U0077384

林昭菁 ◎ 著

**MP3** **超值全彩版**
隨書附贈外師錄製MP3學習光碟

## Bartender的專屬英語特調
調酒師職場與英語的無痕接軌
用英文來學調酒，用調酒來學英文

以「六大基酒＋香甜酒」分類，全書42個單元

🍷 私藏的調酒師日誌
🍸 中英對照調酒
🍸 溫馨提醒＋調酒小故事
 Bartender必看的英語情境對話

# 作者序 Introduction

By the appearance of the glass, it looked like a refreshing drink. It tasted tangy and refreshing, perfect for a day at the bar with friends or on a hot summer's day on your own balcony. The lemon slice on the rim gave it a final touch. It had a sweet, tart, and mild flavor. A nice cocktail just makes your day or night.

Bartending is more complicated than it looks. Bartending is full of techniques and requires a good knowledge of liquors. It is much more than just mixing liquids. There is a whole science of mixology relating to the proper mixing of flavors, colors, temperatures, densities, viscosities, and even textures.

Want to know basic bartending techniques in both Engliash and Chinese? The basic techniques are muddling, building, shaking, blending, mixing, stirring, straining, and floating. Want to know how to make a fabulous drink? This book has many drinks that belong in every bartender's book. New York Sour? It sounds fancy and also looks fancy. Floating is the trick. This book also has good party tricks for drinks. DIY Amaretto, Irish Cream, Drambuie and Worcestershire sauce can be handy if the ingredient cannot be found in a store. What about learning exotic cocktail names in Chinese and English? The historical background of liquors also brings us to learn pieces of history information from several countries.

This is a phrase book for anyone who is interested in learning bartending in English. All recipes in this book have been reviewed by professional bartenders.

光是看著玻璃杯，就知道是一杯清涼的飲品。味道酸酸的卻很爽口，這是一杯在酒吧與朋友一起喝的完美雞尾酒，也是一杯在炎熱夏季在陽台上可以喝的完美雞尾酒。杯子上裝飾的檸檬片更是讓雞尾酒畫龍點睛。這樣一杯喝起來有甜有酸也很溫和的味道。能有一杯很棒的雞尾酒會讓白天或是夜晚感到極為美好。

　　調酒做起來比看起來還複雜。調酒是需要很多技巧，也需要對酒有深度的了解。不是説把酒混在一起就是調酒。調酒背後的科學包括有混合適當的風味、顏色、溫度、密度、特質、甚至口感。

　　想要知道英文和中文的基本調酒技巧嗎？基本技術有搗碎法、注入法、搖盪法、混合法、攪拌法、過濾和漂浮法。想知道如何做很棒的飲料嗎？這本書有屬於每一個調酒師需要知道的很多飲料。紐約酸酒？這聽起來不只很特別，看起來也很花俏。技巧在於漂浮法。這本書也有很好的派對調酒技巧。自己做杏仁香甜酒、愛爾蘭香甜奶酒、蜂蜜香甜酒、甚至英式伍斯特黑醋醬都可能很受用，因為有些香甜酒或材料可能買不到。還有特殊調酒的中英名字？酒的歷史背景也會讓我們學習到有些國家的相關歷史。

　　這是一本對調酒主題有興趣的英文學習書。這本書裡的所有酒譜都有經過專業調酒師審查過。

林昭菁

# 目次 CONTENTS

## Part 1 6 Base Liquors
六大基酒

# Part 2 Liqueur
利口酒

# 使用說明 Instructions

42 種你一定要知道、要學會的調酒 ●

● 六大基酒＋香甜酒篇章分類

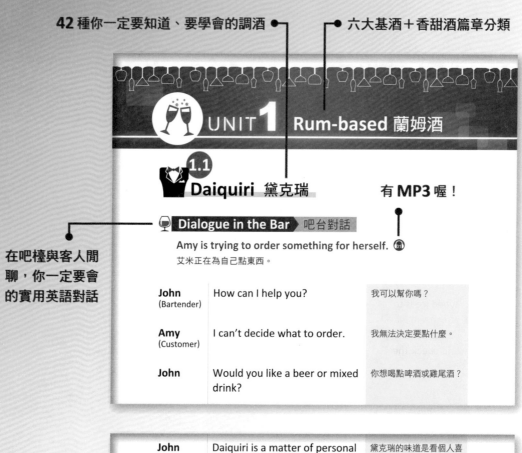

UNIT **1**　**Rum-based** 蘭姆酒

**1.1**
**Daiquiri** 黛克瑞

有 **MP3** 喔！

在吧檯與客人閒聊，你一定要會的實用英語對話

🍷 **Dialogue in the Bar**　吧台對話

Amy is trying to order something for herself. 🎧
艾米正在為自己點東西。

| John (Bartender) | How can I help you? | 我可以幫你嗎？ |
| Amy (Customer) | I can't decide what to order. | 我無法決定要點什麼。 |
| John | Would you like a beer or mixed drink? | 你想喝點啤酒或雞尾酒？ |

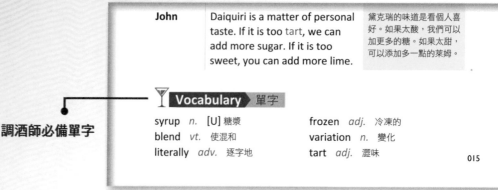

| John | Daiquiri is a matter of personal taste. If it is too tart, we can add more sugar. If it is too sweet, you can add more lime. | 黛克瑞的味道是看個人喜好。如果太酸，我們可以加更多的糖。如果太甜，可以添加多一點的萊姆。 |

🍸 **Vocabulary**　單字

調酒師必備單字

| | | |
|---|---|---|
| syrup *n.* [U] 糖漿 | | frozen *adj.* 冷凍的 |
| blend *vt.* 使混和 | | variation *n.* 變化 |
| literally *adv.* 逐字地 | | tart *adj.* 澀味 |

015

調酒師私藏日誌大公開，
內有不公開的調酒小密技

調酒師的日誌 Bartender's Log Book

用聽的，
更容易記！

Blended cocktails are popular, but it is difficult to get consistent results. Blending the perfect cocktails takes practice and patience that is not hard to learn. It is very easy to make a chunky cocktail or a watery cocktail if not careful. Liquors, juices and fruits should be added to the blender's pitcher first, so these ingredients are mixed properly before adding ice. For fruits, chop them into chunks of about 2.5 cm. Don't put too much ice at first. Ice can always be added later in the blending process. Also, use crushed ice instead of cubed iced. Regular cubed ice is too hard and might shorten the life of the blender's motor and blades. Start blending at a slow speed and then build up the speed gradually. When the blender sounds smooth, stop and check the consistency. If the mix is too watery, add some more ice.

冰沙雞尾酒是很受歡迎，但是要用冰沙調理機攪拌到均勻冰沙的結果不是很容易。要做一杯完美的冰沙雞尾酒需要練習和耐心，但也不難學。如果不小心就很容易做出不均勻或太稀的的冰沙。放入冰塊之前要先把酒、果汁和水果先加入冰沙調理機。先做這一個步驟才能確保材料都有適當的混合。就水果來說，切約兩公分半。開始先不要放太多冰塊。在攪拌過後隨時都可以添加更多的冰。還有，最好是用碎冰，因為方形冰塊太硬可能縮短調理機的馬達和刀片的使用壽命。最要以慢速攪拌，然後再慢慢提高速度。當冰沙調理機的聲音聽起來流暢而沒有冰裂的聲音後，你就應該停下來檢查冰沙的均勻度。如果太稀可以添加更多的冰再攪拌。

調酒師日誌中譯，
加了中文更容易上手

**Useful Sentences** 好好用句型

I cannot decide what to order.
我無法決定要點什麼。

🚲 I don't know how to order.
　我不知道要怎麼點。

🚲 I don't know which to choose.
　我不知道點哪一個。

🚲 I am undecided about what to order.
　我還沒決定要點什麼。

🚲 I have a dilemma here.
　我面臨一個難題。

**decide** 在這裡當動詞表示『做決定』，類似的動詞片語有〈make a decision〉、〈make up your mind〉、〈come to a decision〉、〈choose〉。

It sounds very familiar.
聽起來有點熟悉。

🚲 I heard it before.
　我有聽過這個。

🚲 I knew it from somewhere.
　我在別的地方有聽過。

🚲 That seems familiar to me.
　這對我來說很熟悉。

🚲 It sounds familiar to me. Where have I heard it before?
　這聽起來耳熟。我在哪裡聽過呢？

**familiar** 是形容詞「熟悉的；常見的」，類似的形容詞有 **popular**「流行的」、**well-known**「知名的」、**comparable**「具有可比性」、**related**「相關的」。

017

中英對照酒譜，用英文學
會調酒，用調酒學會英文

## 🍷 Mixology of the day  今日酒譜

### Strawberry Daiquiri
### 草莓黛克瑞

Glassware: Martini glass（馬丁尼杯）
Method: Blend（電動調理機法）

**Ingredients 材料**
2 oz white rum 白蘭姆酒
1 oz lime juice 萊姆汁
1/2 oz Triple Sec 柑橙酒
1/2 tsp. powdered sugar 糖粉（tsp.= 茶匙）
1 cup ice 冰塊
5 strawberries（fresh or frozen）五顆新鮮或冷凍的草莓

## 🍷 Notes  溫馨小提醒

所謂的乾式搖盪法就是要沒有放冰塊的大力的搖盪，有加蛋白的材
料，需要很大力搖盪至少 30 秒，讓蛋白發泡同時也和其他材料完
全融合喝不出蛋白的味道。所謂的搖盪出力，是要搖到手臂有感覺
到疲痛。

魔鬼藏在細
節裡，小小
的技巧可以
大大地提升
調酒的口感

Unit 2
Gin-based

## Short Story of the Cocktail  調酒小故事

沒有人知道紅粉佳人的真正起源。美國在 1920 年至 1933 年有
全國性憲法禁令禁止在美國銷售、生產、進口、運輸酒精飲料，
主要目的是要減少飲酒問題的產生。當時美國社會對美國人的飲
酒行為問題感到震驚，導致美國憲法第十八修正案取消發許可證

有趣的調酒故事，為你創造與
客人或是朋友閒聊時的好話題

# PART 1

6 Base Liquors

# 六大基酒

## UNIT **1** Rum-based 蘭姆酒

### 1.1 Daiquiri 黛克瑞

🍷 **Dialogue in the Bar** ▶ 吧台對話

**Amy is trying to order something for herself.** (01)
艾米正在為自己點東西。

| | | |
|---|---|---|
| **John**<br>(Bartender) | How can I help you? | 我可以幫你嗎？ |
| **Amy**<br>(Customer) | I can't decide what to order. | 我無法決定要點什麼。 |
| **John** | Would you like a beer or mixed drink? | 你想喝點啤酒或雞尾酒？ |
| **Amy** | I want to try a mixed drink. I'd like something sour and sweet. | 我是想試試看雞尾酒。我喜歡酸酸甜甜味道的。 |
| **John** | Do you like Rum? | 你喜歡蘭姆酒嗎？ |
| **Amy** | I guess. I like a Piña Colada and I know it has Rum in it. | 我想是吧。我喜歡椰林風情，我知道那是有蘭姆酒在裡面。 |

| John | Okay. I think you will like Daiquiri. It has rum, lime juice, and simple syrup. It is often served frozen with blended ice. | 好吧。我想你會喜歡黛克瑞。這是有黛克瑞、萊姆汁、和簡單的糖漿。通常是做成冰沙。 |
| --- | --- | --- |
| Amy | Sounds interesting. The name Daiquiri also sounds very familiar. | 聽起來很有趣。黛克瑞聽起來很熟悉。 |
| John | You are right. You might have heard that the most famous Daiquiri lover was Ernest Hemingway. He lived in Havana, Cuba in the 1920's and he loved that drink very much, though he preferred it without sugar. There is even a special variation called a Hemingway Daiquiri. It literally means Hemingway Special in French. | 沒錯。你可能聽說過，名人裡最喜歡黛克瑞是海明威。他在 1920 年時住在古巴的哈瓦那，他當時很喜歡這個雞尾酒，但他比較喜歡沒有加糖。甚至還有另一款雞尾酒就叫做海明威黛克瑞，在法語裡的意思就是「特別的海明威」。 |
| Amy | Okay. I will try that. | 好的。我想試試看。 |
| John | Daiquiri is a matter of personal taste. If it is too tart, we can add more sugar. If it is too sweet, you can add more lime. | 黛克瑞的味道是看個人喜好。如果太酸，我們可以加更多的糖。如果太甜，可以添加多一點的萊姆。 |

## Y Vocabulary 單字

syrup    *n.*   [U] 糖漿
blend    *vt.*   使混和
literally    *adv.*   逐字地

frozen    *adj.*   冷凍的
variation    *n.*   變化
tart    *adj.*   澀味

Blended cocktails are popular, but it is difficult to get consistent results. Blending the perfect cocktails takes practice and patience that is not hard to learn. It is very easy to make a chunky cocktail or a watery cocktail if not careful. Liquors, juices and fruits should be added to the blender's pitcher first, so these ingredients are mixed properly before adding ice. For fruits, chop them into chunks of about 2.5 cm. Don't put too much ice at first. Ice can always be added later in the blending process. Also, use crushed ice instead of cubed iced. Regular cubed ice is too hard and might shorten the life of the blender's motor and blades. Start blending at a slow speed and then build up the speed gradually. When the blender sounds smooth, stop and check the consistency. If the mix is too watery, add some more ice.

冰沙雞尾酒是很受歡迎，但是要用冰沙調理機攪拌到均勻冰沙的結果不是很容易。要做一杯完美的冰沙雞尾酒需要練習和耐心，但也不難學。如果不小心就很容易做出不均勻或太稀的的冰沙。放入冰塊之前要先把酒、果汁和水果先加入冰沙調理機。先做這一個步驟才能確保材料都有適當的混合。就水果來説，切約兩公分半。開始先不要放太多冰塊。在攪拌過後隨時都可以添加更多的冰。還有，最好是用碎冰，因為方形冰塊太硬可能縮短調理機的馬達和刀片的使用壽命。最初要以慢速攪拌，然後再慢慢提高速度。當冰沙調理機的聲音聽起來流暢而沒有冰裂的聲音後，你就應該停下來檢查冰沙的均勻度。如果太稀可以添加更多的冰再攪拌。

## Useful Sentences 好好用句型

I cannot decide what to order.

我無法決定要點什麼。

🍒 I don't know how to order.

　　我不知道要怎麼點。

🍒 I don't know which to choose.

　　我不知道點哪一個。

🍒 I am undecided about what to order.

　　我還沒決定要點什麼。

🍒 I have a dilemma here.

　　我面臨一個難題。

**decide** 在這裡當動詞表示『做決定』，類似的動詞片語有〈**make a decision**〉、〈**make up your mind**〉、〈**come to a decision**〉、〈**choose**〉。

It sounds very familiar.

聽起來有點熟悉。

🍒 I heard it before.

　　我有聽過這個。

🍒 I knew it from somewhere.

　　我在別的地方有聽過。

🍒 That seems familiar to me.

　　這對我來說很熟悉。

🍒 It sounds familiar to me. Where have I heard it before?

　　這聽起來耳熟。我在哪裡聽過呢？

**familiar** 是形容詞「熟悉的；常見的」，類似的形容詞有 **popular** 「流行的」，**well-known** 「知名的」，**comparable** 「具有可比性」，**related** 「相關的」。

## Mixology of the day　今日酒譜

# Strawberry Daiquiri
## 草莓黛克瑞

Glassware: Martini glass（馬丁尼杯）
Method: Blend（電動調理機法）

### Ingredients 材料
2 oz white rum 白蘭姆酒
1 oz lime juice 萊姆汁
1/2 oz Triple Sec 柑橙酒
1/2 tsp. powdered sugar 糖粉（tsp.= 茶匙）
1 cup ice 冰塊
5 strawberries（fresh or frozen）五顆新鮮或冷凍的草莓

### Instructions 作法
Pour all ingredients in a blender and blend at high speed for about 1/2 minute. Pulse the blender a few times to start to break up the ice. If the blender has an "ice" option, use it when pulsing until the ice has been reduced to small pieces. Blend until the beverage is smooth with no large ice pieces. Garnish with a fresh strawberry. For better results, use ice from ice machine or bagged ice for better smoothies. Home freezer ice is much harder and sizes can be irregular.

把所有的材料倒入調理機，用高轉速攪拌約半分鐘。瞬轉幾次把冰塊打散。如果你的調理機有「碎冰」的選項，瞬轉打碎冰塊時，用這個「碎冰」的選項。混合直到所有材料混合均勻並且沒有大小冰塊。用新鮮的草莓做裝飾。為了較好的效果，用製冰機或袋裝冰塊可以打出比較均勻的冰沙，因為家裡冷凍庫的冰塊比較硬，也比較大小不一。

## Notes ▶ 溫馨小提醒

不是每個人都喜歡很濃厚的霜凍黛克瑞，霜凍是用調理器將冰和調酒的材料打碎混合均勻所做成的。如果要有更多的水果味，可以用冷凍水果來取代新鮮水果和冰塊。用同樣的方式在調理器攪拌。酸酸甜甜的味道很受一般女性的歡迎，霜凍黛克瑞（Frozen Strawberry Daiquiri）很適合推薦給女性。

## Historical Background　調酒小故事

位在加勒比海的古巴首先是由克里斯托弗·哥倫布所發現，後來在 1492 年被西班牙佔領。這裡氣候溫和，非常適合種植菸草和甘蔗，這裡的所在地也很適合歐洲人在航海全盛時期的中途停站點包括來自不同地方的海盜，英國和法國的水手。在 17 世紀時，英國的水手喝的都是啤酒，但是後來英國軍隊發現蘭姆酒的後勁較強，不用喝的比啤酒多，但是因為酒精濃度太強，所以軍隊指揮命令蘭姆酒用水和柑橘汁（通常是萊姆）混合稀釋太強的酒精濃度。這不僅讓英國軍隊比喝啤酒要清醒幾分，也比較健康。這是最早所知道的萊姆汁、水和蘭姆酒的混合，也就是後來被成為「黛克瑞」的由來。

# UNIT **1** Rum-based 蘭姆酒

**1.2**

# Mojito 莫希托

## 🍷 **Dialogue in the Bar** ▶ 吧台對話

**Bartender Jenny and John are talking with the** 🔘(03)
**guest about different ways of making Mojito.**
調酒師珍妮和約翰正在與客人談論有關製作莫希托不同的方式。

| | | |
|---|---|---|
| **Allen** | This Mojito tastes a little different from last time I had it, but it is good. | 這杯莫希托的味道和我之前喝的有一點點不同，但是很好喝。 |
| **Jenny** (Bartender) | You are right. It is a little different. We ran out of sparkling water. I used Ginger Ale instead. | 你說得對。這是有點不同。我們的蘇打水用完了。我用薑汁汽水代替。 |
| **Allen** | Not bad at all. It is interesting. | 是不錯。很有意思。 |
| **Jenny** | Nothing is written in stone. That's why I love this job. It gives me space to create something different. John and I make Mojitos differently. I don't muddle, just juiced to avoid bitter oils. | 沒有什麼規則不能變通的。這就是為什麼我喜歡這份工作。我能有空間做不同的雞尾酒。約翰和我做的莫希托就不一樣。我沒有用搗杵的方式，只是榨出萊姆汁但避免皮表面苦味的油。 |

|  | I also like to give it a nice touch by dropping some squeezed lime before I add the last amount of ice. | 在最後加冰塊前，我很喜歡加一點萊姆汁，我覺得這樣更有味道。 |
| --- | --- | --- |
| **Allen** | No wonder. Your Mojito is different from John's. I remember he mentioned about adding a little Angostura to balance the bitterness of the mint. | 難怪。你的莫希托喝起來和約翰的莫希托不一樣。我記得他會加一點安格斯特拉苦精來平衡薄荷的苦味。 |
| **Jenny** | I learned something new from a bartender at a wedding last summer. He added a little bit of fresh raspberries to muddle with the mint. It was amazing. Bartending is not rocket science, but it certainly can create something to impress many people. | 我去年夏天在一個婚禮裡從一個調酒師學到了一些新東西。他會加一點新鮮的紅莓和薄荷一起搗拌。喝起來真的很棒。調酒並沒有這麼困難，但很肯定的是可以創造新的味道打動了許多人。 |

## Vocabulary　單字

| create | vt. | 創造 | touch | vt. | 觸摸 |
| --- | --- | --- | --- | --- | --- |
| drop | v. | 滴下 | bitterness | n. | 苦味 |
| certainly | adj. | 無疑地 | impress | vt. | 印象深刻 |

Mojito is a perfect drink on a hot summer's night or day. It is not hard to learn how to make the perfect mojito. The common way is to first muddle sugar and mint, but mint syrup can be used instead just to save time. Homemade mint syrup is simple. It is just sugar, water, and mints. The sweetness of syrup can balance the sourness of the limes in the mojito. Syrup is infused with mint to add to the flavor of the drink. To make the simple syrup, heat up 1 cup water and 1 cup sugar in a saucepan on the stove. Once the sugar has dissolved in the water, take it off the heat and add about 15 mint leaves and let them infuse. Allow the simple syrup to cool. The longer it infuses, the more flavors it will have in the mojito. For the best result in the Mojito, freshly squeezed lime juice is absolutely necessary.

莫希托是炎熱夏天的夜晚或白天一杯完美的飲料。要做出完美的莫吉托其實不難。常見的方法是將糖和薄荷搗在一起，但這個步驟可以用薄荷糖漿來代替。自製薄荷糖漿是非常簡單的。材料只有糖、水和薄荷。糖漿甜度是用來平衡莫希托裡的酸味。薄荷糖漿則是添加飲料的薄荷味。簡單糖漿的作法是，把 1 杯水和 1 杯糖放入鍋內在爐子上加熱。一旦糖溶解在水中，就可關火，加入約 15 片薄荷葉，讓味道浸出來。讓糖漿冷卻。浸的時間越長，在莫希托裡就越有味道。要做一杯最好的莫希托，放入新鮮擠壓檸檬汁是絕對必要的。

## 🔊 **Useful Sentences** 好好用句型

We ran out of sparkling water.

我們的蘇打水都用完了。

🚲 We are all out of beer.

　　我們的啤酒都沒有了。

🚲 We don't have any of that kind of wine left.

　　我們那種酒都賣完了。

🚲 We have no more bottled water left.

　　我們的瓶裝水都沒有了。

🚲 We are running out of options.

　　我們沒有什麼選擇了。


〈run out of〉是指什麼東西沒有了，所以〈of〉後面要解釋是什麼沒有了。
另外一個〈run out〉則可以以被動的方式來使用。

• Our money eventually ran out.

　　我們的錢最後都花完了。

• Our supplies are all ran out.

　　我的們資源最後都用完了。


It was amazing.

真的很驚人。

🚲 It was unbelievable.

　　這是令人難以置信的。

🚲 It was shocking.

　　這是令人震驚的。

🚲 I can't believe it.

　　我簡直不敢相信。

🚲 It was stunning.

　　這是驚人的。

## Mixology of the day 今日酒譜

# Mojito
# 莫希托

Glassware: Collins glass（可林杯）
Method: Muddle and stir（攪杆法和攪拌法）

**Ingredients 材料**
12 fresh mint leaves 新鮮薄荷葉
4 lime wedges 萊姆角
2 tsp. sugar 糖
1 cup crushed ice 碎冰
2 oz white rum 白蘭姆酒
1/2 cup club soda 蘇打水

**Instructions 作法**
Place mint leaves and 1 lime wedge into a Collins glass. Use a muddler to crush the mint and lime to release the mint oils and lime juice. Add 2 more lime wedges and the sugar, and muddle again to release the lime juice. Fill the glass almost to the top with ice. Pour the rum over the ice, and fill the glass with club soda. Stir, taste, and add more sugar if desired. Garnish with a lime wedge.

首先將全部薄荷葉和一個萊姆角放入杯中用搗棒攪杆讓薄荷油和萊姆汁釋出。再把兩個萊姆角和糖加入杯中，再用搗棒搗出更多萊姆汁後直接將冰塊加入杯子直到幾乎倒滿，之後把白蘭姆酒往冰塊上倒入再加蘇打水。攪拌均勻，試試味道，如果需要添加更多的糖再加糖。用萊姆角裝飾。

## Notes　溫馨小提醒

調製莫希托（Mojitos）一定要用碎冰，碎冰融化的比較快，相對可以提高烈酒的味道。輕輕略搗薄荷和砂糖即可，過度攪杵會搗出薄荷的葉綠素苦味。一定要用白蘭姆酒（white rum）或淡蘭姆酒（light rum），其他的蘭姆酒比較不易調製出莫希托原始配方所呈現的清澈透明顏色也會攪渾莫希托的味道。原始配方中用的就是白蘭姆酒。

## Historical Background　調酒小故事

莫希托最初的發明地是在古巴首都哈瓦那。當時是在找可以醫治熱帶疾病的成分，後來意外發現蘭姆酒對這種疾病很有幫助，加上當地的熱帶材料如青檸檬、甘蔗汁、薄荷變成一種好喝的調酒，在古巴這樣的熱帶氣候，喝萊姆汁本來就對預防痢疾有很大的幫助，加上糖和薄荷就讓這個調酒變成大眾口味，所以有些調酒師做莫希托會加上一根小小的甘蔗。在當地最有名的 mojito 酒吧叫做 "La Bodeguita del Medio"，因為海明威曾說過 "My mojito in La Bodeguita, my daiquiri in El Floridita."，而那家店牆上還保有海明威的所寫下的親筆字跡。

## 1.3
# Cuba Libre / Rum and Coke 自由古巴 / 蘭姆可樂

🍷 **Dialogue in the Bar** 吧台對話

**Paul and John are talking about the** 🔊05
**popularity of Rum and Coke.**
保羅和約翰在談論蘭姆可樂的流行。

| | | |
|---|---|---|
| **John** (Bartender) | I used to work at a college bar. Rum and Coke is very popular among college students in the US. | 我曾經在一所大學附近的酒吧工作。蘭姆可樂在美國大學生之間很受歡迎。 |
| **Paul** | It is also popular in weddings. It is not considered as a high class drink. Rum and Coke is regarded as the "low end" of mixed drinks. | 在婚禮裡也很受歡迎。這不是一個高檔的雞尾酒。蘭姆可樂是屬於非高級類的雞尾酒。 |
| **John** | You are right. It is underrated. Rum and Coke tastes really great if it is made right. | 你説得對。蘭姆可樂是被低估的。如果調得好的話,蘭姆可樂是很棒的。 |
| **Paul** | Is that true that the high-end rum does not really make a better Rum and Coke. | 聽説高檔的蘭姆酒不一定會調出比較好的蘭姆可樂? |

| | | |
|---|---|---|
| **John** | That is true. It is because many types of rum add their own unique flavors, like coconut or vanilla that made the Rum and Coke a different drink entirely. Only a few rums are made directly from sugar cane juice. Most are made from molasses. So each kind of rum has its own distinct characteristics. | 那是真的。因為很多蘭姆酒本身有獨特的味道，像椰子或香草的添加料，這使蘭姆可樂的雞尾酒會有不同口味。只有少數蘭姆酒是直接從甘蔗汁做的，大部分是由糖蜜製成。因此，每款蘭姆酒都有自己鮮明的特色。 |
| **Paul** | I was told that you can make a Rum and Coke with any kind of rum, huh? | 有人跟我說任何蘭姆酒都可以做蘭姆可樂，對吧？ |
| **John** | That's correct. Different types of rum made Rum and Cokes taste differently, but the mixology is the same. | 那是真的。不同的蘭姆酒做的蘭姆可樂會有不同的味道，只是調酒的方式是一樣的。 |
| **Paul** | I have tried Rum and Coke Cheesecake before. The taste was very unique. | 我甚至有吃過蘭姆可樂做的起司蛋糕。味道很獨特。 |
| **John** | A simple Rum and Tonic is also good. I like it best with the dark rum and a squeeze of lime. | 簡單的蘭姆加通寧水也不錯。我最喜歡的是用深色蘭姆酒加上一點萊姆汁。 |

## Vocabulary 單字

unique *adj.* 獨一無二的

distinct *adj.* 明顯的

simple *adj.* 簡單的

entirely *adv.* 全部的

characteristics *n.* 特徵

squeeze *n.* 榨，擠

027

A Rum and Coke is made without lime and a Cuba Libre is made with lime. Rum and Coke is simply mixing rum with coke. Pour the rum in a highball glass filled with ice, top with coke and garnish with a lime wedge. For a Cuba Libre, lime juice is added to the drink. For the rum, use a high-quality rum or any personal favorite rum. Different rums create different unique tastes. Generally, any light, gold, or spiced rum can be used in the Cuba Libre. First squeeze the juice of half a lime into a chilled glass, add ice cubes, then pour the rum and cola into a glass. Both a Rum and Coke and Cuba Libre are supposed to be easy to make. Regardless, the recipe for a Cuba Libre is a little bit complicated. It requires muddling the squeezed-out lime shell in the bottom of the glass to extract a little of the rind's bitter oil before adding the rest of the ingredients.

蘭姆可樂沒有加萊姆，自由古巴有加萊姆。蘭姆可樂只是直接混合蘭姆酒與可樂。在高球杯中裝滿冰塊，加入蘭姆酒後再加可樂，用萊姆片裝飾後就是蘭姆和可樂。自由古巴則是把萊姆汁直接添加到飲料。可以使用高品質的蘭姆或任何個人最喜歡的蘭姆。不同的蘭姆酒做出來的雞尾酒會有各自獨特味道。一般而言，任何淡色、金色或有香味的蘭姆酒都可以用來做自由古巴。首先擠半個萊姆汁放入冰鎮玻璃，加入冰塊，倒入蘭姆酒後再倒入可樂。蘭姆和可樂和自由古巴都是很容易做的。然而，自由古巴有另外一個比較複雜的酒譜，在加入所有材料之前需要在杯子裡先搗杵萊姆，以提取外皮的一點苦油。

**Useful Sentences** 好好用句型

I used to work at a college bar.

我以前在大學附近的酒吧工作過。

🍒 I worked at a college bar before.

　　我之前在大學附近的酒吧工作過。

🍒 I had a job at a college bar before.

　　我以前在大學附近的酒吧工作過。

🍒 I was hired by a college bar before.

　　我以前在大學附近的酒吧工作過。

That's correct.

那是對的。

🍒 That's right.

　　那是對的。

🍒 That's true.

　　那是真的。

🍒 That's accurate.

　　那是正確無誤的。

〈correct〉形容詞，同義字有 **proper**、**appropriate**，用法都一樣。

● **It is proper.**

　　那是正當的。

● **It's appropriate.**

　　那是正當的。

## Mixology of the day　今日酒譜

# Cuba Libre
# 自由古巴

Glassware: Collins glass（可林杯）
Method: Stir（攪拌法）

### Ingredients 材料
2 oz gold rum 金色蘭姆酒
4 oz Coke 可樂
2 lemon wedges 檸檬角
Ice 冰塊

### Instructions 作法
Add ice to about half of the cup, add Rum, pour rum in a Collins glass filled with ice. Top with coke. Stir. Squeeze the lemon in, and drop the wedge in the glass. 蘭姆酒倒入裝滿冰塊的可林杯。倒入可樂加至八分滿，攪拌均勻。將檸檬汁擠入，再將檸檬角丟入杯中做裝飾。

## Notes 溫馨小提醒

自由古巴只有兩種材料組合，調製方法簡單所以廣受歡迎。酒杯隨意、份量也可不拘，而冰塊可多加，如此更能凸顯碳酸類飲料的特色。因為可樂是深色，可以選自己喜歡的任何顏色的蘭姆酒來調製。雖然簡單，但是萊姆在這杯雞尾酒扮演很重要的角色。萊姆讓整個味道更有多層次，酸酸的萊姆也平衡了可樂的甜味。

## Historical Background 調酒小故事

自由古巴（Cuba Libre）的由來是有很深的歷史意義的。有名的百加得蘭姆酒家族在 1890，在古巴就參與反西班牙殖民的社會運動。在 1900 初，美國的可口可樂進軍了古巴市場的同時美軍也駐守古巴支持反西班牙殖民的解放古巴 "Free Cuba"，之後古巴共和國誕生。在這段古巴的社會和政治動盪的時候，第一杯調出來的自由古巴就是用正統的可口可樂加百加得蘭姆酒。之後可口可樂加百加得蘭姆酒的自由古巴也在美軍裡漸漸傳開來。Cuba Libre 就是 Free Cuba 的意思。時事的變化，朋友也可以一夕間變敵人，古巴在 1959 年在卡斯楚的統治下變成了共產黨，也因此成為美國在加勒比海的頭號敵人。自由古巴隱約訴說著資本主義和共產主義的不融合卻也融合。

## **1.4**
## Mai Tai 邁泰

### 🍷 Dialogue in the Bar ▶ 吧台對話

**Bartender Jenny and customer Lewis are talking** 🔘07
**about the techniques for making a Mai Tai.**
調酒師珍妮和客人路易斯在談論做邁泰雞尾酒的技巧。

| | | |
|---|---|---|
| **Jenny**<br>(Bartender) | A Mai Tai is a well-crafted cocktail. If you want to do it right, you must put in a lot of effort. | 邁泰是一種精心製作的雞尾酒。如果你想要做好的話，你必須下很大的功夫。 |
| **Lewis** | You are right. I've had bad ones and good ones as well. | 你說得對。我曾喝過不好的，也有喝到不錯的。 |
| **Jenny** | Each bartender makes it differently. Different drinks call for different techniques. For a Mai Tai, there are two crucial techniques, one is floating the rum and the other is shaking the ice. | 每個調酒師做的不一樣。不同的飲料需要不同的技巧。對於邁泰，有兩個關鍵的技術，一種是蘭姆酒的漂浮法，另一個是搖盪冰塊。 |
| **Lewis** | Do you shake crushed ice? Or you just shake in the regular way and pour it over crushed ice? | 你有搖盪碎冰塊嗎？或者先一般的搖盪然後再倒在碎冰上？ |

**Jenny**　A good bartender never shakes a drink with crushed ice, 'cause the ice will melt too quickly. You shake it with cubed ice and strain it to a glass filled with fresh crushed ice, as it doesn't dilute the cocktail too fast. Always shake with cubes to keep the dilution of the drink at minimum, then strain it into a glass with crushed ice.

一個優秀的調酒師絕對不會搖盪碎冰塊，因為這樣會把飲料稀釋了。你要用冰塊來搖盪，然後過濾到有加碎冰的杯子，這樣才不會讓雞尾酒稀釋太快。一定要先搖盪冰塊，以保持飲料最少的稀釋，然後再過濾到有碎冰的杯子裡。

**Lewis**　I've learned a valuable lesson here. I also heard that for the Mai Tai, you only put the white rum in the shaker, not the dark rum.

我又學到一課了。我也聽說做邁泰時，只需要把白蘭姆酒放在雪克杯搖盪，不要放深色的蘭姆酒在雪克杯裡。

**Jenny**　The mixed drink is designed to focus on the dark rum, so some people see it as a great way to enjoy their favorite rums. The method is to put a splash of dark rum on top or even serve flaming. Although the dark rum float is not the original, but it is a common addition. It adds hints of spice and vanilla to the drink. To float, put the spout of the liquor up against the glass and pour. A higher percent alcohol of volume should be used for floating.

這款雞尾酒主要是把深色的蘭姆酒當作焦點，所以有一些人把這款的雞尾酒當作是用來喝自己喜愛的蘭姆酒。方法是在最後倒入一些深色蘭姆酒，有的甚至在調酒上點火。深色蘭姆酒漂浮法不是原始酒譜的一部分，但卻是一種常見的方式，這可以讓調酒中的香料和香草的香氣較為濃郁。漂浮法就是把酒嘴靠沿著杯子倒入。漂浮在上層的酒要選用酒精濃度較高的酒。

DIY Grenadine? No problem. Grenadine is just pomegranate juice mixed with sugar then boil until it becomes syrup. Grenadine is derived from the French word "grenade" which means "pomegranate". There is a good reason to DIY grenadine. A typical bottle of the store-bought grenadine consists of high fructose corn syrup, water, citric acid, sodium citrate, sodium benzoate, different food colors, artificial flavors, and preservatives. Homemade grenadine only has sugar and pomegranate juice. It only takes a few minutes to make grenadine with bottled pomegranate juice. Combine 1/4 cup sugar and 1 cup 100% unsweetened pomegranate juice. In a sauce pan, combine the sugar and juice. Place over medium heat on the stovetop and stir. Bring to a boil and cook until slightly thickened. Cool and add lemon juice (optional). Pour into a clean bottle. It can be stored in the refrigerator for up to one month. Be sure to use 100% unsweetened pomegranate juice. If the result is not sweet enough, just stir in more sugar or even just don't add lemon juice.

自己做紅石榴糖漿？其實不難。紅石榴糖漿只是石榴汁與糖加在一起煮沸變成糖漿。Grenadine 是從法語的紅石榴 "grenade" 衍生出來的。有一個好的原因，讓自己做紅石榴糖漿。一般商店買來的紅石榴糖漿都有含果糖、玉米糖漿、水、檸檬酸、檸檬酸鈉、苯甲酸鈉、不同食品色素、人造香料和防腐劑。自製紅石榴糖漿只有糖和石榴汁，而且用瓶裝的石榴汁只需要幾分鐘的時間就可以做成紅石榴糖漿。把 1/4 杯糖和 1 杯 100% 不含糖的紅石榴汁放平底鍋加熱用中火煮。攪拌均勻，煮至濃濃的糖漿狀即可。放涼後可以添加檸檬汁（可省略）。倒入一個乾淨的瓶子。放在冰箱中可以保存長達一個月。一定要使用 100% 不加糖的石榴汁。如果煮完後的糖漿不夠甜，再加入糖熬煮，或者可直接省略檸檬汁。

## 🍵 **Useful Sentences** 好好用句型

Each bartender makes it differently.

每個調酒師做的都不同。

🍸 We all have our own different techniques.

我們每個人都有自己不同的技巧。

🍸 We have different recipes.

我們有不同的食譜。

🍸 We have different ways of making the same drink.

我們用不同的方式做同樣的雞尾酒。

🍸 He makes it his way, and I make it my way.

他有他的方式，我有我自己的方式。

〈**differently**〉副詞，不同地，形容動詞。

〈**different**〉形容詞，不同，不一致，形容名詞。

I am learning a lesson here.

我正在這裡學了一課。

🍸 I am learning a lot here.

我在這裡學到了很多東西。

🍸 I am learning something new.

我正在學習新的東西。

🍸 This is new for me.

對我來説這是新的。

## Mixology of the day 今日酒譜

# Mai Tai
# 邁泰

Glassware: Highball glass（高球杯）
Method: Shake and strain（搖盪和過濾）

**Ingredients 材料**
1 oz light rum 淺色蘭姆酒
1/2 oz Curacao 柑橘酒
1 1/2 oz pineapple juice 鳳梨汁
1 1/2 oz orange juice 柳橙汁
1/4 oz lemon juice 檸檬汁
Dash of grenadine 紅石榴糖漿
Ice cubes 冰塊
1/2 oz dark rum 深色蘭姆酒
1 orange wedge and 1 Maraschino cherry 柳橙角和酒漬櫻桃

**Instructions 作法**
Pour all the ingredients except the dark rum into a shaker with ice cubes. Shake well. Strain into a Highball Glass and half filled with ice. Top with the dark rum. Garnish with an orange wedge and Maraschino cherry。
除了深色蘭姆酒外，將其他材料倒入雪克杯搖勻後過濾到高球杯，加一半的冰塊在杯裡。把深色蘭姆酒倒在上面，用柳橙角和酒漬櫻桃裝飾。

## Notes 溫馨小提醒

邁泰酒譜有些會用橙味利口酒（Triple Sec），有些會用柑橘酒
（Curacao）。對酒外行的人來說，這樣種的替換應該喝不出差
別。這兩種就都是甜橙味的酒，但是兩種不同的酒。橙味利口酒是
穀類做的酒，柑橘酒是白蘭地做的。如果想要有一點苦味或顏色，
可以加柑橘酒。如果比較喜歡甜味，那就用橙味利口酒。

## Historical Background 調酒小故事

在雞尾酒的分類裡有一類型叫 Tiki Cocktail，這類型的雞尾酒都
是以新鮮果汁為主。Tiki 是一種風格，是指夏威夷、大溪地、復
活島、斐濟等南太平洋群島，充滿熱帶風情，相關裝飾品的擬人
雕像、面具及火炬
更是讓人感覺原始也很有活力，此
風格就統稱為 Tiki。Tiki 風格是二
次大戰時期間由士兵帶回美國，餐
廳的裝飾以熱帶風情的木、石、圖
騰和棕櫚樹等裝飾為主，展現原始
而自然。說是誰發明 Mai Tai 有
很多版本，其中以 Trader Vic's
（偉克商人餐廳）在 1944 年所最
初調製的最廣為接受。當時這裡的
調酒師有兩個朋友來自大溪地，他
臨時起意特調製了一杯雞尾酒，他
的大溪地朋友喝了之後就說 "Mai
Tai- Aoa Ae"（Out of this
world- the best），之後這杯雞
尾酒就被稱為 Mai Tai。（取自英
文 Wikipedia）

## 1.5

# Pina Colada 椰林風情

### 🍷 Dialogue in the Bar ▶ 吧台對話

Customers and John are talking about the [09]
ingredients in a Pina Colada.

顧客和約翰在討論「椰林風情」裡的材料。

| | | |
|---|---|---|
| **Elisa** | Do you have Piña Coladas? | 你有椰林風情嗎？ |
| **John** (Bartender) | Of course. Would you like one? | 當然有。妳想要來一杯嗎？ |
| **Elisa** | Yeah, but can you make it without coconut cream? I heard that the coconut cream contains a lot of calories. Can you use coconut water instead? | 是的，但是你可以做沒有加椰漿的嗎？我聽說椰漿裡有很多的卡路里。你可以用椰子水代替嗎？ |
| **John** | I certainly can. Without it, the drink will be less creamy, but it is still good. Coconut cream is made from mature coconut flesh that is preserved in sugarcane juice and is totally natural, but it is very fattening. | 當然沒問題。沒有加椰漿的雞尾酒比較不濃，但還是不錯的。椰漿是成熟的椰子肉做的，然後加甘蔗汁保存，完全是天然的，但是脂肪非常高。 |

| Elisa | Do you use white rum? | 你用白蘭姆酒？ |
| --- | --- | --- |
| John | Yes I do. I use Bacardi white rum. Rum with no flavor in Piña Colada is better. Gold rum has flavor, and white rum does not. | 是的，沒錯。我用的是百加得白色蘭姆酒。椰林風情用沒有味道蘭姆酒是比較好的。金色蘭姆酒有味道，白色蘭姆酒沒有。 |
| Anna | I would like to order one too, but I don't like to have alcohol in it. Piña Colada is very refreshing. I love it, but it's a relatively sweet drink and with alcohol, and it can be very strong. Also, I will have to drive later, so I would rather not have any alcohol. | 我想點一杯，但我不喜歡有加酒的味道。椰林風情喝起來很清爽。我很喜歡，但是這是比較甜的雞尾酒也有酒精，所以後勁可能很強。還有，我需要開車，所以我寧可不要喝任何酒精。 |
| John | No problem. I'll make you a Virgin Piña Colada. | 沒問題。我幫你做一杯無酒精的椰林風情。 |

## Vocabulary 單字

instead　adv　反而
flesh　*n.*　果肉
natural　*adj.*　自然的
relatively　*adj.*　相對地
drive　v.　開車
rather　*adv.*　倒不如

The secrets to making the best Piña Colada is just getting the right key ingredients. If good and fresh pineapple is hard to get, bottled pineapple juice is not a bad choice. Fresh pineapple does not always mean good pineapple. A great pineapple shows some distinct signs. It should have fresh green leaves and a strong sweet smell. If you have a juicer, that's great. If you don't have a juicer, that's fine, too. Chop the pineapple into chunks, mash it with a potato masher, then squeeze the juice out of the mashed pulp. Cream of coconut is the other signature ingredient of the Piña Colada. Make sure you get the right kind. Not coconut milk (it's too thin), not coconut cream (it's not sweet), but cream of coconut which is a mixture of coconut cream and sugar. Coco López is the only one worth buying. Both dark and light rum can be used, but light rum brings out the bright flavor of the pineapple and coconut.

做一杯好喝的椰林風情有什麼秘密呢？好的材料是關鍵因素。如果好又新鮮鳳梨很難買得到的，罐裝鳳梨汁是不錯的選擇。新鮮鳳梨並不全都是很好的鳳梨。挑好的鳳梨有幾個特徵。好的鳳梨應該有新鮮的綠葉和濃濃的香味。如果你有一台榨汁機，當然很不錯。如果你沒有一台榨汁機，那也沒關係。把鳳梨切成塊，用搗碎器搗爛，然後擠出汁。椰奶也是椰林風情的重要材料。但是要確保買的是正確的椰漿。不是椰子汁（太稀），不是椰子奶油（不甜），要買的是椰漿，這是椰子奶油和糖的混合物。可可洛佩茲是唯一值得購買的品牌。深色和淺色蘭姆酒都可以使用，但是淺色蘭姆酒比較能帶出鳳梨和椰子的鮮明的味道。

## Useful Sentences　好好用句型

Would you like one?

你想要嗎？

🦑 **Do you want to try one?**

　　你想試試嗎？

🦑 **How about trying this one?**

　　試試這個如何？

🦑 **Maybe you should give it a try.**

　　也許你應該試試看。

I would rather not have any alcohol.

我寧願沒有任何酒精的。

🦑 **I prefer not to have any alcohol.**

　　我不希望有含任何酒精。

🦑 **I should not have any alcohol.**

　　我不應該喝酒的。

🦑 **I'd better not to have any alcohol.**

　　我最好不要喝任何含酒精的飲料。

## Mixology of the day　今日酒譜

# Frozen Pina Colada
# 椰林風情霜凍

Glassware: Chilled hurricane cocktail glass（冰鎮颶風杯）
Method: Blend（電動調理機法）

**Ingredients 材料**
2 oz aged rum 蘭姆酒
1 1/2 oz coconut cream 椰漿
6 oz pineapple juice 鳳梨汁
1 oz heavy cream 鮮奶油
Pineapple wedge, for garnish 裝飾用鳳梨角
1 Maraschino cherry 酒漬櫻桃
Ice 冰

**Instructions 作法**
Combine all the ingredients in a blender cup. Add 1 cup of ice. Blend at a high speed until smooth. Pour contents into a chilled hurricane glass. Garnish with the pineapple wedge and Maraschino Cherry. Coconut cream can be substituted with lower calories coconut milk.

將所有的成分放入調理機杯。加入 **1** 杯的冰塊。用高速度攪拌，打至所有材料都混合均勻後，再倒入冰鎮颶風杯。用鳳梨角和酒漬櫻桃裝飾。椰漿也可以用熱量較低的椰子水來代替。

## Notes 溫馨小提醒

椰林風情雖然可以用各種蘭姆酒調製，但是用不同蘭姆酒的組合也會有驚人的結果。鳳梨和椰子搭配是椰林風情最具代表性的味道。這兩樣可以用新鮮水果，也可以用罐頭。如果有新鮮的冷凍鳳梨其實更好，這樣在調理機混合時就不需要加冰塊，因為加冰塊會讓味道較淡。

## Historical Background 調酒小故事

到底是誰發明椰林風情（**Piña Colada**）其實是一個謎。傳說是 **1800** 年的加勒比海的海盜為了要提高海盜內部的士氣，就讓同行的海盜喝蘭姆酒、椰子和鳳梨混合的酒。但是沒有人真正知道那是什麼樣的配方，後來在 **1950** 年代在波多黎各的聖胡安（**San Juan, Puerto Rico**）的調酒師開始調出椰林風情（**Piña Colada**），之後這一直是很受歡迎的經典的特調雞尾酒。椰林風情主要是希望捕捉波多黎各的陽光明媚和熱帶風情。

## 1.6
# Anejo Highball 安蘭海波杯

### 🍷 Dialogue in the Bar 吧台對話

**John and Jenny are talking about different liquors**  ⑪
**used in an Anejo Highball.**

約翰和珍妮在討論安蘭海波杯裡的不同酒。

| | | |
|---|---|---|
| **John**<br>(Bartender) | Three people ordered the Anejo Highball tonight. We don't normally have many orders for that at one night, it was unusual. | 今晚有三個人點安蘭海波杯。我們在一個晚上通常不會有很多人點這個,這不太尋常。 |
| **Jenny**<br>(Bartender) | You are right. The Anejo Highball is not quite popular in Taiwan yet. I know it is gaining popularity in the US. It is becoming a classic cocktail, but it is still only found in chic and hip bars and nightspots. Do you make them with a particular recipe? | 你說得對。安蘭海波杯在台灣還不是很流行。我知道在美國是越來越受歡迎,也慢慢在成為一種經典的雞尾酒,但仍然是只在比較時尚和時髦的酒吧和夜店才會有。你有一個特定的酒譜嗎? |

| John | Yes. I do. I use the original Dale DeGroff's recipe. But I like to use Jamaican aged rum instead of Bacardi rums. It also works very well with rum from Martinique, or Martinique Rhum Agricole. Rhum Agricole is the French term for cane juice rum. | 是的。我有。我用的是原來的戴爾·地格夫的酒譜。但我喜歡用牙買加朗蘭姆酒而不是百加得蘭姆酒。用馬提尼克島生產的蘭姆酒，或馬提尼克農業蘭姆酒也不錯。Rhum Agricole 在法語中是指以甘蔗汁為發酵原料製成的蘭姆酒。 |
|---|---|---|
| Jenny | Yeah, of course. | 是的，當然。 |
| John | For this recipe, an Anejo tequila works well, too. | 對於這個酒譜，用安蘭龍舌蘭酒也不錯。 |
| Jenny | I like Anejo Highballs very much, too. The interaction of the bitters and orange curacao is very unique. The subtle spice of the ginger beer and lime juice make it complex. | 我很喜歡安蘭海波杯。苦味和柑橘香甜酒的結合是非常獨特的。生薑啤酒的香料和青檸汁也讓這樣的雞尾酒喝起來很有層次。 |

## Vocabulary 單字

normally *adv.* 正常地
classic *adj.* 典型的
Jamaican *adj.* 牙買加的、牙買加人
Martinique *n.* 馬丁尼克島
interaction *n.* 互動
ginger *n.* 薑

# 調酒師的日誌 Bartender's Log Book ⑫

Curaçao is basically an orange liqueur, and it is not difficult to DIY. Combine 1/4 cup oranges zest, 1 tablespoon of dried bitter orange peel, 1 cup brandy, and 1 cup vodka in a small container. Seal and shake. Let it infuse for 19 days at room temperature. On day 20, add 4 whole cloves, then seal and shake. Let it infuse for an additional two days. Bring 2 cups sugar and 1 1/2 cups water in a small saucepan over high heat and stir to dissolve. Let the syrup cool. Strain out the alcohol liquid through a filter into a jar. Discard the zest and cloves. Mix the strained mixture with the syrup in a bottle. Shake and let it rest for a minimum of one day before use. Store in a sealed container at room temperature for up to three months. For a Blue Curaçao, add blue food coloring a few drops at a time until desired color is reached.

拉索島橙皮甜酒基本上是柑橘類的香甜酒，這個自己做其實不難。把 1/4 杯橙皮（新鮮的）、1 匙乾燥苦橙皮、1 杯白蘭地和 1 杯伏特加全部加在一個小密封容器。密封和搖盪。在室溫下浸泡 19 天。第 20 天時加入 4 個丁香，然後密封和搖晃再讓其浸泡兩天。另外把 2 杯糖加 1 杯半水在一個小鍋裡煮高火沸煮，攪拌溶解。讓糖漿冷卻。把浸泡後的酒過濾到瓶中後可以把橙皮和丁香丟棄。將過濾後的酒與糖漿混合並搖晃，讓所有材料融合後放置最少一天即可使用。在室溫下儲存在密封容器中可以長達三個月。如果要做藍色橙皮甜酒，加入幾滴藍色的食用色素，直到顏色看起來適量即可。

## Useful Sentences 好好用句型

We don't normally have many orders for that at one night.

我們通常一個晚上不會有很多人點這個。

🍒 Not many people order that at one night.

不會有很多人在一個晚上點這個。

🍒 Most of time, people don't order that very often.

大部份的人不會點這個。

🍒 Usually we don't have many orders for that.

通常我們沒有很多人點這個。

It also works very well with rum.

這個和蘭姆酒很配。

🍒 It goes well with rum, too.

這個和蘭姆酒很配。

🍒 It is very good with rum.

這個和蘭姆酒很配。

🍒 You can use it with rum instead.

你可以用蘭姆酒來替代。

🍒 It works together with rum.

這個和蘭姆酒很配。

## Mixology of the day　今日酒譜

# Anejo Highball
# 安蘭海波杯

Glassware: Chilled highball glass（冰鎮高球杯，海波為 highball 的譯音）
Method: Shake and stir（搖盪法和攪拌法）

**Ingredients 材料**

1 1/2 oz. Añejo rum 安蘭蘭姆酒
1/2 oz. orange curacao 柑橘香甜酒
1/2 oz. lime juice 萊姆汁
2 dashes Angostura bitters 兩滴苦精
2 oz. ginger beer 薑汁啤酒
1 orange wedge 柳橙角

*1 dash=1 ml=3-4 滴

**Instructions 作法**

Fill a cocktail shaker with ice. Add the rum, orange curacao, lime juice and bitters and shake well. Strain into an ice-filled highball glass. Next, add ginger beer, and give the mixture a good stir. Garnish with the orange wedge.

在雪克杯裡裝滿冰塊，注入蘭姆酒、柑橘香甜酒、萊姆汁和兩滴的苦精。均勻搖晃後過濾到冰鎮高球杯。接下來，加入薑汁啤酒並攪拌均勻。最後以萊姆角和柳橙角做裝飾。

## Notes　溫馨小提醒

所謂的海波杯（highball）又可稱是高球杯，是指在混合雞尾酒裡含有基本的酒精成分，再加上不含酒精成分的例如果汁所混合。這個名字的來由是因為這樣的混合雞尾酒通常是放在有高度的杯子，所以就演變成一種調酒的名詞。市面上有很多不同高度的高球酒杯，高球酒杯還是有一些的規則，要至少是 12 盎司，細口玻璃（這樣可以保留汽泡）。有名的長島冰茶，用的就是高球酒杯。

## Historical Background　調酒小故事

Añejo Rum 有很溫柔的中文翻譯名，叫安蘭蘭姆酒，安蘭蘭姆酒的特色是有豐富醇厚的口感和濃郁的香氣。這個名字是來自一個古老的西班牙語單詞，意思是「陳年過的」。陳年過的酒更顯出高雅品味。市面上的蘭姆酒幾乎都是在存放過威士忌或波本威士忌的橡木桶裡陳年，這樣的陳年時間從 1 到 30 年或是更久的時間都有。在陳年過程中，隨著時間長久，蘭姆酒慢慢從金色的變為深褐色。

# UNIT **2** Gin-based 琴酒

## 2.1
## Pink Lady 紅粉佳人

### 🍷 Dialogue in the Bar ▶ 吧台對話

**Emily is talking about the drink she had on Valentine's Day.** 🔊
艾米莉在談論有關她在情人節所喝的雞尾酒。

| | | |
|---|---|---|
| **Jenny**<br>(Bartender) | Did you and Jason go out for Valentine's Day? | 妳和傑森在情人節有出去嗎？ |
| **Emily** | We sure did. Guess what we had for the drink? The Pink Lady. | 當然有。妳猜我們點了什麼雞尾酒？紅粉佳人。 |
| **Jenny** | Wow, perfect choice. Who can resist the Pink Lady? It is retro and romantic. | 哇，這是很完美的選擇。誰可以抗拒紅粉佳人？這是一杯很復古和浪漫的雞尾酒。 |
| **Emily** | It was really gorgeous and elegant. It is beautiful. I love the lovely color. It was very refreshing, but I had to sip very slowly to enjoy it. | 那是很華麗也很典雅。真的很美。我很喜歡那個優雅的顏色。感覺也很清新，但需要慢慢啜飲來享受那個味道。 |

**Jane**

I heard about this drink long time ago, but did not have any chance to try it until last year in my company's New Year's party. My colleague recommended I order a Pink Lady. It was impressive and gorgeous. Later, I was surprised to find out there are egg whites in the drink. I chatted a little with the bartender there, he said that egg whites don't really add flavor to the drink, but they give a frothy head that's quite attractive. Luckily, I am not allergic to eggs. The bartender said he could also use heavy cream instead.

我很久以前有聽說過這種飲料，但一直沒有任何機會喝，直到去年在公司的新年晚會才喝到。我的同事推薦我點紅粉佳人。確實是令人印象深刻也很華麗。後來我很驚訝地發現雞尾酒裡有蛋白。我當時和那時工作的調酒師聊了一點，他說，蛋白在雞尾酒裡其實沒有添加味道但是那個泡沫看起來相當有吸引力的。幸運的是，我對雞蛋沒有過敏。調酒師說，鮮奶油可以代替蛋白。

**Jenny**

Egg whites are interesting in drinks. You'll find egg whites in some other sours too, like the Whiskey Sour. If you are allergic to eggs, it is okay to leave them out.

在雞尾酒裡蛋白這個材料是很特別。其他有一些雞尾酒也有蛋白，像威士忌酸酒。如果妳對雞蛋過敏，沒有加蛋是沒有關係的。

---

## Ｙ Vocabulary 單字

romantic *adj.* 浪漫的

slowly *adv.* 慢慢地

attractive *adj.* 吸引人的

gorgeous *adj.* 華麗的

impressive *adj.* 令人印象深刻的

instead *adv.* 作為替代地

Egg whites and grenadine are the two special ingredients in this frothy, pink, sour, and sweet Pink Lady. Be careful with eggs. There are always risks to make food or drinks with raw eggs. Few things can be done to ensure the freshest and safest eggs for drinks. Buy eggs out of refrigerated cases only. Choose eggs with no cracks or damaged shells. Buy pasteurized eggs because the pasteurization should have killed any bacteria in the egg. As soon as brought home from the store, refrigerate the raw eggs right away. Store eggs in the coldest part of the refrigerator where the temperature is 7 degrees Celsius or lower. Do not store eggs in the door which is the hottest part of the refrigerator. Also, keep the eggs in the original carton. If one prefers no egg whites in the Pink Lady, it is okay to leave it out. The egg white does not really affect the flavor of the drink, but does give it a luxuriously frothy texture.

酸甜的紅粉佳人裡有豐富的泡沫和粉紅的顏色是因為加了蛋清和紅石榴糖漿的成分。使用雞蛋要小心。用生雞蛋來做吃的或是喝的總是有風險。對於雞尾酒裡的生雞蛋有幾件事情可以做到以保證最新鮮和最安全。只買有冷藏的雞蛋。要選雞蛋蛋殼外沒有裂紋或破損。要買殺菌雞蛋，因為殺菌雞蛋可以殺死雞蛋裡任何細菌。從商店買後就應該馬上回家放在冰箱裡。雞蛋要在冰箱裡溫度低於 7 攝氏或更低的地方。不要把雞蛋放在冰箱的門，這是冰箱的最熱的部分。此外，要把雞蛋放在原始的雞蛋紙盒保持新鮮。如果有客人不喜歡紅粉佳人裡的蛋清，也沒關係，這是可以省略的。蛋清並沒有真正影響雞尾酒的味道，只是讓紅粉佳人雞尾酒有豪華的泡沫質感。

## 🖥 **Useful Sentences** ▶ 好好用句型

Perfect choice.

完美的選擇。

🎻 Good choice. 好的選擇。

🎻 Excellent choice. 很棒的選擇。

🎻 Smart choice. 聰明的選擇。

🎻 Great choice. 對的選擇。

🎻 Wonderful choice. 很棒的選擇。

〈choice〉：名詞；選擇，抉擇，同義字有 selection, preference, pick, decision.

It is okay to leave it out.

沒有放沒有關係。

🎻 You don't have to have it. 你不一定要放。

🎻 You can omit it. 可以不要放。

🎻 You can take it out. 你可以把它拿掉。

〈leave〉動詞，離開，保留，不少有關〈leave〉口語的動詞片語都很好用：

• leave it as it is 就照原狀

I don't mind. Please just leave it as it is.

我無所謂，就請照原狀。

• leave it at that 就這樣算了

Just leave it at that. Someone will take care of it later.

就這樣就可以，等一下會有人來處理。

• leave it out 算了吧，不用，沒有關係

I like my coffee black. Please leave the sugar out.

我喜歡原味的咖啡，請不要加糖。

## 🍷 Mixology of the day ▶ 今日酒譜

# Pink Lady
# 紅粉佳人

Glassware: Cocktail glass（雞尾酒杯）
Method: Dry Shake then shake（乾式搖盪法加搖盪法）

**Ingredients 材料**
1 1/2 oz gin 琴酒
1 oz apple brandy 蘋果白蘭地
1/2 oz freshly squeezed lemon juice 新鮮檸檬汁
1/3 oz syrup 糖漿
1 dash grenadine 紅石榴糖漿
1/2 egg white, preferably pasteurized 一顆蛋蛋白，最好是殺菌過的蛋
Maraschino cherry for garnish 裝飾用酒漬櫻桃
Ice 冰

**Instructions 作法**
Add all ingredients (except garnish) to a cocktail shaker with no ice (dry shake). Shake really hard so the egg white will foam and has as much volume as possible, at least 30 seconds. Once foamy and voluminous, add ice (regular shake) to the shaker until it's half full. Shake vigorously about 20 seconds. Strain the contents of the shaker into a cocktail glass. Garnish with a maraschino cherry.
除了裝飾材料外，把所有材料放入雪克杯，但不要放冰，這種方式就是乾式搖盪法，大力搖盪讓蛋白可以發泡也有足夠多的量，至少要搖 30 秒。一旦蛋白發泡後，加入雪克杯一半的冰（加冰後就是一般搖盪法）。大力搖盪直到雪克杯內材料是冰涼的，約 20 秒，之後把材料過篩到雞尾酒杯。用酒漬櫻桃裝飾。

## Notes　溫馨小提醒

所謂的乾式搖盪法就是要沒有放冰塊的大力的搖盪，有加蛋白的材料，需要很大力搖盪至少 30 秒，讓蛋白發泡同時也和其他材料完全融合喝不出蛋白的味道。所謂的搖盪出力，是要搖到手臂有感覺到痠痛。

## Historical Background　調酒小故事

沒有人知道紅粉佳人的真正起源。美國在 1920 年至 1933 年有全國性憲法禁令禁止在美國銷售、生產、進口、運輸酒精飲料，主要目的是要減少飲酒問題的產生。當時美國社會對美國人的飲酒行為問題感到震驚，導致美國憲法第十八修正案取消發許可證給啤酒製造商、釀酒商、葡萄酒商和酒精飲料的批發和零售賣家。紅粉佳人在那期間反而受到很多人的歡迎，主要是在禁酒時期，琴酒的品質不是很好，所以有必要添加額外的風味，以補償杜劣等琴酒的不良味道。

一般據信，Pink Lady 的起源是為了獻給在 1911 年時曾紅極一時的百老匯歌舞劇 "The Pink Lady" 的女主角 Hazel Dawn。這一種調酒在此劇落幕之後，經過第一次世界大戰，一直到了美國 1920 至 1933 年之間的禁酒期間，卻愈來愈受歡迎。因為在禁酒時期的琴酒品質不好，而 Pink Lady 中加有紅石榴糖漿及奶油，能掩蓋劣等琴酒的味道。

## 2.2
# **Singapore Sling** 新加坡司令

🍷 **Dialogue in the Bar** 吧台對話

**Charlie is talking about his experience in Singapore.** ⑮
查理在述說在新加坡的經驗。

| | | |
|---|---|---|
| **Charlie** | I don't really drink alcohol, but I had a chance to try a Singapore Sling last month while I stayed in Singapore for a conference. | 我其實是不喝酒的，但我上個月在新加坡開會時有機會喝到新加坡司令。 |
| **John** (Bartender) | It is a great place. I visited Singapore a couple of times before. | 那是很棒的地方。我去過新加坡好幾次。 |
| **Charlie** | We had the conference at Raffles Hotel. At the end of the day, we had dinner there. My colleague recommended that I try a Singapore Sling, 'cause it's the drink of the country. So we went to the Long Bar, the place where a Chinese bartender invented the Singapore Sling in 1951. | 我們的會議是在萊佛士酒店。那天會議結束後，我們就在那裡吃晚餐。我的同事說，我一定要試試看新加坡司令。那是他們的國酒。我們就在長吧吃晚餐，據說在 1951 年時，一位華裔的調酒師就是在長吧發明新加坡司令。 |

| John | Raffles Hotel is very famous. If you don't visit the hotel, you can't say you've visited Singapore. There's also a shopping center inside the hotel. I really love the tradition at the Long Bar that the littering is encouraged, and everyone can just brush the peanut shells onto the floor. | 萊佛士酒店是非常有名的。如果沒有去這家酒店，不算去過新加坡。在酒店裡還有一個購物中心。我愛死了長吧那個可以邊吃邊丟的傳統，每個人可以就這樣將花生殼都撥到地上。 |
|---|---|---|
| Charlie | So do I. The bartender there told us that they sell more than two thousand Singapore Slings every day. | 我也是。調酒師有告訴我們，他們每天賣的新加坡司令有超過 2000 杯。 |
| John | The sweet sour and other tropical flavors make the Singapore Sling very popular. | 新加坡司令的甜酸味和其他熱帶風味加起來的味道很受歡迎。 |
| Charlie | You are right. I tasted pineapple in the drink and I love it. | 沒錯。我有喝到鳳梨的味道，我很喜歡這個味道。 |

## Vocabulary 單字

conference *n.* 會議
famous *adj.* 有名的
tropical *adj.* 熱帶的

great *adj.* 很棒的
thousand *n.* 千位
popular *adj.* 受歡迎的

Triple sec is a clear, strong, and sweet orange flavored liqueur. DIY triple sec can make many drink recipes taste better. There are popular drinks with triple sec, such as the Cosmopolitan, Margarita, Hurricane, Mai Tai, Singapore Sling and many more. So it is worth it to make DIY triple sec. Place the rind of 3 oranges and rind of 3 lemons (not the white part) into a glass jar and fill it with 24 oz. vodka. Secure the lid tightly. Let the vodka and rinds sit for at least 4 days in a cool place to infuse. When the infusion is complete, pour 2 cups sugar and 2 cups water into a saucepan and bring it to a boil, reduce to a simmer and cook until slightly thickened. Remove from the heat and let cool completely. Pour the syrup in a glass jar. Strain all liquid ingredients through a fine strainer into the jar to combine it with the syrup. Seal with the lid. Shake for 30 seconds. Bottle it up and it keeps in the refrigerater for about a month.

橙味利口酒是一個濃度高，清澈和甜甜有柑橘味的利口酒。自己做的橙味利口酒可以讓雞尾酒喝起來口感更好。有很多雞尾酒都有加橙味利口酒，如柯夢波丹、瑪格麗塔、颶風、邁泰、新加坡司令等等。所以值得 DIY 橙味利口酒。作法是將 3 個橙子皮和 3 個檸檬皮（不包含白色部分）放入一個玻璃瓶後倒 24 盎士伏特加。緊緊地蓋好蓋子。讓伏特加和皮在陰涼處浸泡至少 4 天。當浸泡完畢後，另外在鍋中倒入 2 杯糖和 2 杯水，煮沸後降火再慢慢熬煮到有糖漿濃度。熄火後等到完全冷卻。把糖漿倒入一個廣口玻璃瓶，再用過濾的方式把橙子皮和檸檬皮伏特加的浸泡液過濾到有糖漿的玻璃瓶。密封。搖動 30 秒。裝瓶後可以冷藏約一個月。

## Useful Sentences 好好用句型

It is a great place.

很棒的地方。

🚲 It's a wonderful place.

很棒的地方。

🚲 It's exceptional.

非常特別。

🚲 It's extraordinary.

非常特別。

I love it.

我很喜歡。

🚲 It appeals to me.

這很吸引我。

🚲 It's a good idea.

這是好主意。

🚲 I'm fond of it.

我很喜歡。

🚲 I'm crazy about it.

我非常喜歡它。

🚲 I just can't get enough of it.

給我再多也不夠。

# Mixology of the day ▶ 今日酒譜

# Singapore Sling
# 新加坡司令

Glassware: Chilled Collins glass（冰鎮可林杯）
Method: Shake（搖盪法）

## Ingredients 材料

1 1/2 oz dry gin 琴酒
1/2 oz cherry liqueur 櫻桃香甜酒
1/4 oz Cointreau liqueur 君度橙酒
1/4 oz Bénédictine 班尼狄克丁藥草酒
4 oz pineapple juice 鳳梨汁
1/2 oz lime juice 萊姆汁
1/3 oz grenadine 紅石榴糖漿
1 dash Angostura bitters 安格斯特拉苦精數滴（**1dash** 約等於 **3-4** 滴）
1 slice of pineapple and cherry 鳳梨片和櫻桃

## Instructions 作法

Combine all ingredients in a shaker. Shake well then strain into a chilled Collins. Garnish with pineapple slice and cherry.
將所有材料倒入雪克杯加滿冰塊，均勻搖盪，在過濾冰塊後倒入冰鎮可林杯，用鳳梨片和櫻桃裝飾。

## Notes 溫馨小提醒

新加坡司令的酒譜可以有很多變化，不過基本上是保留琴酒做為基酒，然後以手邊可用的食材或根據酒客的口味，加入各種不同的熱帶水果果汁做調味，整體口味是偏酸甜，顏色也很鮮豔，也用水果切片做裝飾，但不要太誇張，不要做出好看但不好喝的新加坡司令。

## Historical Background 調酒小故事

新加坡最著名的調酒便是新加坡司令 "Singapore Sling"，這杯調酒是由華裔的海南人嚴崇文（**Ngiam Tong Boon**）所發明，約在1910～1915年間所發明，當時他正在萊佛士酒店（**Raffles Hotel**）工作。新加坡司令這個名字很有趣，雖然本意確實是「新加坡的司令」，但是英文名稱卻是直譯 "Singapore Sling"，此調酒誕生的故事其實很單純的，當時有一個顧客喝膩了琴通寧（**Gin Tonic**），要求喝點不一樣的，調酒師就變出了這個新加坡司令，後來就成為新加坡的國酒。如果搭乘新加坡航空，無論什麼艙等都可以免費點「新加坡司令」（但都是預先調好的）。

## 2.3
# Alexander Cocktail 亞歷山大雞尾酒

### 🍷 Dialogue in the Bar ▶ 吧台對話

**New server Amy is chatting with Jenny,** 🄗
**who is getting the bar ready.**
新來的服務生艾米跟正在做準備工作的珍妮聊天。

| | | |
|---|---|---|
| **Amy** | When I first tried Alexander Cocktail, it was at a friend's wedding. All my girlfriends at the wedding loved it. The taste is unlike any cocktail I have ever had. Is it hard to make it? | 我第一次喝到亞歷山大雞尾酒是在一個朋友的婚禮。在婚禮上，所有的女性朋友都很喜歡此款雞尾酒。味道喝起都不像我以前喝過任何的雞尾酒。此款雞尾酒很難做嗎？ |
| **Jenny** (Bartender) | It is what we called a "dessert cocktail". It is actually a quite basic mixology. The main ingredients are gin, chocolate liqueur, and cream. The goal for this drink is to effectively combine the dense cream with the other ingredients, and all you need to do is to shake it long enough. | 這是一種我們所說的「甜點雞尾酒」。這其實是一個很基本的調酒。其主要成分是琴酒、巧克力甜酒和奶油。做這杯雞尾酒的目標是要有效地把濃濃奶油與其他配料完全的結合起來，所需要的技巧就是要搖盪足夠長的時間。 |

| | | |
|---|---|---|
| **Amy** | So, it is not hard to make? | 那麼，這不是很難做嗎？ |
| **Jenny** | No, not really. The original Alexander Cocktail was made with Gin, but now the common variation of the Alexander is the Brandy Alexander. Is that what you had at the wedding? | 真的不是很難。亞歷山大雞尾酒的原始酒譜是用琴酒做的，但是現在一般受歡迎的是白蘭地亞歷山大。妳在婚禮上喝的是白蘭地亞歷山大嗎？ |
| **Amy** | Probably. I am not sure. I don't really know much about liquors. I had it again last week at a friend's house. It was a cold night and the drink seemed perfect. | 也許吧。我不知道。我對酒真的不知道很多。我上週在朋友的家也有喝到。那天很冷，所以那杯雞尾酒喝起來感覺很對。 |
| **Jenny** | That's true. Cold weather is the perfect time for a rich drink like the Brandy Alexander. There are other variations including the Coffee Alexander, which replaces the gin with coffee liqueur, and the Blue Alexander, which uses blue curacao instead of the crème de cocoa. | 這是真的。像白蘭地亞歷山大這種雞尾酒在寒冷的天氣是一個完美的選擇。還有其他的作法，包括咖啡亞歷山大，這是用咖啡利口酒和琴酒做的，另外一款是藍色亞歷山大，這是用藍色柑香酒取代咖啡利口酒做的。 |

**Unit 2**
Gin-based

 **Vocabulary** 單字

| | | | |
|---|---|---|---|
| effectively | *adv.* 有效的 | really | *adv.* 真的 |
| common | *n.* 普通的 | variation | *n.* 變化的 |
| weather | *n.* 天氣 | | |

A golden rule for Alexander cocktail ratio is 1:1:1 for a base liquor, liqueur and cream. If using cream, make sure to use real cream, not half-and-half cream. The original recipe for the Alexander cocktail is made with gin, but a Brandy Alexander is also common. Another variation is a Coffee Alexander in which cream is replaced with crème de cacao. Third one is the Blue Alexander where Blue Curacao is used in place of gin. There are many other variations of this cocktail. If served over crushed ice, the Brandy Alexander becomes a frappé which is similar to a milkshake. Vanilla ice cream can be used instead of heavy cream for a Brandy Alexander. One variation is Alexander's Sister, which has gin, heavy cream and sweet and mint-flavored crème de menthe (instead of creme de cacao). Crème de menthe is usually made from Corsican mint. Volare Alexander is made from 1 oz. Volare crème de cacao, 1 oz. cognac and 1 oz. light cream, and served in a chilled cocktail glass garnished with chocolate powder.

亞歷山大雞尾酒的黃金比例是 1：1：1 的基酒、利口酒和鮮奶油。使用的鮮奶油，務必使用真正的鮮奶油，而不是半鮮奶油（一半鮮奶油和一半牛奶，含脂量 10-12％，無法打發）。亞歷山大雞尾酒的原始酒譜是用琴酒，但白蘭地亞歷山大也很常見。另一個變化是咖啡亞歷山大，這是用可可酒替換奶油。第三個是藍色亞歷山大，基酒用的是藍色柑香酒取代琴酒。這種雞尾酒還有許多其它變型。如果雞尾酒上面加碎冰，白蘭地亞歷山大基本上就變成了像奶昔的冰咖啡。香草冰淇淋可以代替鮮奶油，就成了白蘭地亞歷山大。其中一個變化是亞歷山大姐妹，這是用白蘭地和鮮奶油，但是用薄荷酒代替利口酒，這是一個甜甜有薄荷味的雞尾酒。這個薄荷酒主要是科西嘉島薄荷所做的。Volare 可可酒也可以用來做亞歷山大雞尾酒，用 1 盎士 Volare 可可酒、1 盎士干邑白蘭地和 1 盎士淡奶油，飲用時上面加可可粉。

## Useful Sentences 好好用句型

Is it hard to make it?

很困難做嗎？

🍒 Is it not easy to make it?

不簡單做嗎？

🍒 Is it difficult to make it?

很難做嗎？

🍒 Is it complicated to make?

很複雜做嗎？

🍒 Is it challenging to make?

很有挑戰性嗎？

I am not sure.

我不確定。

🍒 Maybe.

或許。

🍒 Perhaps.

可能。

🍒 I am not certain.

我不確定。

🍒 It depends.

看狀況。

# Alexander Cocktail
# 亞歷山大雞尾酒

Glassware: Cocktail glass（雞尾酒杯）
Method: Shake and strain（搖盪法加過濾法）

## Ingredients 材料

1 oz. gin 琴酒
1 oz. white crème de cacao 白可可香甜酒
1 oz. light cream 鮮奶油
Ice 冰
nutmeg 豆蔻粉

## Instructions 作法

Add all ingredients (except nutmeg) with ice in a mixing cup. Shake well and strain into a cocktail glass. Sprinkle nutmeg on top and serve. The cream can be substituted with milk or even ice cream to make an after meal treat.

把所有的材料（除了豆蔻粉外）和冰加入雪克杯。均勻搖盪然後再過篩到雞尾酒杯，把豆蔻粉灑在上面即可。鮮奶油可以用牛奶來替代，甚至可以加冰淇淋成為飯後甜點。

## 🍸 Notes 溫馨小提醒

有許多加奶製品的飲料會加荳蔻粉，荳蔻粉有去腥的作用，通常都會撒一點，或加一點混合，但是荳蔻粉還可以減少脹氣，助消化，舒緩焦慮，也能淨化體內有害細菌。如果飲料中加的是奶油球或一般牛奶，奶味比較不重，可以省略荳蔻粉。

## Historical Background 調酒小故事

真正第一杯亞歷山大雞尾酒是特洛伊·亞歷山大（Troy Alexander），在 1915 年慶祝一個虛構卡通人物的創建所調製出來的雞尾酒，他就以自己的名字命名這個雞尾酒，當初用的基酒是琴酒。後來在 1922 年的皇家婚禮有調製亞歷山大雞尾酒，但是所用的基酒是白蘭地而不是琴酒，但是後來成為流行的是以白蘭地調製的亞歷山大雞尾酒（the Brandy Alexander）。

# UNIT 2 Gin-based 琴酒

## 2.4
# Around the World 環遊世界

### 🍷 Dialogue in the Bar ▸ 吧台對話

**Bartender John and Jenny are talking about** 🔊19 **how to make Crème de Menthe with customer.**
調酒師約翰和珍妮跟客人正在談論如何做薄荷酒。

| | | |
|---|---|---|
| **Jimmy** | Around the World cocktail not only has a strange name, but it really does not taste very good. I think it has Gin in it. | 環遊世界的雞尾酒不僅有奇怪的名字，而且味道喝起來也沒有那麼好。我覺得裡面有加琴酒。 |
| **John** (Bartender) | The original recipe has Gin, Crème de Menthe (green), and pineapple juice. Many people don't like the taste of Crème de Menthe (green) and pineapple juice mixed together. | 環遊世界的原始酒譜是琴酒、綠薄荷酒和鳳梨汁。很多人不喜歡綠薄荷酒和鳳梨汁的搭配。 |
| **Jimmy** | I heard it is not popular in Taiwan. | 我聽說這款雞尾酒在台灣不是很受歡迎。 |
| **John** | You are right. Most bartenders in Taiwan think that Around the World cocktail is just a mix of different liquors. | 你說得對。大多數在台灣的調酒師認為環遊世界的雞尾酒只是混合大量基酒在一起。 |

| | | |
|---|---|---|
| **Jimmy** | Where does the green color come from? | 這杯雞尾酒裡的綠色是從何而來？ |
| **John** | It is the Crème de Menthe, which is a sweet mint-flavored liqueur. | 那是綠薄荷酒，是種甜甜薄荷味的甜酒。 |
| **Jenny** (Bartender) | Have you ever tried to make homemade Crème de Menthe? It tastes and smells like fresh mint. It is definitely better than the commercial one, and it's totally simple to make. Since it's made with real mint, the liqueur is a greenish-yellow. You can add food coloring if you'd like it to be greener. | 你有沒有自己嘗試做過薄荷酒？味道和氣味很像新鮮的薄荷。絕對比市面上買的還要好，而且非常容易的做。因為是用真正的薄荷做的，所以這個薄荷酒利口酒是黃綠色的。如果想要看起來更綠，可以添加食用色素。 |
| **Jimmy** | What's the base liquor? | 這是用什麼是基酒做的呢？ |
| **Jenny** | Vodka. It is just vodka, fresh mint leaves, sugar, and water. | 伏特加。只是伏特加，加新鮮的薄荷葉，糖和水。 |

## Vocabulary 單字

taste  *n.*  味覺

flavored  *adj.*  味道

homemade  *adj.*  自製的、家裡做的

mint  *n.*  薄荷

build  v.  注入（調酒中的注入方式，將酒經酒嘴直接倒入杯中）

There are several methods of making the Around the World cocktail: shake and strain, build, or blend. Building a cocktail is adding one ingredient after the other directly into the glass and no shaking or straining is necessary. Building is a quick and easy way to make cocktails. Built drinks are often long drinks that are served in a Highball or Collins glass. It normally has only a few ingredients that will mix together easily. Start by adding the non-alcoholic ingredients (lemon or lime juice, syrups etc.) to the glass first. Once the non-alcoholic ingredients are in the glass, it's time to add the spirits and liqueurs. Always use a measure to be correct with the amount. Then it's time to add ice. For most drinks in Highball or Collins glasses, as much ice as possible should added to slow down the dilution and also stop from adding to much mixer such as soda, coke, or fruit juices.

環遊世界雞尾酒的作法有幾種：搖盪和過濾法、注入法或電動攪拌機法。雞尾酒的注入法就是把材料分次的直接倒入玻璃杯中，過程無需搖盪和過濾。這是做雞尾酒最快速和簡便的方法。使用注入法調製的雞尾酒往往是使用較大的杯子，例如高球杯或是可林杯，並且只有一些很容易混合在一起的成分。首先倒入杯裡的是非酒精成分的材料（檸檬或酸橙果汁，糖漿等）。一旦非酒精成分倒完後，就倒入烈酒和甜酒。一定要用量杯以確保正確的量。再來是加冰塊的時候。要注意的是，對於高球杯或可林杯來說，冰塊應添加到盡可能最滿，這樣會減慢稀釋的速度，也可以避免加入太多的蘇打水、可樂或果汁。

## Useful Sentences　好好用句型

It really does not taste that good.

這個吃起來沒有那麼好吃。

&#x1F6B2; The taste is awful.

　　吃起來很難吃。

&#x1F6B2; I hate that taste.

　　我很不喜歡那個味道。

&#x1F6B2; It really tastes bad.

　　吃起來真的很難吃。

&#x1F6B2; The taste is bad.

　　味道很不好。

〈taste〉可當名詞，可當動詞。

• Do you want to have a taste of this dessert?

　　你要嚐嚐看這個甜點嗎？〈taste〉在這裡是當名詞。

• Do you want to taste this dessert?

　　你要嚐嚐看這個甜點嗎？〈taste〉在這裡是當動詞。

Have you ever tried to make homemade crème de menthe?

你有沒有試過自己做薄荷酒呢？

&#x1F6B2; Have you thought about making homemade crème de menthe?

　　你有沒有想過自己做薄荷酒呢？

&#x1F6B2; Have you ever considered about making homemade crème de menthe?

　　你有沒有想過自己做薄荷酒呢？

&#x1F6B2; Do you think you would like to make crème de menthe?

　　你有沒有想要做薄荷酒呢？

**Mixology of the day** ▶ 今日酒譜

## Around the World
## 環遊世界

Glassware: Cocktail glass（雞尾酒杯）
Method: Shake（搖盪法）

### Ingredients 材料
40ml Gin 琴酒
10ml Crème de menthe (green) 綠薄荷酒
10ml Pineapple juice 鳳梨汁
Ice 冰塊

### Instructions 作法
Fill the shaker with ice, and pour in Gin, pineapple juice and crème de menthe. Cover and shake, until the outside of the shaker is frosty, and strain into cocktail glass, and serve. Warning, this is the original recipe of Around the World, and it's what we called short drink cocktail. However, in Taiwan, we prefer to make Around the World with several different kinds of liquors.

將雪克杯中裝滿冰塊，倒入琴酒、鳳梨汁和綠薄荷酒。蓋上並搖盪雪克杯，直到雪克杯外層呈霜狀，過濾倒入雞尾酒杯中。警告，這是原始的環遊世界配方，是一般所稱的短飲型雞尾酒。然而在台灣，我們較喜歡在「環遊世界」中加入好幾種的酒。

## Notes 溫馨小提醒

常見的環遊世界有三層漸層的顏色，伏特加、琴酒、龍舌蘭、蘭姆酒、柑橙酒、威士忌這六款酒都可以用來調製環遊世界，這是酒精濃度偏高的雞尾酒，一杯之後可能獲得天旋地轉的快感，就有如環遊世界一般。豪華版的還會增加視覺特效會在杯中點上火，但是為了安全起見，大部份還是以果雕來裝飾。

## Historical Background 調酒小故事

世界上賣的最好的琴酒是菲律賓的 Ginebra San Miguel。在菲律賓以外的大多數人從來沒有聽說過，是因為 Ginebra San Miguel 最大的市場是在菲律賓，而這也是世界知名的生力啤酒的姊妹產品，同屬於 San Miguel Corporation（生力集團）。該琴酒在全世界的佔有率有 46%，在菲律賓的市場佔有率則高於 60%。生力酒廠是西班牙人於 1834 年在菲律賓建立的東南亞地區最早的一家啤酒廠。目前生力啤酒是菲律賓第一大啤酒廠。

## 2.5
# Gin Tonic 琴通寧

### 🍷 Dialogue in the Bar ▶ 吧台對話

**Bartender John and Jenny are talking about** ㉑
**techniques for making a Gin and Tonic.**
調酒師約翰和珍妮在談論做琴通寧的技巧。

| | |
|---|---|
| **John** | Gin and Tonic is really a no brainer. There are only two ingredients. Sometimes, little tricks can make a big difference. For example, I always wash my ice. Do you? |
| **Jenny** | I do too. That's one of first techniques I learned about ice. Ice from the home freezer has a smell, so washing ice is a must. But mostly, after the ice is washed, the edges of the ice can be more smooth which can slow down the melting speed. |

琴通寧真的很容易做。這款雞尾酒只有兩種材料。但是有時候，小技巧也會讓容易做的東西有很不同的口感。例如，我都會先洗冰。妳呢？

我也會。這是我第一次學有關冰時所學到的技巧。家裡冰箱的冰有異味所以一定要先洗。但大致而言，洗冰之後，稜角會被去掉，融化速度會稍慢。

| John | You are right. Also, from my experience, "washed" ice makes a carbonated drink lose less bubbles. | 你説的沒錯。還有，我的經驗告訴我，洗過的冰可以讓碳酸飲料留住較多的氣泡。 |
| Jenny | Tonic water also has to be cold too. | 通寧水也一定要用冰過的。 |
| John | Another common technique is to pour the tonic water close to the edge of the glass, very close to the top of the ice so it can reduce bubble loss as well. This is called "pouring it down along the edge of the cup". | 另一種常見的方法是沿著杯壁倒入冰過的通寧水可以減少泡沫的損失。這種倒酒法有人稱為「杯壁下流」。 |
| Jenny | No matter how easy the drink is to make, there is always a little technique to make one drink better than the others do. | 不管雞尾酒是多麼容易做，一點點技術的使用，總會讓做出來的雞尾酒比別人做得好喝。 |

 **Vocabulary** 單字

freezer   *n.*   冰庫
mostly   *adv.*   大致上
carbonated   *adj.*   有汽泡的，含二氧化碳的
less   *adj.*   較小的，較少的
bubbles   *n.*   汽泡
pour   *vt.*   倒入

Some brands of tonic water are more expensive than others. An expensive one does not mean better, at least when mix with gin. Some brands have complex citrus and herbal flavors and some brands don't. Tonic water should be bitter or even a little aggressive. The bitterness should be balanced by sweetness. Canada Dry and Schweppes are common brands that can be found in regular retailer stores. Canada Dry is not an expensive brand, but it has enough bitterness and good citric flavor to offset the sweetness. Some think the Canada Dry's lemony flavor is artificial. In general, Canada Dry is refreshing, and it is sweet with smooth bitterness on the drink. It also is vigorously carbonated. Schweppes is also not highly priced. Many think Schweppes lacks complexity, and it is too sweet when mix with gin. It is more like a Sprite soda. Still, some found it bittersweet and refreshing, with good carbonation and clear quinine and citrus flavor.

有一些通寧汽水的價格比其他品牌的貴。昂貴的通寧汽水並不意味是比較好，至少是指在與琴酒做調酒時。有些品牌帶有多重的柑橘和香草口味，而有些沒有。奎寧水應該是苦的，甚至有點嗆的味道。這樣的苦味應該由細膩甜味來平衡。加拿大通寧汽水和舒味思通寧汽水是一般大買場可以買到的品牌。加拿大通寧汽水不是一個價格高的品牌，但它有足夠的辛酸和檸檬酸味可以平衡甜味。但是有人會覺得品牌的檸檬味太假。由加拿大通寧汽水所做的琴通寧喝起來很清爽，甜甜的也有點酸。而且碳酸氣很足夠。比較起來，舒味思通寧汽水缺少多重性，而且太甜。用這個品牌做的通寧汽水比較像是雪碧汽水。但是還是有人覺得舒味思通寧汽水苦甜各半，也很爽口，有良好的碳酸氣，也有很清晰的奎寧和柑橘的味道。

## 🔲 **Useful Sentences** ▶ 好好用句型

I always wash my ice.

我都會先洗我的冰。

🍒 I wash my ice all the time.

　我常常會先洗我的冰。

🍒 I wash my ice every time.

　我每次都會先洗我的冰。

🍒 I am used to washing my ice.

　我有習慣先洗我的冰。

**always** 副詞〈總是，經常；一直〉，形容動詞的動作。

• I wash my ice.

　我會洗一下冰。

• I always wash my ice.

　我都會先洗一下冰。

• I always wash my ice when I make cocktails.

　如果我在做雞尾酒時，我都會先洗冰。

I do too.

我也是。

🍒 Me too.

　我也是。

🍒 I am the same way.

　我也是那樣的。

🍒 So am I.

　我也是。

🍒 Same here.

　我也是。

🍒 Myself as well.

　我自己也是。

# Mixology of the day ▶ 今日酒譜

## Gin Tonic
## 琴通寧

Glassware: Chilled highball glass（冰鎮高球杯）
Method: Stir（攪拌法）

### Ingredients 材料
3 oz. gin 琴酒
4 oz. tonic water 通寧水
Ice cube 冰塊
Freshly squeezed lime juice 新鮮萊姆汁
1 lime wedge 萊姆角

### Instructions 作法
Place the ice cubes in a chilled Highball glass. The ice should come near the top of the glass. Add the gin first, then the tonic water second, then the lime juice last. Stir well. Garnish with lime wedge, and serve. Try tonic water ice cubes; simply fill an empty ice cube tray with tonic water. After freeze, it is tonic water ice cubes.

把冰塊放入冰鎮高球杯。冰塊應該放到接近玻璃的上面。加入琴酒、通寧水，然後萊姆汁，攪拌均勻。用萊姆角裝飾，即可供應。可以試試不一樣的冰塊，將通寧水倒入冰盤，結冰後就是通寧水冰塊。

## Notes 溫馨小提醒

琴通寧很夏天,很像汽水,喝起來都可以感受到整個夏天沁涼的氣氛!黃瓜是夏天的蔬菜,琴酒製作時就有黃瓜萃取物,所以做琴通寧時可以切 1/4 條的小黃瓜,黃瓜條放入杯中後,琴酒倒入杯中同時可以沖刷黃瓜條,將清新的味道帶入酒中,黃瓜條還可以在杯內當攪拌棒,清透有汽泡的琴通寧,加上淡淡綠色的黃瓜條,視覺味覺都滿分!

## Historical Background 調酒小故事

琴酒據說是由荷蘭人在 16 世紀發明的,最初是作為處方藥物治療,認為可以促進血液循環。琴酒後來傳到了英國,在英國的製作成本較低,也漸漸成為首選飲品。英國皇家在 1857 年時接管治理印度,之後就有更多的英國人開始去印度。然而,早期的移民對熱帶氣候的瘧疾感到非常困擾。早期的通寧水含有很高量的奎寧,奎寧是從南美金雞納樹皮(South American cinchona tree)萃取的。這種樹皮能阻止寒顫,可以治療和預防瘧疾。那時的通寧水是非常苦澀。英國人很快發現,通寧水加了琴酒、糖、冰和柑橘就可以減輕通寧水的苦味,這樣的喝法不止可以治癒、治療和預防瘧疾,加了萊姆汁後也可以治療漫長海上旅途造成的壞血病,因此琴通寧也成了英國大帝擴展殖民主義(Britain's colonialism)成功的一個重要功臣。

# UNIT **2** Gin-based 琴酒

## 2.6
## Martini 馬丁尼

🍷 **Dialogue in the Bar** 吧台對話

**Carol is asking the ingredients used in a Martini.** (23)
卡羅在問有關馬丁尼的成分。

| | | |
|---|---|---|
| **Carol** | Is a Martini made with vodka or gin? | 馬丁尼是用伏特加或琴酒做的？ |
| **John:** | Nowadays, when someone orders a Martini in a bar, it is usually house vodka with dry vermouth and garnished with green olive or a lemon twist. House vodka is a common brand of vodka that bars use, but it can be any vodka. | 一般當我們向調酒師點杯馬丁尼，通常就是特種品牌的伏特加加香艾酒然後用綠橄欖或螺旋形檸檬皮裝飾。每個吧台會自己選定特種品牌的伏特加來當基酒，因此可以是任何品牌的伏特加。 |
| **Carol** | I was told Martinis are made with gin. | 有人告訴過我馬丁尼是以琴酒為基酒的。 |

| | | |
|---|---|---|
| **John** | You are right. The original Martini is made with gin and the method of making the cocktail is to stir, not shake. Martini is James Bond's favorite drink. In the movie, when he orders a Martini, he would say, "Shaken, not stirred." | 是沒錯，原始的馬丁尼酒譜是以琴酒為基酒，並以攪拌的方式調製而非現今的搖盪。馬丁尼是 007 詹姆斯·龐德最喜歡的雞尾酒。在電影裡，當他點馬丁尼時，他會說「請用搖盪法，不是攪拌法。」 |
| **Carol** | What does a Dry Martini mean? | 所謂的辣味馬丁尼是什麼意思呢？ |
| **John** | Dry refers to dry vermouth. There are three different types of vermouth. The classic Martini is made with dry vermouth。 | 辣味指的是所加的香艾酒。香艾酒有三種，標準的馬丁尼就是用 dry vermouth 所做的。 |
| **Carol** | What's difference between Martini Dry and Dry Martini? | 那 Martini Dry 和 Dry Martini 有什麼不同呢？ |
| **John** | Good question. Martini Dry is a name of a wine made in Italy. Dry Martini is a name of the cocktail. | 這是一個好問題。Martini Dry（馬丁尼純香艾酒）是一款義大利酒的名稱。而 Dry Martini 則是調酒的一種。 |

## Vocabulary　單字

original　*adj.*　最初的　　　　method　*n.*　方法
stir　*vt.*　攪拌　　　　　　　shake　*vt.*　搖動
between　prep.　在……之間

A real Martini has to have dry vermouth. "Wet" or "Dry" Martini actually refers to the amount of vermouth added to the mix. Vermouth is a fortified wine made with herbs and spices. Because the alcohol content of the vermouth is relatively low, vermouth has a limited shelf life. Once it is opened, its flavor will go off over time. To keep it at very best, store opened bottles in the refrigerator for no longer than three month. If you are not sure about the freshness of the vermouth, it is always a good idea to discard that bottle and buy a fresh one. Some bartenders think that that if good quality vodka or gin is used, don't use vermouth. Years ago the vodkas were not as pure, so vermouth was used to cover up the not so great taste of the vodka. Now, vodkas are so pure and only have a little taste. They are easier to drink. Classically, a martini has vermouth because it is just a beautiful mixture of vermouth and gin or vodka.

一杯真正的馬丁尼一定要有香艾酒。所謂 "Wet" 或 "Dry" 馬丁尼,指的是香艾酒的添加量的多少(**wet** 加較多的香艾酒)。香艾酒是一種加香草和香料所做的強化葡萄酒。因為香艾酒的酒精含量比較低所以有保持期限。一旦打開,味道過了一段時間會漸漸消失。為了保持其最好的味道,開瓶後應該要存儲在冰箱裡三個月內。如果不確定手中的香艾酒是好是壞,那就丟了買另外一瓶新鮮的。有些人會建議如果調酒時用的是很好的伏特加或琴酒,就不必加香艾酒。很久以前的伏特加酒不是很純,所以調酒時會加香艾酒來掩蓋了伏特加不純的味道。現在的伏特加酒可以做得很純,味道沒有那麼濃也比較容易喝。傳統上來說,馬丁尼有加香艾酒,因為是香艾酒和琴酒或伏特加酒就是一個美麗的結合。

## Useful Sentences 好好用句型

I was told Martini is made with Gin.

有人告訴我，馬丁尼是用琴酒做的。

❧ I learned that Martini is made with Gin.

我了解的是馬丁尼是用琴酒做的。

❧ I was informed that Martini is made with Gin.

我所知道的是馬丁尼是用琴酒做的。

❧ I was taught that Martini is made with Gin.

我所學到的是，馬丁尼是用琴酒做的。

There are three different types of vermouth.

有三種不同類型的香艾酒。

❧ Vermouth comes in three different types.

香艾酒有三種不同的類型。

❧ There are three variations of vermouth.

香艾酒有三種不同的變化。

❧ There are three types of vermouth.

有三種不同類型的香艾酒。

Unit 2
Gin-based

## Mixology of the day 今日酒譜

# Martini
# 馬丁尼

Glassware: Chilled Martini glass（冰鎮馬丁尼杯）
Method: Stir and strain（攪拌法和過濾法）

**Ingredients 材料**
2 oz gin 琴酒
1 oz dry vermouth 香艾酒
Ice 冰
1 olive 橄欖

**Instructions 作法**
Stir gin and vermouth with ice in a mixing glass. Strain into a chilled cocktail glass, add the olive, and serve. Pour the ingredients into a mixing glass filled with ice cubes. Stir for 30 seconds. Strain into a chilled cocktail glass. Garnish with 1 olive.

在雪克杯裡加入琴酒和香艾酒，加滿冰塊，攪拌約 30 秒。過濾到冰鎮雞尾酒杯，配上一個橄欖。馬丁尼的原始酒譜是用琴酒做的，根據喜好，香艾酒可加多加少，如果喜歡辛辣味道，就可加較少的香艾酒。馬丁尼的裝飾也不一定要用橄欖欖，可以用螺旋形檸檬皮（lemon twist）或者用珍珠洋蔥（cocktail onion）來搭配！

## Notes 溫馨小提醒

在調酒裡使用的橄欖前，要先把橄欖洗一洗以防止油在雞尾酒內混濁的視覺。一般要把橄欖放在冰箱，要用前再適量的拿出來洗一洗。但是有一種骯髒馬丁尼（Dirty Martini）是用鹽醃製做的橄欖（olive in brine）則不需要先洗過，因為骯髒馬丁尼就要有那種混濁感。有些骯髒馬丁尼的酒譜會建議加入少滴醃製橄欖的鹽汁。

## Historical Background 調酒小故事

馬丁尼由來的說法有很多種。其中一個說法是在加州的淘金期（the Gold Rush），有一個礦工挖到黃金，他走入一家酒吧，請酒保調製一杯特別的調酒來慶祝他新發現的財富。那個酒保隨手把現有的材料混合成一杯，香艾酒（vermouth）加琴酒再加上一點點綴，就隨便稱這一杯為馬丁內斯（Martinez），這個名稱是當時酒店所在的小鎮。後來這杯馬丁內斯很受歡迎。但是，有人說馬丁尼是在舊金山發明的，也有人說馬丁尼是 1911 年時在紐約發明的。更有一個說法是，馬丁尼是生產香艾酒的一個義大利酒廠發明的。

## 3.1

# Bloody Mary 血腥瑪莉

### 🍷 Dialogue in the Bar ▷ 吧台對話

**Mrs. Johnson and Mr. Johnson are learning** ㉕ **some facts about a Bloody Mary from Jenny.**

強生太太和先生正在向珍妮學習有關血腥瑪麗的一些事實。

| | | |
|---|---|---|
| **Mrs. Johnson** | I don't like Bloody Marys very much. It just sounds so crazy, and I don't like celery. | 我真的不是很喜歡血腥瑪麗。這款雞尾酒聽起來太瘋了，我不喜歡芹菜。 |
| **Mr. Johnson** | It does have a strong taste. Not everyone likes a strong drink, but I am just about to order one. | 確實有很強的味道。不是每個人都喜歡味道重的飲料，但我正要點一杯呢。 |
| **Jenny** (Bartender) | The drink's critical ingredients are relatively simple, vodka, and tomato juice. | 這款雞尾酒最關鍵的材料其實很簡單，就是伏特加和番茄汁。 |
| **Mrs. Johnson** | Tomato juice should be put in soup, not in drinks. | 番茄汁應該是加在湯裡面，不是加在雞尾酒裡。 |

| | | |
|---|---|---|
| **Jenny** | Actually, the drink usually has more ingredients. The more common additions to the juice base are, salt, horseradish, hot sauce (such as Tabasco), citrus juices (especially lemon or lime), and Worcestershire sauce. | 其實，這款雞尾酒通常會加更多的成分。比較常見的有加鹽、辣根、辣椒醬（如塔巴斯哥辣醬）、柑橘類果汁（尤其是檸檬或萊姆）和英式伍斯特醬。 |
| **Mrs. Johnson** | It sounds like some ingredients for a pot of soup. | 聽起來好像就是一鍋湯。 |
| **Jenny** | You are very funny. | 妳很會說笑。 |
| **Mr. Johnson** | Do you shake or just stir the drink? | 你的作法是搖盪或只是攪拌呢？ |
| **Jenny** | I shake all ingredients in a shaker with ice and then fine strain it into an ice-filled glass. | 我通常會把所有的材料放在雪克杯，加冰一起搖盪，然後在過濾到有放冰塊的杯子。 |
| **Mr. Johnson** | There are other choices for garnishing, right? | 還有其他的裝飾，對不對？ |
| **Jenny** | A common garnish is a celery stalk. Other common garnishes include olives or lemon wedges. | 一般常見的裝飾是芹菜條，其他常見的裝飾還有包括橄欖和檸檬角。 |

**Unit 3** Vodka-based

## Vocabulary 單字

critical *adj.* 關鍵性的
garnish *n.* 裝飾物

common *adj.* 普通的
wedge *n.* 角、楔形物

The unique combination of ingredients in a Bloody Mary creates different flavor compounds. Some like the salty sweetness of tomato juice and celery. Others like the horseradish or the hot bite of black pepper. Others like the olive juice in the drink. There are a few basic rules for making a decent Bloody Mary. Tomato Juice is the most important ingredient in a Bloody Mary, so make sure to get a high quality, flavorful tomato juice. Tomato juice is good enough on its own, but there are other ingredients that could be added to the drink, such as Worcestershire sauce, anchovies, tamarind, beef consommé, and soy sauce. A Bloody Mary should always be shaken vigorously with plenty of ice in order to properly chill and dilute the mixture. Use lots of ice in the shaker, so it can water down the drink. Make sure the glass is well-chilled before pouring the drink into it. A squeeze of lemon juice, lime juice, pickle juice, or olive juice can balance the flavors in the drink.

血腥瑪麗裡其成分的獨特組合創造出不同變化的味道。有些人喜歡番茄汁和芹菜的鹹鹹甜甜味道。也有人喜歡辣根或黑胡椒的辣味。有些人則喜歡血腥瑪麗裡的橄欖汁。調製正統的血腥瑪麗是有幾個基本規則。番茄汁是血腥瑪麗最重要的材料，所以一定要用高品質和美味的番茄汁。只要番茄汁其實就夠好了，其他特別的成分也可以被添加到血腥瑪麗裡，如英國伍斯特醬、鯷魚、羅望子、甚至牛肉清湯和醬油。調製血腥瑪麗一定要劇烈搖動而且要用大量冰塊，這樣才可以稀釋調酒。在雪克杯裡要用很多的冰，這樣可以淡化調酒。裝調酒的杯子也一定要先冰過後才倒入調酒。用新鮮擠檸檬汁、萊姆汁、醃製汁和橄欖汁都可以平衡調酒的味道。

## Useful Sentences 好好用句型

I don't like Bloody Mary very much.

我不是很喜歡血腥瑪麗。

🚲 I hate Bloody Mary.

我就是討厭血腥瑪麗。

🚲 I dislike Bloody Mary.

我不喜歡血腥瑪麗。

🚲 I am totally disgusted with Bloody Mary.

我對血腥瑪麗完全反感。

🚲 I don't care for it.

我不太在乎這個。

It sounds like ingredients for a pot of soup.

聽起來像是煮湯的材料。

🚲 It seems like ingredients for a pot of soup.

很像是煮湯的材料。

🚲 It sounds as if you are making a pot of soup.

聽起來好像你是在煮一鍋湯。

🚲 Apparently, it's like a pot of soup.

很明顯的,這很像一鍋湯。

🚲 It looks like a pot of soup.

看起來很像一鍋湯。

🚲 It looks as if you are making a pot of soup.

看起來很像你是在煮一鍋湯。

## Mixology of the day　今日酒譜

# Bloody Mary
# 血腥瑪麗

Glassware: Highball glass（高球杯）
Method: Stir（攪拌法）

**Ingredients 材料**

1 oz vodka 伏特加

4 oz tomato juice 番茄汁

0.5 oz Worcestershire sauce 英國伍斯特醬

0.25 oz dashes Tabasco 塔巴斯哥辣醬

Pinch salt and black pepper 鹽及黑胡椒

1 cup ice cubes 冰塊

1 lemon wedge 檸檬角

**Instructions 作法**

In a highball glass, stir together tomato juice, vodka, Worcestershire sauce, Tabasco, salt, and pepper. Fill glass with ice, then pour mixture into second glass. Pour back and forth 3 to 4 times to mix well, then squeeze the lemon juice in. Garnish with a lemon wedge.

將材料倒入高球杯杯中，加滿冰塊，稍加攪拌，然後將混合物倒入第二杯，在兩個杯子中來回倒 3～4 次，擠入檸檬汁，用檸檬角裝飾。

很多酒譜會指定用塔巴斯哥辣醬，因為香氣比較夠，但是如果沒有，也可灑上一點現磨黑胡椒。

## Notes 溫馨小提醒

典型的血腥瑪麗通常會放一條芹菜，不只可以加味，也有攪拌作
用。選用的芹菜條要看起來沒有爛爛黑黑的，芹菜條的長度也要幾
寸高於杯子，芹菜條的切法通常是有角度，主要是視覺目的，芹菜
條可以有葉子，也可以沒有葉子，但是芹菜條整體看起來就是要青
青脆脆，綠色的芹菜條和紅色的血腥瑪麗就成為視覺上的對比。

## Historical Background 調酒小故事

伏特加的原產國是俄羅斯，這是以穀物所釀造的，在俄羅斯家家
戶戶都會有伏特加，任何場合都會有伏特加清澈如水的伏特加也
被俄羅斯人稱為「生命之水」。甚至還有俄羅斯詩人把伏特加比喻
如流水一樣源源不
絕，可想而知，伏特加所代表的俄
羅斯的靈魂和精神。俄羅斯人喜歡
直接用小酒杯喝伏特加烈酒，伏特
加酒也因為沒顏色、沒甜味，也沒
有植物的天然香氣，反而成為調酒
中最好的基酒。

# UNIT **3** Vodka-based 伏特加酒

## 3.2 White Russian 白色俄羅斯

### 🍷 Dialogue in the Bar 吧台對話

**John and Jenny are talking about different kinds** ㉗
**of White Russian and Black Russian.**
約翰和珍妮在談論不同的黑色俄羅斯和白色俄羅斯雞尾酒。

| John | Both Black Russians and White Russians are easy to make, but each has its own distinct characteristics. | 黑色俄羅斯和白色俄羅斯雞尾酒都很容易做的，各有鮮明的特色。 |
| --- | --- | --- |
| Jenny | You are right. Using the words black and white in names to contrast with each other is brilliant, and the names are easy to remember. | 你説得對。在名字上用黑色和白色會有很清楚的互相對比，而且名字很容易記住。 |
| John | I like the White Russian very much. It's a simple, creamy vodka mixed drink with a nice coffee flavor that makes a great after dinner drink. The related drink list to the White Russian is almost endless. | 我非常喜歡白色俄羅斯。這是一個簡單的，濃濃奶味的伏特加加咖啡酒所做的雞尾酒，這是一杯很不錯的飯後飲料。和白色俄羅斯有關的雞尾酒有一大堆。 |

If you skip the cream, it will be a Black Russian. Give the White Russian a shake at the end and it is a Dirty Bird. Add amaretto then it is called Roasted Toasted Almond. You can even add coke to the drink and it is a Colorado Bulldog. Another option is to float the cream on top. It looks amazing and is a good way to perfect your layering skills.

如果不加奶油，就是一杯「黑色俄羅斯」。如果在雪克杯裡搖盪白色俄羅斯的材料，就成了一杯「髒鳥」。加入杏仁酒就成了「烘烤杏仁」。甚至加入可樂，就變成一杯「科羅拉多州的鬥牛犬」。另一種作法則是在酒上面加鮮奶油。這看起來是很特別的，也是練習雞尾酒層次感的很好的方式。

**Jenny**

I am not too crazy about cream, so I actually like Black Russian. It is a nice dessert cocktail, perfect to end the night. Someone told me that the Russian people tend to think this is a drink for tourists. Russians just prefer a good pure vodka.

我沒有很迷鮮奶油，所以我比較喜歡黑色俄羅斯。這是一個很好的甜點雞尾酒，可以對夜晚做一個完美的結束。有人告訴我，俄羅斯人普遍認為這是觀光客的飲品。俄羅斯人只是喜歡喝純的伏特加。

## Ⓨ Vocabulary 單字

contrast　*n.*　懸殊差別

almond　*n.*　杏仁

layering　*n.*　分層

creamy　*adj.*　似乳脂的

perfect　*n.*　完美的

tourist　*n.*　觀光者

Some people like the idea of a milk or cream cocktail and feel the drink is comforting and relaxing. However, dairy products are not for everyone. Bartenders need to be aware of customers who have allergies or an intolerance to lactose. There are people who simply do not like milk. If a diary ingredient needs to be substituted, soy milk, rice milk, almond milk, or cashew milk can be used. Be careful to read the ingredients listed in these types of "milk". Unlike regular milk or cream, many non-dairy product substitutes have sugar, salt, and other ingredients that might change the flavors in drinks. For warm milk in a drink, heat the milk gently and just enough so that it is steaming, stir it constantly and avoid boiling. If the milk gets up too hot, don't use it. For a busy bartender, warming milk takes extra patience and constant attention.

有些人喜歡雞尾酒裡有加牛奶或奶油，喝起來的感覺就是很舒服和放鬆，但是乳製品並不適合每一個人。調酒師需要知道誰有過敏體質，或是誰不能有乳糖。或者有些人就是根本不喜歡雞尾酒裡有牛奶。如果雞尾酒裡的奶製品必須被換掉，可以考慮用豆漿、米漿、杏仁乳或腰果牛奶。但是要小心閱讀這些東西的成分。與普通牛奶或奶油不同的是，許多非乳製品的替代品裡本身有加白糖、鹽等其他成分，這樣可能會改變雞尾酒的味道。如果雞尾酒裡需要用到溫牛奶，如熱牛奶需要慢慢加熱到熱氣騰騰，且要不斷攪拌，並避免沸騰。如果牛奶太熱，就不能用在雞尾酒。對於一個忙碌的調酒師來說，加熱牛奶需要額外的耐心和不時的注意。

## Useful Sentences　好好用句型

If you skip the cream, it is a Black Russian.

如果沒有用鮮奶油，就是黑色俄羅斯。

🍒 If you take out the cream, it is a Black Russian.

　　如果你沒有放鮮奶油，就成了黑色俄羅斯。

🍒 If you don't use the cream, it is a Black Russian.

　　如果你沒有使用鮮奶油，就成了黑色俄羅斯。

〈skip〉是及物動詞，也是不及物動詞，用法很多，可以作為〈跳來跳去〉、〈掠過〉、〈不出席〉。

• **Don't skip class anymore.**

　不要再曠課了。

• **I don't like onion. Please skip onion when you cook the dish.**

　我不喜歡洋蔥，你煮那道菜時請不要放洋蔥。

I am not too crazy about cream.

我沒有很迷鮮奶油。

🍒 I don't like cream very much.

　　我不是很喜歡鮮奶油。

🍒 Cream is not my favorite.

　　鮮奶油不是我最喜歡的。

🍒 It's not my first choice.

　　那不是我的第一選擇。

🍒 Cream is not that special to me.

　　鮮奶油對我來說不是很特別。

🍒 I am not passionate about cream.

　　我不是很喜歡鮮奶油。

## Mixology of the day 今日酒譜

# White Russian
# 白色俄羅斯

Glassware: Old Fashioned Glass（古典酒杯）
Method: Build（直接注入法）

**Ingredients 材料**
2 oz Vodka 伏特加
1 oz coffee liqueur 咖啡香甜酒
Light cream 鮮奶油
Ice 冰

**Instructions 作法**
Pour vodka and coffee liqueur over ice cubes in an old fashioned glass. Fill with light cream.
把伏特加及咖啡香甜酒倒入裝滿冰的古典酒杯裡，再倒入鮮奶油（約八分滿即可）。

## Notes 溫馨小提醒

一些需要加奶製品的雞尾酒其實都只使用一點點，奶製品的味道可以增加飲料在喝起來時豐富的質感。白俄羅斯是以奶製品為主，還有其他以白俄羅斯為主所調製的雞尾酒。但是你可以決定是要使用牛奶，新鮮奶油或奶油球。

## Historical Background 調酒小故事

很多酒的小故事都和時事、政治有關聯。黑色俄羅斯雞尾酒在 1947 年由調酒師 Gustave Tops 專門為當時駐盧森堡的美國大使珀爾·里德·梅斯塔（Perle Reid Mesta）所調製的。珀爾當時是美國社交名流，熱衷參與政治也加入婦女黨，她也是一個平等權利修正案的早期支持者。後來當時的美國總統哈里·杜魯門派她擔任盧森堡的美國大使。調酒師 Gustave Tops 當時在布魯塞爾的飯店酒吧工作，當大使珀爾到該飯店的時候，他想要為大使調出一杯特別的雞尾酒，當時冷戰剛開始，調酒師覺得這杯雞尾酒的定調應該是有黑暗神秘的感覺，所以就用伏特加與卡魯哇咖啡酒調出黑色俄羅斯。

Unit 3
Vodka based

097

## 3.3
# Moscow Mule 莫斯科騾子

### 🍷 Dialogue in the Bar ▶ 吧台對話

**Andy, John and Jenny are talking about variations** 🔘29
**of the Moscow mule.**

安迪，約翰和珍妮在討論莫斯科騾子的不同酒譜。

| | | |
|---|---|---|
| **Andy** | I love Moscow Mules. | 我很喜歡喝莫斯科騾子。 |
| **John** (Bartender) | It is very refreshing. | 那是非常讓人感到清爽的雞尾酒。 |
| **Andy** | I sometimes make it at home, but I am tired of the same thing. Do you have other variations? | 我有時會在家裡自己做，但我現在想喝不一樣的。你有不同款的莫斯科騾子嗎？ |
| **Jenny** (Bartender) | Actually, there are many variations. It is summer, and there are many summer fruit versions of the Moscow Mule. | 其實有很多不同款的莫斯科騾子。現在是夏天，有很多夏季水果版本的莫斯科騾子。 |
| **John** | I saw one online, and it was so unusual that I actually tried it. It was pretty good. It's just that the name will throw you off, Peach Basil Moscow Mule. | 我在網路上看過一個非常不一樣的酒譜，我也試了一下，相當的不錯。只是你會覺得名字很奇怪，水蜜桃巴西利莫斯科騾子。 |

| | | |
|---|---|---|
| | He took the traditional cocktail (vodka + ginger beer + lime juice) and gave it a refreshing summer twist with peach vodka, fresh basil, and lemon juice! The Moscow Mule was originally created with lemon juice instead of lime juice. | 他將傳統的酒譜（伏特加＋薑汁啤酒＋萊姆汁），以水蜜桃伏特加，新鮮巴西利和檸檬汁替代變化成清爽的夏天味道！莫斯科騾子最初發明時是用檸檬汁做的而不是用萊姆汁。 |
| Andy | Peach Vodka? | 水蜜桃伏特加？ |
| John | Yes. It is very summer-ish. | 是的。這是非常的有夏天氣息。 |
| Jenny | Do you have the recipe? | 你有酒譜嗎？ |
| John | I do, but the recipe makes four servings. Add 2 oz. vodka and 6 oz. ginger beer to each glass. Squeeze one quarter of a lemon into each glass, and then add a couple pieces of fresh basil. Stir all of the ingredients together. Fill four glasses with ice, preferably copper cups, but any cocktail glasses will work. | 有的，我的配方是 4 人份。每一杯用 2 盎司伏特加和 6 盎司薑汁啤酒加在一起。每杯裡擠入四分之一檸檬汁，然後加一點新鮮九層塔。把所有成分攪拌一起。杯裡加滿冰塊，最好是用銅杯，但任何雞尾酒杯都可以。 |

 **Vocabulary** 單字

| | | | | |
|---|---|---|---|---|
| actually | *adv.* | 事實的 | peach *n.* | 桃子 |
| serving | *n.* | （食物、飲料等）一份 | quarter *n.* | 四分之一 |
| basil | *n.* | 巴西利 | preferably *adv.* | 較喜歡的 |

The copper mug is the signature of the Moscow Mule drink. Copper mugs should be 100% copper, and they are not cheap. Don't waste money on mugs that aren't 100% copper. What are the benefits of a copper mug? It keeps the drinks cold for a very long time, especially if the cocktail is consumed outdoors. The handle of the mug helps maintain drink temperature because it keeps away the high body heat of the hand. It actually provides some taste benefits. Vodka can cause the copper to oxidize, slightly boost the aroma, and enhance the taste of the vodka. Ultimately, the copper mug is just unique, and looks cool and fun. The Moscow Mule is very cool, refreshing and tasty. It is ideal for warm weather at the pool, beach, cook-outs, etc. Of course, if no copper mugs are available, any cup, glass or mug can be used.

銅杯是莫斯科騾子的代表。銅杯應該是 100％的銅，銅杯是不便宜的。不要花冤枉錢買不是 100％的銅。銅杯有什麼好處呢？銅杯可以讓飲料冷卻很長的時間，特別如果是在戶外喝雞尾酒這是很有好處的。杯子的手柄有助於保持飲料的溫度，因為手柄讓高體溫的手遠離雞尾酒。實際上，銅杯對味道也是有好處。伏特加在銅杯裡可導致銅氧化，可以略微提高伏特加的香氣，增強伏特加的味道。最後，銅杯就是看起來不一樣，就是很酷、也很有趣。莫斯科騾子是非常清爽可口的雞尾酒。非常適合在溫度高的天氣時，在游泳池、海灘、或是烤肉時等等場合來喝。當然，如果沒有銅杯，也沒關係，任何的杯子、玻璃杯、馬克杯都可以。

## Useful Sentences 好好用句型

It is very refreshing.

非常令人清爽。

**It's revitalizing.**

讓人感到恢復元氣。

**It's stimulating.**

很有刺激性。

**It's energizing.**

讓人很有活力。

**It's exhilarating.**

這是令人振奮的。

〈refreshing〉形容詞，通常是指精神上讓人清爽的，有精神的，另人耳目一新的。

It was originally created with lemon juice instead of lime juice.

最初是用檸檬汁做的而不是用萊姆汁。

**It was first created with lemon juice instead of lime juice.**

第一次做的時候是用檸檬汁做的而不是用萊姆汁。

**At first, it was created with lemon juice instead of lime juice.**

起初做的時候是用檸檬汁做的而不是用萊姆汁。

**In the beginning, it was created with lemon juice instead of lime juice.**

一開始做的時候是用檸檬汁做的而不是用萊姆汁。

〈create〉及物動詞，有〈創建，發明〉之意，原本沒有的東西或事情，因為〈create〉的動作而出現實質的東西或事情，可以是負面，也可以是正面。

- Please don't create any more problem. 請不要再製造麻煩了。
- The chef created the amazing seafood dish that everyone loves.

那個廚師創造了一道很棒的海鮮料理大家都很喜歡。

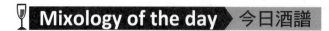

## ▾ **Mixology of the day** ▸ 今日酒譜

# Moscow Mule
# 莫斯科騾子

Glassware: Copper mug（銅杯）
Method: Build（直接注入法）

**Ingredients 材料**
Ice cubes 冰塊
1.5 oz vodka 伏特加
1 tablespoon fresh lime juice 新鮮萊姆汁
4 oz ginger beer 薑汁啤酒
1 lime wedge 萊姆角

**Instructions 作法**
Fill the mug with ice. Add vodka and lime juice, then ginger beer; stir to mix. Garnish with lime wedge.
杯中加入冰塊，先倒入伏特加，再倒入薑汁啤酒和檸檬汁，輕輕攪拌，用檸檬片裝飾。

＊薑汁啤酒可以用雪碧半瓶（約 **150ml**）代替。

### Notes 溫馨小提醒

原始酒譜其實是用薑汁啤酒,以前在台灣買不到薑汁啤酒,但是隨著美式的大賣場的盛行,薑汁啤酒可以比較容易買的到,如果買不到薑汁啤酒,薑汁汽水也是不錯的選擇。更清涼但比較甜。薑汁汽水是清涼跟酸甜所以比較不適合口味偏向辛辣的白蘭地、威士忌、龍舌蘭使用。

### Historical Background 調酒小故事

莫斯科騾子是在 1941 年在洛杉磯的一間酒吧發明的,當時一個烈酒和食品經銷商和酒吧老闆相遇,他們在吧台把薑汁啤酒和思美洛伏特加(Smirnoff Vodka)混合後加入了萊姆。後來他們還特別定製了銅杯,烈酒和食品經銷商就開始在美國各地推銷這個莫斯科騾子。他當時也買了一台剛發明上市的拍立得(Polaroid),在不同的酒吧推銷給客人時,他會拍照,一張留在酒吧,然後到另一家酒吧推銷時,把另一張照片給另一家酒吧看說附近的酒吧都在喝莫斯科騾子。原本只是單純的宣傳促銷手法,莫斯科騾子卻意外引起極大的迴響!從 1947 年到 1950 年間也因為莫斯科騾子的受歡迎,思美洛伏特加銷售量增加了三倍多。

Unit 3
Vodka-based

## 3.4

# Screwdriver 螺絲起子

## 🍷 Dialogue in the Bar ▶ 吧台對話

**Adam and Jenny are talking about different ㉛ kinds of Screwdrivers.**

亞當和珍妮在談論不同款的螺絲起子

| | | |
|---|---|---|
| **Adam** | That orange drink over there looks very refreshing. What is it? | 那杯橙色的雞尾酒看起來非常清爽。那是什麼？ |
| **Jenny**<br>(Bartender) | It's a Screwdriver. | 那是螺絲起子。 |
| **Adam** | What's in it? | 裡面是什麼？ |
| **Jenny** | It is just vodka and orange juice. It's one of the easiest cocktails to make and is very popular. | 這只是伏特加和柳橙汁。這是最簡單的雞尾酒之一，也非常受歡迎。 |
| **Adam** | May I try some? | 我可以來一杯嗎？ |

| Jenny | Sure. The cocktail looks quite orange in color. It's a little sweet and a little sour. It is easy to drink fast, but it has vodka in it, so be careful. | 當然。這杯雞尾酒看起來非常像柳橙汁。這是有點甜甜酸酸的。很容易就喝的很快，但是因為有伏特加在裡面，所以要小心。 |
|---|---|---|
| Adam | Yes. Thanks for reminding me. | 是的。謝謝妳的提醒。 |
| Jenny | If you like, and next time you can try a Harvey Wallbanger. It's a different kind of Screwdriver. What gives it its kick is the Galliano- a golden liqueur from Italy that's flavored with herbs. Galliano has a complex flavor, with hints of sweetness, vanilla and the licorice-like anise. | 如果你喜歡這款的雞尾酒，下次你可以試試看 Harvey Wallbanger。這是一個不同類型的螺絲起子。這裡面味道很特別是因為加了加利亞諾酒，這是來自義大利加香草的黃色酒。加利亞諾有很不同層次的香味，甜味，香草和甘草般的八角味道。 |
| Adam | You just pour Galliano in? | 妳就直接加入加利亞諾酒嗎？ |
| Jenny | Well, we actually float the Galliano on top. | 我們其實讓加利亞諾酒漂浮在酒的上層。 |

**Unit 3**
Vodka-based

## Y Vocabulary 單字

orange   *adj.*   橙色的、橘色的
hint   *n.*   暗示
sweetness   *n.*   甜美
vanilla   *n.*   香草
licorice   *n.*   甘草
anise   *n.*   大茴香

# 調酒師的日誌 Bartender's Log Book ㉜

There are many variations of the Screwdriver. Here are few fun and easy recipes to try. If you know the history or origin of the liquor, you might find the names entertaining. A screwdriver with equal parts of vodka and Mountain Dew is a "Dew Driver". A screwdriver with one part Tequila and two parts orange juice is a "Mexican Screw". A screwdriver with one part Bourbon and two parts orange juice is an "American Screw". A screwdriver with one part Cognac and two parts orange juice is a "French Screw". A screwdriver with one part Galliano and two parts orange juice is an "Italian Screw". A screwdriver with one part Rum and two parts orange juice is a "Cuban Screw". A screwdriver with one part Schnapps and two parts orange juice is a "German Screw". A screwdriver with one part Brandy and two parts orange juice is a "Rusty Screw". A screwdriver with one part Cointreau and two parts orange juice is a "Double Screw".（取自英文 Wikipedia）

螺絲起子酒譜可以做出許多變化。這裡有一些有趣和容易的酒譜可以嘗試。如果你知道這些烈酒的歷史或起源，你可能會會心一笑。一比一的伏特加和山露汽水（在中國名為「激浪」）的調酒就變成「伏特加激浪」。一比一的伏特加和橘子汁的調酒就是「墨西哥螺絲」。一比二的波旁酒和橘子汁的調酒就是「美國螺絲」。一比二的干邑白蘭地和和橘子汁的調酒就是「法國螺絲」。一比二的加利亞諾酒和橘子汁的調酒就是「義大利螺絲」。一比二的蘭姆酒和橘子汁的調酒就是「古巴螺絲」。一比二的杜松子酒和橘子汁的調酒就是「德國螺絲」。一比二的白蘭地和橘子汁的調酒就是「生鏽的螺絲」。一比二的君度酒和橘子汁的調酒就是「雙螺絲」。

## Useful Sentences 好好用句型

What's in it?

裡面有什麼？

🍒 What are the ingredients?

材料是什麼？

🍒 What is it made with?

是什麼做的呢？

🍒 How is it made?

是如何做的呢？

It is easy to drink fast.

很容易就喝很快。

🍒 It's not hard to drink fast.

要喝很快不難。

🍒 You will have no problem to drink it fast.

要喝很快不會有問題的。

🍒 You will drink it in a second.

很快就喝完的。

〈easy〉形容詞，簡單，相反詞是〈difficult, hard〉

## Mixology of the day 今日酒譜

# Screwdriver
# 螺絲起子

Glassware: Collins glass（柯林杯）
Method: Build（直接注入法）

**Ingredients 材料**
1.5 oz vodka 伏特加
6 oz orange juice 柳橙汁
Ice 冰塊
1 slice of orange or lemon for garnish 柳橙片或檸檬片

**Instructions 作法**
Add ice in a Collins glass. Add vodka and orange juice and stir to combine. Garnish with a lemon or orange slice.
將伏特加倒入裝滿冰塊的杯中，然後倒入柳橙汁。以檸檬或柳橙片做裝飾。

## ⚇ Notes 溫馨小提醒

裝飾用柳橙片的柳橙最好是用外皮沒有打蠟的柳橙所切的，當然也要選顏色鮮橙色，沒有棕色斑點，也要完全清洗乾淨。通常會切約3/8吋，可以切好放在冰箱，但是存放時間最好不要超過四個小時後才使用，最好還是要用時再切才會達到水果新鮮的最高效果。

## Historical Background 調酒小故事

Unit 3<br/>Vodka-based

誰發明杯中洋溢著柳橙汁香味的螺絲起子有很多種說法，最廣為人知的小故事是在伊朗油田工作的美國工人隨意將伏特加倒入罐裝的柳橙汁，用隨手拿到的螺絲起子攪勻後飲用。螺絲起子後來被廣為接受，也是全球賣得第二好的雞尾酒（Screwdriver，又被稱做是"vodka and orange"）。

這樣的場景不難想像，就像台灣的勞工界，流行以維士比加入養樂多或其他碳酸飲料（如雪碧、蘋果西打）後飲用。

# UNIT 3 Vodka-based 伏特加酒

## 3.5
## Chi Chi 奇奇

### Dialogue in the Bar 吧台對話

**Paul is asking John to recommend him a perfect** ③③
**drink for a hot day.**
保羅請約翰推薦一杯適合炎炎夏日的完美飲品。

| **Paul** | It's so hot today. What's a good drink for a hot day? | 今天天氣這麼熱。有什麼是在熱天氣喝的雞尾酒呢？ |
| **John** (Bartender) | How about a Margarita or Daiquiri? | 要不要來一杯瑪格麗特或黛克瑞？ |
| **Paul** | I am not too crazy about Margaritas. Do you have anything with coconut? | 我不是很喜歡瑪格麗特。你有什麼是加椰子的呢？ |
| **John** | You'll probably like a Chi-Chi. It is a wonderful tropical cocktail. It's made with vodka. | 你可能會喜歡奇奇。這是一個很棒的熱帶雞尾酒。是用伏特加調的。 |
| **Paul** | Actually, I've had it before. It is good. Sure. Please make me one. I remember it's a little blue in color. | 其實，我以前有喝過。這個不錯。請幫我做一杯吧。我記得是有一點藍藍的顏色。 |

| | | |
|---|---|---|
| **John** | The blue color comes from the blue curacao and the flavor is very similar to a Pina Colada. Think of it as the blue vodka version. | 藍色顏色來自藍色柑香酒，味道和椰林風情很相似。就把這杯想成是藍色伏特加版本。 |
| **Paul** | I've never had blue vodka before. | 我以前從來沒有喝過藍色伏特加。 |
| **John** | It is pretty recent in the market. There are many more possibilities for flavored vodkas as well such as raspberry, citrus, or one of the whipped cream vodkas. | 這是比較新的產品。有很多不同味道的伏特加，以及如紅莓，柑橘，甚至有奶油伏特加呢。 |
| **Paul** | That sounds superb. I like anything with vodka. | 這些聽起來都不錯。我喜歡有伏特加的雞尾酒。 |

## Vocabulary　單字

coconut　*n.*　椰子
remember　v.　記得
version　*n.*　版本
recent　*adj.*　最近的
citrus　*n.*　柑橘
whipped　*vt.*　攪打

The original Chi Chi is made with cream of coconut. Similar names, such as coconut water, coconut milk, coconut cream and cream of coconut can be confusing. Coconut water is clear liquid inside a coconut. Cut open the top of a coconut, and the liquid can be drunk straight from the coconut. Coconut milk is made from the flesh of the coconut simmer with water. Coconut milk is commonly used for cooking curries, sauces, soups, and desserts. Coconut cream is much thicker than coconut milk. The creamy liquid comes from pressing the fresh coconut meat. Cream of coconut is the thickest. Sugar is added, so it is very sweet and commonly used in mixed drinks and desserts. If cream of coconut cannot be found, there is a substitution. Skim the top layer off an unshaken can of coconut milk. Without shaking, the sweeter part goes to the top. Mix sweetened condensed milk with 1/2 teaspoon of coconut extract. Also, cream of coconut is not the same as the crème de coconut, which is a rum-based liqueur.

奇奇的原始酒譜是用椰子奶油做的。有很多相似的名稱如椰子水、椰汁、椰子奶油和椰漿會讓人搞混。椰子水是椰子裡面透明的液體。剖開椰子頂部，就可以直接喝椰子汁。椰奶則是椰子的果肉與水製成的。椰奶是常用在咖哩烹調、醬料、湯和甜點。椰子奶油比較濃厚。濃濃的液體是來自新鮮椰子肉的壓榨。椰漿非常濃，也有添加糖所以是非常甜，通常用在雞尾酒和甜點。如果你找不到椰漿可以有另一個替代品。用一罐椰奶但不要搖動，比較甜的部分會浮在上面，把上面撈起混合 **1/2** 茶匙的量加上煉乳即可。此外，椰漿和可可酒是不一樣，可可酒是一種以蘭姆酒為基礎的甜酒。

## 🎙 Useful Sentences 好好用句型

I had it before.

我以前有喝過。

🍒 I tried it before.

我以前試過。

🍒 I tasted it before.

我以前吃過。

🍒 I sampled it before.

我以前試過。

〈before〉是副詞，在句子裡形容動詞的時間〈以前〉

• **We met before.**

**我們以前見過。**

That sounds superb.

聽起來很棒。

🍒 It sounds interesting.

聽起來很有意思。

🍒 Great idea!

很不錯的意見！

🍒 It sounds great.

聽起來不錯。

〈superb〉是形容詞，是〈堂皇的，華麗的，極好的〉，和〈excellent〉有同等意思。

## Mixology of the day 今日酒譜

# Chi Chi
# 奇奇

Glassware: Collins glass（可林杯）
Method: Blend（電動攪拌機法）

**Ingredients 材料**
2 oz vodka 伏特加
5 oz pineapple juice 鳳梨汁
1.5 oz cream of coconut 椰子奶油
2 thin slices pineapple 兩個鳳梨片
2 maraschino cherries on toothpicks 穿叉酒櫻桃

**Instructions 作法**
Combine the vodka, pineapple juice, cream of coconut, and ice into a blender, blend on high speed until well combined, about 30 seconds. Pour into a Collins glass, decorate with two slices of pineapple and cherries, and serve immediately.
將伏特加、鳳梨汁、椰子奶油和冰放入攪拌機用高速攪拌直到均勻，約 30 秒。
倒入柯林斯杯，用兩片鳳梨和兩個酒櫻桃裝飾，立即飲用。

## 🍸 Notes 　溫馨小提醒

奇奇或椰林風情一定少不了椰奶，在台灣，有些調酒師會用莎莎亞椰奶（Sasaya coconut drink），但是這種品牌在大賣場、7-11、全家、家樂福、全聯社都沒有，很多酒吧會自己進，如果臨時要買，雜貨店和檳榔攤一定可以買的到，因為很多勞工朋友最愛「阿B+莎莎亞」。在美國的酒吧，通常會用的是來自波多黎各的 Coco Lopez，也是公認最好的品牌。目前在台灣，也有許多酒吧是用這一個牌子。

**Unit 3**
Vodka-based

## Historical Background 　調酒小故事

奇奇是一種以伏特加為基酒，加上鳳梨汁，椰奶和檸檬汁綜合起來甜甜的雞尾酒，如果是以蘭姆酒為基酒加上同樣水果材料就是椰林風情。椰林風情是在 1950 年最初調出的，但是奇奇自 1978 年以就一直代表波多黎各（Puerto Rico）的雞尾酒。波多黎各被西班牙統治了四百年，在 1898 年古巴獨立戰爭（Cuban War of Independence）之下因為美國干預的結果使西班牙和美國之間有戰爭衝突（the Spanish–American War）。在 1898 年，西班牙把波多黎各割讓給美國，波多黎各成為美國的領土，波多黎各是自治區但是在波多黎各出生的人可領有美國護照。英文的 Chi-Chi 其實是一種所謂的洋涇浜語言（pidgin），Chi-Chi 在所謂的英文洋涇浜是指母奶。洋涇浜不屬於任何語言，主要是不同語言的人在一起時透過文字、聲音或多種其他語言和文化的肢體語言構建的，主要目的就是相互溝通。這從波多黎各的殖民地歷史來看，奇奇這杯雞尾酒的洋涇浜語言也就更有歷史背景了。

## 3.6

# Salty Dog  鹹狗

### 🍷 Dialogue in the Bar ▶ 吧台對話

**Melissa is asking Jenny about cocktails with grapefruit juice.** ③⑤
梅麗莎在問珍妮有關有葡萄柚汁的雞尾酒。

| | | |
|---|---|---|
| **Melissa** | Are there any good cocktails with grapefruit juice? | 有什麼好的雞尾酒是有加葡萄柚汁的？ |
| **Jenny**<br>(Bartender) | If you like grapefruit, you will like the Salty Dog. It is simple to make. It is just a very refreshing mix of vodka and freshly squeezed grapefruit juice. | 如果妳喜歡葡萄柚，妳會喜歡鹹狗雞尾酒。這個調酒方式很簡單。這是很清爽的搭配，只是伏特加酒加新鮮榨的葡萄柚汁。 |
| **Melissa** | It sounds great. | 聽起來不錯。 |
| **Jenny** | There are not many customers right now, so I can make you one. Hand juicing is time-consuming, but the refreshingly rewarding, tangy drink is worth it. | 現在沒有很多客人，我可以做一杯給妳。手榨果汁非常耗時，但是喝起來就是很不一樣，口感清新、香氣濃郁是很值得的。 |

| | | |
|---|---|---|
| **Melissa** | Sure. I love grapefruit and freshly squeezed juice. | 好啊。我很喜歡葡萄柚，也喜歡新鮮現榨的果汁。 |
| **Jenny** | I sometimes add a touch of simple syrup if the grapefruit is a bit too tart. You actually have a choice here. This drink called a Salty Dog is served in a salt-rimmed Martini glass. It is called a Greyhound, if it is served in a chilled glass without salt. These two drinks are both great. Salting or not salting can make it into two different drinks. | 如果葡萄柚有點太酸，我有時會加一點糖漿。實際上有兩種選擇。這款飲料是叫鹹狗，在馬丁尼酒杯杯口有沾鹽。如果是用冰鎮、沒有製作鹽圈的杯子，這款雞尾酒就叫做灰狗。這兩種飲料都很不錯。杯口沾鹽或不沾鹽就變成兩款不同的飲料。 |
| **Melissa** | I want to try the Salty Dog. | 我想嘗嘗鹹狗。 |
| **Jenny** | Yes, sure. Here you are and enjoy it! Just a warning, it is vodka-based. | 好的，當然。這就是妳點的鹹狗，好好享用吧！只是先警告妳，這是用伏特加為基酒做的。 |

 **Vocabulary** 單字

refreshing　*adj.*　令人精神煥發的

squeeze　*vt.*　壓榨

salt-rimmed　杯口抹鹽圈

Martini glass　*n.*　馬丁尼杯

chilled glass　*n.*　冰杯

different　*adj.*　不同的

How to rim a cocktail glass with salt or sugar? The basic steps to rim a cocktail glass are simple. First, pour sugar or salt on a plate. Make sure to use plenty, so the rim gets covered. Also make sure the circle of powder is bigger in diameter than the rim of the glass. Then moisten the rim with a wedge of lime, lemon or orange. Turn the glass upside down and dip it. Twist (or not to twist) the glass to get more salt or sugar on the rim. Try it both ways to see what works the best. For salt, use coarse sea salt or kosher salt. Any salt other than table salt works. Table salt just doesn't have the right texture for rimming glasses. Regular white sugar, brown sugar, or powdered/confectioner sugar will work. Depending on the cocktail recipe, there are other options that can be used to rim the glass, such as cocoa, cinnamon-sugar, hot & spicy mix, onion powder, and garlic powder, celery salt, crushed candy, or even cookies.

如何用鹽或糖做雞尾酒鹽杯？雞尾酒鹽杯基本步驟其實很簡單。把糖或鹽倒在一個盤裡。儘量倒很多以確保杯緣能完全沾到，鹽或糖的面積要比杯口直徑大。用萊姆、檸檬或橘子把杯口外邊沾溼。杯子上下倒掛沾在鹽或糖上。此時可以轉轉杯口，不轉也可以，這是憑個人喜好的動作。鹽的話可以用粗海鹽，食鹽因為口感不對，所以食鹽以外的鹽幾乎都可以用。糖的話用純白色或紅糖皆可，糖粉也可以。依照不同的調酒酒譜，杯口可以沾用不同的材料，如可可粉、肉桂糖、混合香辣粉、洋蔥粉和大蒜粉、芹菜鹽、碎糖果或碎餅乾。

## 🔊 **Useful Sentences** 好好用句型

It sounds great.

聽起來不錯。

🚲 I love that idea.

　我喜歡這個主意。

🚲 That sounds wonderful. It would be my pleasure to have it.

　這聽起來很不錯，我會很高興喝喝看。

🚲 Excellent. I would love to have it.

　不錯。我很想試試看。

Unit 3
Vodka-based

〈sound〉是及物動詞，後面要接補語才能表示句子完整的意思

● It sounded really bad. 聽起來很不好。

Just a warning.

警告。

🚲 Be aware.

　請注意。

🚲 Be mindful.

　要留意。

🚲 Just remember.

　要記住。

〈warning〉是可數名詞，所以要用單數或複數。

● I am giving you a last warning. Don't do it again.

　我在給你最後警告，不要再犯同樣的錯了。

慣用語〈warning against〉,〈warning of〉警告

● This is a warning against drinking under influence.

　這是對酒醉駕駛的警告。

● This is a warning of speeding.

　這是超速警告。

## Mixology of the day ⟩ 今日酒譜

# Salty Dog
# 鹹狗

Glassware: Old-fashioned glass（古典酒杯）
Method: Shake（搖盪法）

**Ingredients 材料**
1 oz vodka 伏特加
1.5 oz freshly squeezed grapefruit juice 新鮮葡萄柚汁
Salt to rim the glass 杯口 鹽
Ice cubes 冰塊
Lemon wedges 檸檬角

**Instructions 作法**
Rub the lemon along the rim of the glass, then salt rim. Combine vodka and grapefruit in a shaker with ice. Shake well and fine strain grapefruit and vodka mixture into a chilled glass which filled with ice cubes. It is also popular to substitute gin for vodka.

以檸檬片沾濕杯口，以滾動方式於杯口沾上一圈鹽巴。在雪克杯中裝入六分滿冰塊，倒入伏特加和葡萄柚汁，搖盪後過濾到裝滿冰塊的冰杯中就完成。這個酒譜也可以將琴酒取代伏特加，也是很受歡迎。

# Notes 溫馨小提醒

馬丁尼杯鹽口製作：可以用點檸檬汁先塗在杯口，這樣鹽粒才會容易附著在杯口上，沾鹽時也要小心，應該只把鹽沾在杯口外，不能把鹽沾在杯口內。飲料中含有果汁及冰塊因此可選用較大的玻璃杯，倒入飲料時要特別小心，不要破壞完整的鹽口。最佳選擇是岩鹽因為比較細且鹹度不會太高。

## Historical Background 調酒小故事

「鹹狗」是調酒師喬治‧傑塞爾（George Jessel）發明的，他也是發明「血腥瑪麗」的調酒師。傑塞爾在 1950 年代調製出「鹹狗」，當時他是要在一杯調酒裡加強酒精含量，因為他的立場是反對美國共和黨（Republican）。他說，"這是我自己發明的小東西，"他說，"只要半個新鮮的葡萄柚汁，半伏特加和少許鹽，喝了你就覺得任何民主黨人（Democrat）都可以贏選戰。"他立即把這杯調酒叫做鹹狗。而"Salty Dog"在英文俚語中，一般意指為經驗豐富的水手或船友。也可以用以指稱對方具有良好的信譽。另外也意味著最好的朋友。因為在很久以前，狗主人會用鹽擦狗的皮膚作為防蚤蟲劑，所以，"salty dog"也可以被用來形容是一個人最愛、最好的朋友。

## 4.1
## Old Fashioned 古典雞尾酒

### 🍷 Dialogue in the Bar ▶ 吧台對話

**Annie is asking Jenny's opinion about how to ⑶⑺ make a real Old Fashioned.**

安妮正在問珍妮怎麼樣調製出一杯正統的古典雞尾酒。

| | | |
|---|---|---|
| **Annie** | What's a real Old Fashioned whisky cocktail? I believe I've tried one before, but I am not sure if what I had was a real one. The one I had had orange and cherry in it. Is that a real one? | 什麼是真正的古典雞尾酒？我覺得我有喝過，但我不知道我喝的是不是正統的。我喝過的是有柳橙和櫻桃。這是正統的嗎？ |
| **Jenny** (Bartender) | Personally, I prefer no fruit. An Old Fashioned should be strong and simple. I would like to recommend you try the classic version at least once, if you like. | 就個人而言，我是比較喜歡沒有水果。古典雞尾酒的味道濃烈卻簡單。如果妳有興趣，我想推薦妳至少試一次傳統的作法。 |
| **Annie** | I would love to. | 我很樂意試試。 |

| Jenny | A traditional Old Fashioned is really simple. It only has three ingredients, plus ice. The key is to maximize each of the ingredients. | 傳統作法的古典雞尾酒非常簡單。材料只有三種，再加上冰塊。關鍵是要讓每個成分發揮最大的效果。 |
|---|---|---|
| Annie | Do you use crushed ice in an Old Fashioned? | 在古典雞尾酒裡妳會加碎冰嗎？ |
| Jenny | Oh no. Definitely not. Big ice cubes are one of the signature ingredients of this drink. We call that "on the rocks". For a slow sipper, the bigger the ice you use the better. It will melt slower, and keep your drink cold without watering it down. | 當然不會。絕對不會。此款雞尾酒的特色之一是加大冰塊。我們稱這一種酒是「加在冰塊上」（加冰）。如果是慢慢的品飲的雞尾酒，冰塊要越大會越好，這樣融化的比較慢，同時雞尾酒也不會越喝越淡。 |

 **Vocabulary** 單字

personally   *adv.*   就個人而言
version   *n.*   [C] 版本
definitely   *adv.*   絕對的
signature   *n.*   簽名

Unit 4
Whisky-based

There are always ways to make a better Old Fashioned even though it is a very simple drink. Following a few principles can help make a good Old Fashioned cocktail. For a Whiskey Old Fashioned, rye is sharper and less sweet so use rye whiskey instead of bourbon. As for sugar, use dark and less processed sugar. Semerara or turbinado sugar is recommended. If white sugar is the only choice, it works too. However, brown sugar does not work. If using sugar cubes, make sure to muddle the sugar and bitters until mixed completely. Add a teaspoon of water or seltzer to help the muddling. Simple syrup works well and is convenient at busy bars. For the bitters, Angostura bitters are an absolute must and additional bitters can be added, such as orange bitters. Try other bitters to experiment with getting different results. This drink is served on the rocks and the ice cubes should be big to minimize dilution.

古典雞尾酒是一個非常簡單好做的雞尾酒，可是，就算簡單還是有不同的方法可以讓這雞尾酒調出來更好喝。只要遵循幾個原則就可以做出好喝的古典雞尾酒。對於威士忌做的古典雞尾酒，裸麥比較嗆也不甜所以用裸麥威士忌代替波本會比較好。糖的話要使用深色和加工少的糖。最好的選擇是 Semerara 或 turbinado 品牌的糖。如果白糖是唯一的選擇也是可以。但是就是不要用紅糖。如果使用的是方糖，要先把糖和苦精搗拌在一起直到完全混合。搗拌時可以加水或蘇打水。糖漿也可以，吧台在忙時，糖漿是好的材料選擇。苦精的話，一定要用安哥斯特拉苦精，之後再加上其他不同的苦酒也可以，如橙味苦精。也可以嘗試其他不同苦精。此款雞尾酒是要加冰塊，但是冰塊要用大的冰塊，這樣才能將稀釋程度降到最小。

## Useful Sentences 好好用句型

I prefer no fruit.

我比較喜歡沒有水果的。

🚲 I don't want fruit in it.

　我不要加水果。

🚲 I want it without fruit.

　我不要加水果。

🚲 Please don't add fruit in it.

　請不要加水果。

The bigger the ice you use the better.

冰塊越大越好。

🚲 As far as I am concerned, I like the bigger cube.

　就我個人而言，我喜歡大的冰塊。

🚲 The larger cube works better.

　較大的冰塊效果會更好。

🚲 It is better to have a big cube.

　最好是有大冰塊的。

## Mixology of the day 今日酒譜

## Old Fashioned
## 古典雞尾酒

Glassware: Old fashioned glass（古典酒杯）
Method: Muddle and stir（攪杵法和攪拌法）

### Ingredients 材料

1 sugar cube 方糖
2-3 dashes Angostura bitters 安格斯特拉苦精
2 orange slices 柳橙片
3 ounces bourbon whiskey 波本威士忌
Maraschino cherry for garnish 酒漬櫻桃

### Instructions 作法

Add sugar, bitters and one orange slice in the cup. Muddle the ingredients. Add ice and bourbon in the glass and stir. Garnish with one orange slice and cherry.

把方糖放入古典酒杯，把苦精滴在方糖上，加入一片柳橙在杯子內，用搗棒把杯內材料一起搗碎。加入冰塊後再倒入波本威士忌攪拌均勻。用第二片柳橙片和酒漬櫻桃裝飾。

## Notes 溫馨小提醒

蘇打水的氣泡可以帶出雞尾酒的香氣，但是要注意不要加太多，不然喝起來就會像是蘇打酒。苦精不僅提升雞尾酒的口感，香氣也會大大加分。多滴點苦精基本上不會對口感有太大的影響。在台灣的吧台界，常用的是安格斯特拉苦精或是費氏兄弟威士忌桶苦精。

## Historical Background 調酒小故事

位於肯塔基州路易斯維爾的潘登尼斯俱樂部（the Pendennis Club in Louisville, Kentucky）自 1880 年左右就開始提供古典雞尾酒（The Old Fashioned），有些專家認為這很可能是史上第一杯被稱為雞尾酒的調酒，但是這個觀點是有爭議性。古典雞尾酒在 1870 到 1890 之間的美國本土是很流行的一種調酒，在第二世界大戰之後，很多商人非常喜歡在酒吧點這款雞尾酒。在那些時代，古典雞尾酒的流行也只限於美國和英國境內，也往往是特定的年齡和身份的人才會點此款雞尾酒。

# UNIT 4 Whisky-based 威士忌

## 4.2 Whiskey Sour 威士忌酸酒

### Dialogue in the Bar 吧台對話

John and Jenny are talking about their favorite **39**
Whiskey Sour recipes.

約翰和珍妮正在討論他們最喜歡的威士忌酸酒的作法。

| John | Simplicity is what a true sour is all about. It is just whiskey, sugar, and citrus. | 簡單才是酸酒真正的味道。這樣的雞尾酒裡僅僅有威士忌、糖和柑橘味。 |
|------|------|------|
| Jenny | What's your favorite recipe for a Whiskey Sour? | 你最喜歡威士忌酸酒酒譜是哪一個？ |
| John | My recipe is very simple. It is 1 oz. whiskey, 1 oz. lemon juice, 1 tsp. powdered sugar, a handful of ice, and a lemon slice for garnish. | 我的酒譜很簡單。用的是1盎司威士忌、1盎司檸檬汁、1小匙糖粉，一些冰和一片檸檬做裝飾用。 |
| Jenny | Have you tried other variations? | 你有沒有嘗試過其他的變化？ |

| John | I've tried a New York Sour, and it's not bad. It uses bourbon, lemon juice, simple syrup, and dry red wine. My favorite is the recipe I use though. | 我有做過紐約酸酒，還不錯。這是用波旁酒，檸檬汁，糖漿水，和乾紅葡萄酒調製的。我最喜歡的酒譜還是我目前用的配方。 |
|---|---|---|
| Jenny | I had an Egg White Whiskey Sour before and was very impressed with the last splash of orange liqueur. | 我有喝過蛋清威士忌酸酒，讓人印象非常的深刻，尤其是最後用橙味利口酒灑在上面。 |
| John | I had one that had dry red wine floated over the drink. | 我喝過的是有乾紅葡萄酒漂浮在上面。 |
| Jenny | The beauty of this cocktail is that it can be made with any whiskey. | 這款雞尾酒的美妙之處在於是可以用任何威士忌酒調成。 |
| John | Have you ever heard the advice of the great Harry Craddock about drinking a cocktail? It's a perfect idea to heed his suggestion when enjoy a glass of Whiskey Sour. He said: "The way to drink a cocktail is quickly, while it's still laughing at you." | 你有沒有聽説過偉大的哈里·克拉多克對於喝雞尾酒的建議？在享受一杯威士忌酸酒時照他所建議的做是相當不錯的主意。他説：「喝雞尾酒的方式是要很快的喝，在這杯酒還在嘲笑你之前就要喝完。」 |

Unit 4
Whisky-based

## Vocabulary　單字

powdered　*adj.*　粉末的
variation　*n.*　變化
splash　v.　飛濺

handful　*n.*　少量
impress　*vt.*　印象深刻
laugh　vi.　笑

Egg white adds a light and frothy texture to the cocktail. When egg white is used for cocktails, both dry shake and regular shake are used to thoroughly combine an egg white and the other ingredients. Dry shake is shaking ingredients without ice. Regular shake is shaking ingredients with ice added. To do it right, all of the ingredients, except the ice, are shaken first. After the dry shake, add ice, shake as normal then strain. Dry shake takes time. For a busy bartender, dry shake can be a nightmare. However, there are a few ways to shorten the dry shake time. Throw the spring from a Hawthorne strainer into the tin. The spring acts like a whisk, helping coagulate the egg's proteins. Also, add sugar cubes to egg white before a dry-shaking can help break up the egg and half the shaking time. Another way is using a small electric whipper to easily make a good foam.

蛋白會讓雞尾酒喝起來輕柔有泡沫。當雞尾酒裡用到蛋白時,做的方法會用到乾式搖盪和一般搖盪以徹底結合雞尾酒裡蛋白和其它成分。乾式搖盪法是在雪克杯裡搖盪時沒有加冰塊。一般搖盪法是在雪克杯裡搖盪時有加冰塊。首先除了冰塊以外,所有的材料放入雪克杯後搖盪均勻。乾式搖盪後,加入冰塊,正常搖勻然後過濾。乾式搖盪法是需要時間。如果調酒師很忙時,乾式搖盪法會是一個噩夢。然而,有幾種方法可以縮短乾式搖盪法的時間。把霍桑濾網裡的彈簧放入雪克杯。彈簧有打發發泡的作用,可以幫助雞蛋裡的蛋白質凝聚。此外,在乾式搖盪法之前加入方糖可以打散蛋白,這樣可以縮短一半的搖盪時間。另一種方法是使用小型電動攪拌器可以輕鬆的打好泡沫。

## Useful Sentences 好好用句型

What's your favorite recipe for Whiskey sour?

你最喜歡什麼樣的威士忌酸酒酒譜？

Which recipe do you like the most for Whiskey sour?

你最喜歡哪一個威士忌酸酒酒譜？

Which recipe do you prefer to use for Whiskey sour?

你比較喜歡用哪一個威士忌酸酒酒譜？

What's your best-loved recipe for Whiskey sour?

你最喜愛的威士忌酸酒酒譜是哪一個？

Have you tried other variations?

你是否有試過其他的變化？

Have you had other variations?

你有沒有試過其他的變化？

Did you try other variations?

你有沒有試過其他的變化？

Have you ever had other variations?

你有沒有試過其他的變化？

Have you ever drank other variations?

你有沒有試過其他的變化？

## **Mixology of the day** 今日酒譜

# Whiskey sour
# 威士忌酸酒

Glassware: Chilled cocktail glass（冰鎮雞尾酒杯）
Method: Shake and float（搖盪法，漂浮法）

**Ingredients 材料**
2 oz bourbon 波本威士忌
1 oz lemon juice 檸檬汁
0.5 tsp. superfine sugar 砂糖（tsp.＝茶匙）
Ice 冰
0.5 oz dry red wine 紅酒

**Instructions 作法**
Add the bourbon, lemon juice, sugar, and ice in the shaker. Shake well. Strain into a chilled cocktail glass. Use back of a barspoon and gently disperse red wine on the back of the spoon to allow it float on drink.
在雪克杯中加入波本威士忌、檸檬汁、砂糖和冰。搖盪均勻。過濾到冰鎮雞尾酒杯，然後將紅葡萄酒輕輕倒在勺子背面讓其漂浮在雞尾酒上。

## Notes 溫馨小提醒

使用漂浮法時要很小心的不要讓酒和其他材料有太多的混合。一定要使用無甜味酒，像梅洛紅酒（Merlot），如果使用糖份含量較高的葡萄酒，這樣所作出的威士忌酸酒會太甜。漂浮法的理論是比重，比重低的可以漂浮在比重高的液體上，而比重則與酒精及糖份含量有關，一般為放入的順序會是糖漿→香甜酒→果汁→基酒。

## Historical Background 調酒小故事

金氏世界紀錄裡最古老的瓶裝威士忌是在 1851 年和 1858 年之間在蘇格蘭的 Glenavon Distillery，一般人所熟悉的威士忌是蘇格蘭威士忌、愛爾蘭威士忌、美國的波本威士忌，但是加拿大，德國，芬蘭，丹麥，英國和澳洲都有自己生產威士忌，日本威士忌由 1920 年代由三得利（Suntory）和 Nikka 兩大品牌主導日本威士忌市場。不管來自哪一個國家，所有的威士忌都有共同點，那就是以穀類為原料（如：大麥，玉米或裸麥）。威士忌基本上以原料來分可分為：麥芽威士忌、穀物威士忌和調合威士忌。

Unit 4
Whisky-based

# UNIT4 Whisky-based 威士忌

## 4.3
## Manhattan 曼哈頓

🍷 **Dialogue in the Bar** ▷ 吧台對話

**John and Jenny are talking about how to make a Manhattan.** 🎧
約翰和珍妮在討論如何做曼哈頓雞尾酒。

| John | The Manhattan is one of my favorite drinks. | 曼哈頓是我最喜歡的雞尾酒之一。 |
|------|---------------------------------------------|-------------------------------|
| Jenny | I like them, too. A good Manhattan can be every bit as good as a decent Martini. A bad Manhattan will always be much worse. | 我也很喜歡。好的曼哈頓喝起來和好的馬丁尼不相上下。但是不好的曼哈頓真的是會難喝到不行。 |
| John | Do you like it with Rye or Bourbon? | 妳喜歡的曼哈頓是用裸麥威士忌做的還是波旁酒做的？ |
| Jenny | I think Rye is the best, but I know Rye Whiskey is difficult to buy in Taiwan. The vermouth should be the sweet red kind. The bitters should be Angostura. | 我覺得裸麥做的會是最好的，但我知道裸麥威士忌在台灣很難買的到。香艾酒應該用的是甜甜紅色的那種。苦精應該用的是安格斯特拉苦精。 |

| | | |
|---|---|---|
| **John** | How long do you chill your glass? | 妳會冰鎮杯子多久呢？ |
| **Jenny** | I place the glass in the freezer for 30 minutes. It has to be very cold for better results since a Manhattan is served straight up, like Martini. | 我會把杯子放在冷凍庫30分鐘。一定要很冰才會有好的效果。因為曼哈頓和馬丁尼一樣，調好後直接飲用，不加冰塊的。 |
| **John** | I agree. Some recipes for the Manhattan say it can be served either straight up or on the rocks. I believe if you pour the ingredients for a Manhattan over ice, it isn't a Manhattan. | 我同意。有些酒譜說曼哈頓可以不加冰塊，有些則是有加冰塊。我覺得，如果有加冰塊就不是曼哈頓。 |
| **Jenny** | What do you like to use for the garnish? | 你喜歡用什麼來裝飾？ |
| **John** | Lemon twist or maraschino cherry can be used for the garnish. But you can basically use whatever garnish you want. | 螺旋型檸檬皮或酒釀櫻桃都可以用來裝飾。但基本上可以使用任何你想要的來裝飾。 |

**Unit 4**
Whisky-based

## ▼ Vocabulary ▶ 單字

bit　　*n.*　少量
rye　　*n.*　裸麥、黑麥
twist　*n.*　彎曲

decent　*adj.*　正統的
straight　*adj.*　平直的

Bourbon is a particular type of whiskey. "All bourbon is whiskey, but not all whiskey is bourbon." Whiskey is made with wheat, rye, barley, and corn, then aged in wooden barrels. At least there are more than 10 countries make whiskey. Bourbon, however, must be made in the US. It has to meet its own specific definition. Bourbon must contain 51 percent corn. The barrel used for storing Bourbon can only be used once. The used barrels are then used for other whiskeys. Also, bourbon must have no flavoring, coloring, or other additives. Bourbon has to be between 80 and 160 proof. The proof is double of the percentage of the volume of alcohol in the spirit. So a spirit with 45 % alcohol by volume (or ABV) is a 90-proof spirit. The proof is used for tax purposes. Distillers pay taxes based on the proof of a gallon of their products.

波本威士忌是一種特殊類型的威士忌。內行人的說法是,「所有的波本酒都是威士忌,但不是所有的威士忌是波本。」威士忌是用小麥、裸麥、大麥和玉米所做的。然後,是在木桶裡發酵。全世界至少有 10 個以上的國家有出產威士忌。但是波本一定要在美國製造才能叫波本,而且一定要遵守嚴格的規定。波本必須含有 51％以上的的玉米。用於存儲波旁桶也只能使用一次。用過的波旁桶則回收用於其它的威士忌。還有,波本酒不能加任何的香料,色素或其他添加劑。波本酒也必須是 80 和 160 之間的製酒精度。製酒精度是以 proof 為單位,如果酒液體積的是 45% ,proof 的算法就是酒精量的百分比加倍,這樣的製酒精度就是 90-proof。製酒精度的目的是稅收。釀酒商會根據製酒精度的多少來納稅。

## Useful Sentences 好好用句型

I like it too.
我也喜歡。

🔊 Me too.
　我也是。

🔊 I love it too.
　我也非常喜歡。

🔊 Same here.
　我也是。

🔊 I hear you.
　我同意。

🔊 Myself as well.
　我自己也是如此。


I agree.
我同意。

🔊 I agree with you.
　我同意你的看法。

🔊 I do that too.
　我也是這樣做。

🔊 We are in accord.
　我們有同樣的看法。

🔊 My thoughts exactly.
　我的想法和你的完全吻合。

🔊 I have no objections.
　我沒有異議。

🔊 We are of one mind.
　我們的想法是一樣的

🔊 Our thoughts are parallel.
　我們的想法是一樣的

Unit 4
Whisky-based

## Mixology of the day 今日酒譜

# Manhattan
# 曼哈頓

Glassware: Chilled cocktail glass（冰鎮雞尾酒杯）
Method: Stir（攪拌法）

### Ingredients 材料
2.5 oz rye whiskey 裸麥威士忌
0.75 oz sweet vermouth　甜香艾酒
3 dashes Angostura bitters 安格斯特拉苦精
Cracked ice 裂冰
1 cherry

### Instructions 作法
Add all ingredients and cracked ice to shaker. Stir well. Strain to a chilled cocktail glass. Garnish with a cherry.
將材料連同裂冰注入攪拌杯後攪拌，攪拌均勻後濾掉冰塊倒入冰鎮的雞尾酒杯。以櫻桃做裝飾。

## Notes 溫馨小提醒

用攪拌法時，如果要讓雞尾酒很冰冷，一定要先敲破冰塊（crack the ice）讓液體增加接觸冰塊的表面積。可以把冰塊放在塑膠袋內，用廚房棒棍在塑膠袋表面敲打讓冰塊破裂。一開始不要加太多冰塊在塑膠袋內，敲破冰塊後，再添加一些冰塊，再敲打。

## Historical Background 調酒小故事

波本酒的製造法規很嚴格，是因為在 1800 年有很多的酒廠在威士忌裏摻假的、稀釋過的或者是篡改原料。終於在 1897 年時，美國政府決定以「1897 年債券法酒瓶規則」（the Bottle in Bond Act of 1897）對波本酒設置一些標準。基本上，此規則要求波本酒要在同一酒廠內的一個蒸餾季節和一個蒸餾器生產。 波本酒必須在 4 年內並經美國政府監督下裝瓶及儲存。此法案成為美國威士忌品質的保證。

## UNIT **4** Whisky-based 威士忌

### 4.4
# The New York Sour 紐約酸酒

🍷 **Dialogue in the Bar** ▸ 吧台對話

**Talking about how to "float".** 🔊
討論如何做「漂浮法」。

| | | |
|---|---|---|
| **Peter** | The New York Sour sounds fancy, and it looks even fancier. | 紐約酸酒聽起來很華麗，看起來更炫。 |
| **Jenny**<br>(Bartender) | It does. It's the kind of drink that belongs in every repertoire: balanced, fancy, good on its own, and also with food. | 是的。這是每個雞尾酒單裡都會有的，因為此款調酒很順口、華麗、好喝，和其他食物也很搭。 |
| **John**<br>(Bartender) | Basically, it's a whiskey sour, but always made with rye whiskey, and finished with a red wine "float". | 基本上，這是一種威士忌酸酒，但一般是用裸麥威士忌酒製成，最後會用紅葡萄酒「漂浮」在上面。 |
| **Peter** | Float? | 漂浮？ |

140

| Jenny | A float is a small amount of wine poured carefully into the glass at the very end, so that it floats in a tidy layer on top. The float method is what makes the New York Sour look fancy. It just looks different. | 漂浮法是在雞尾酒調好後很小心的把少量的葡萄酒傾入在上面,這樣視覺上會有一層不同顏色漂浮在上面。讓紐約酸酒的外觀看起來很花俏就是因為漂浮法。就是看起來很不一樣。 |
|---|---|---|
| Peter | Is it hard to do the float? | 漂浮法很難做嗎? |
| John | It is not hard to do the float. The easiest way to do it is to hold a spoon upside down over the glass, carefully pour the red wine over the back of a bar spoon, so it forms a layer atop the drink, and it cascades gently into the drink without sinking. | 漂浮法不難做。最簡單的方法是倒拿湯匙後在背部慢慢的把紅酒從背部滑下,慢慢讓紅酒一層的漂浮在雞尾酒上面,紅酒會輕輕飄在上面而不會下沉。 |

**Unit 4** Whisky-based

## ▼ Vocabulary 單字

fancy      *adj.*   別緻的
balanced   *adj.*   平衡的
basically  *adv.*   根本上
carefully  *adv.*   小心地
spoon      *n.*    湯匙
cascade    v.    瀑布似地

What are the basic differences between Rye, Scotch and Bourbon? All whisky is grain alcohol. Scotch whisky must be made and bottled in Scotland. Bourbons must be made in the US. Types of grain and countries of origin are largely the key to differentiate whiskies. Scotch is barley based. Scotland Rye is rye based. The US Bourbon is corn based and from the US. Rye whiskey sold in the United States must meet the requirements made by the US government. Rye has to be made from a grain mixture that is at least 51% rye. The rest of the grain mixture can be combinations of corn, wheat, malted rye, and malted barley, rice, oats, and other grains. It has to be aged in new charred-oak barrels. Scotch generally uses second-hand barrels. Different name brands rye whiskey uses different recipes. One can have 60% rye, 35% corn, and 5% barley. One has 51% rye, 39% corn, and 10% barley. One has 80% rye, 15% malted barley, and 5% malted rye. One has 65% rye, 20% malted barley, and 15% corn.

裸麥、蘇格蘭和波本威士忌之間的基本區別是什麼？所有的威士忌都是穀類做的。蘇格蘭威士忌必須是在蘇格蘭生產和瓶裝。波本酒必須在美國製造。不同的威士忌在最大程度上的區分是穀類的使用和產地國。蘇格蘭威士忌是大麥做的，蘇格蘭裸麥則是裸麥做的。波本酒玉米做的，也一定要在美國國內生產。在美國銷售的裸麥威士忌必須符合由美國政府的規定。裸麥威士忌的原料是穀物混合物，其中其至少要有 51% 的裸麥，其他的混合物可以用玉米，小麥，麥芽裸麥和大麥麥芽，大米，燕麥和其它穀物。裸麥威士忌一定要在碳烤過的橡木桶內發酵。蘇格蘭威士忌一般是在回收過的木桶做發酵。不同裸麥威士忌品牌會使用不同的配方。如有的裸麥威士忌有 60% 裸麥，35% 的玉米，和 5% 的大麥。有的裸麥威士忌有 51% 的裸麥，39% 的玉米，10% 的大麥。也有些裸麥威士忌是有 80% 的裸麥，15% 發芽大麥和 5% 發芽裸麥。或者裸麥威士忌有 65% 的裸麥，20% 麥芽和 15% 的玉米。

## Useful Sentences 好好用句型

Is it hard to do the float?

漂浮法很難做嗎？

🚲 Is it difficult to do the float?

漂浮法很難做嗎？

🚲 Is it challenging to do the float?

漂浮法很有挑戰性嗎？

🚲 Is it a difficult task to do the float?

漂浮法很難做嗎？

🚲 Is it complicated to do the float?

漂浮法很複雜嗎？

It is not hard to do the float.

漂浮法不難做。

🚲 It's easy to do the float.

漂浮法很容易做。

🚲 It's piece of cake to do the float.

漂浮法很簡單。

🚲 It's not a big deal to do the float.

漂浮法並不難。

## Mixology of the day 今日酒譜

# The New York Sour
# 紐約酸酒

Glassware: Chilled cocktail glass（冰鎮雞尾酒杯）
Method: Shake & float（搖盪法和漂浮法）

### Ingredients 材料
2 oz rye whiskey 裸麥威士忌
1 oz fresh lemon juice 新鮮檸檬
1 oz simple syrup 糖漿
1/2 oz dry red wine 紅酒
Ice 冰

### Instructions 作法
Add whisky, lemon juice, syrup, and ice to a cocktail shaker and shake well for 10 seconds. Strain into a chilled cocktail glass. Carefully pour the red wine over the back of a bar spoon, so it forms a layer atop the drink.

把威士忌、檸檬汁、糖漿、紅石榴糖漿和冰倒入雪克杯，均勻搖盪 **10** 秒鐘。過濾到冰鎮雞尾酒杯。小心地把紅酒從酒吧勺的背面倒入雞尾酒上讓其漂浮在上面。

## Notes 溫馨小提醒

威士忌是有高酒精濃度的烈酒,也有強烈味道,要調出好喝的威士忌雞尾酒是不簡單的,摻蘇打水或加香甜酒可以沖淡辛辣味,也可以噴附橙皮油在杯口增加香氣。

## Historical Background 調酒小故事

根據雞尾酒權威大衛·汪德李奇(David Wondrich),紐約酸飲實際上不是來自紐約,而是來自芝加哥。在 1880 左右的芝加哥,有一個調酒師用紅葡萄酒調製酸酒(sours)。但這樣的酸酒在禁酒期間的紐約特別流行,當時因為檸檬和糖都是隨手可得的材料,這樣調製的酸酒可以蓋過威士忌的香氣,以躲避禁酒期間的查緝。

**Unit 4**
Whisky-based

## 4.5

# Godfather 教父

### 🍷 Dialogue in the Bar ▸ 吧台對話

**Several people are discussing the variations** 🔊
**of the Godfather drink.**
有幾個人在討論關於教父飲料的不同酒譜。

| | | |
|---|---|---|
| **Ken** | Some of the cocktail names are very intriguing. | 有些雞尾酒的名字是非常耐人尋味的。 |
| **Nate** | That's true. Have you ever heard of the Godfather? It's made with whiskey and amaretto. The drink is served on the rocks in an old fashioned glass. | 這是真的。你有沒有聽過教父？那是威士忌加杏仁香甜酒。這種雞尾酒是裝在古典酒杯裡有冰塊的那種。 |
| **John** (Bartender) | There are several variations of the Godfather. The Godmother cocktail uses vodka in place of whiskey. It's 1 1/2 oz. vodka and 3/4 oz. amaretto almond liqueur. Just pour vodka and amaretto into an old fashioned glass over ice and serve. | 教父是有幾種變化。教母雞尾酒用的是伏特加而不是威士忌。用 1 1/2 盎司伏特加和 3/4 盎司杏仁香甜酒。將伏特加和杏仁香甜酒倒入有冰塊的古典酒杯就是了。 |

| **Nate** | Isn't there one called the Godchild? | 不是有一種叫「教子」的嗎？ |
| --- | --- | --- |
| **John** | Yes. It's the same recipe, but adds some cream. For the cream in cocktails, you have to vigorously shake the mixture for at least 35 seconds and then strain into a cocktail glass with ice. | 是的。這是同樣的配方，但有加了一些奶油。對於有奶油的雞尾酒，你一定要大力搖晃混合物至少35秒鐘，然後過濾到有加冰的雞尾酒杯裡。 |
| **Jenny** (Bartender) | I know there is one called a Goddaughter. It's the same recipe as the Godchild but has vodka instead of whiskey. | 我知道有一個叫「教女」。這和「教子」是相同的配方，但使用的基酒是伏特加不是威士忌。 |
| **Nate** | There is one called the French Connection and it uses cognac instead. | 還有一種叫「法國通」，基酒是用干邑白蘭地。 |
| **John** | There is one more, called the Rusty Nail, made with Scotch and Drambuie. | 還有一種叫「鏽丁」，這是用蘇格蘭威士忌和蜂蜜香甜酒所做的。 |

**Unit 4**
Whisky-based

## Vocabulary 單字

intriguing  *adj.*  令人感興趣的
vigorously  *adv.*  精神旺盛地
instead  *adv.*  作為替代

almond  *n.*  杏仁
mixture  *n.*  混合液
connection  *n.*  連接

Although it is easy to buy amaretto almond liqueur, a DIY version might result in a unique taste in drinks. DIY amaretto almond liqueur is not hard to make. Soak 1/2 cup coarsely chopped apricots in bottled water for about 4 hours. Add 2cups vodka, 1 and 3/4 cups coarsely chopped almonds, 1 cup brandy and 1/4 cup coarsely chopped unsweetened, dried cherries to the jar, cover, and shake. Place in a cool place for 4 weeks, shaking once per week. After 4 weeks, filter the mixture to collect the liquid.  Finely filter the liquid one more time. Add 1 cup vodka, 2 teaspoons almond extract, 1 teaspoon vanilla extract to the filtered liquid and stir to combine. Make the sugar syrup. Heat 1/2 cup dark brown sugar, 1/2 cup granulated sugar and 1/2 cup bottled water until dissolved. Remove from the heat and let cool to room temperature. Add about half of the sugar syrup and taste the liqueur. Add more syrup if necessary. Stir to combine. Bottle and store in a cool, dark place for up to 6 months.

雖然杏仁利口酒很容易買的到，**DIY** 版本的杏仁利口酒會讓雞尾酒有獨特的風味。**DIY** 杏仁利口酒是不難做的。把半杯的的杏子切碎浸泡在瓶裝約 4 小時後過濾，在瓶子內加入浸泡後杏子、2 杯伏特加、1 又 3/4 杯切碎的杏仁、1 杯白蘭地以及 1/4 杯不加糖切碎的乾櫻桃，蓋好搖勻。連續 4 週 放置在陰涼的地方，每週搖晃一次。 4 週後，過濾混合物分開液體後，再次精細過濾液體後，在過濾液體加入 1 杯伏特加、2 茶匙杏仁精、1 茶匙香草精，就是杏仁利口酒。做糖漿水。加熱 1/2 杯黃砂糖、1/2 杯砂糖和 1/2 杯瓶裝水，直至溶解。從火上移開，放涼至室溫。把約一半的糖漿加入杏仁利口酒。適度添加糖漿。混合攪拌。放在陰涼處可以處存放長達 6 個月。

## Useful Sentences 好好用句型

It is intriguing.

這是很耐人尋味的。

🍒 It is fascinating.

　　這是很迷人的。

🍒 It is so different.

　　這是如此的不同。

🍒 It is interesting.

　　這是很有趣的。


Isn't there is one called Godchild?

是不是有一種是叫教子雞尾酒？

🍒 I think there is one called Godchild, isn't it?

　　我覺得有一種是叫教子雞尾酒，不是嗎？

🍒 There is one called Godchild, right?

　　有一種是叫教子雞尾酒，對不對？

🍒 I heard there is one called Godchild.

　　我聽過是有一種叫教子雞尾酒。

## Mixology of the day 今日酒譜

# Godfather
# 教父

Glassware: Old fashioned glass（古典酒杯）
Method: Build（直接注入法）

### Ingredients 材料
2 oz Scotch whisky 蘇格蘭威士忌
1 oz amaretto almond liqueur 杏仁香甜酒
big ice 大冰塊

### Instructions 作法
Add ice in an old fashioned glass. Pour all ingredients directly into old fashioned glass.
把大冰塊放在古典酒杯裡。用直接注入法將材料加入已放好冰塊的杯中攪勻。

\* 如果將基酒換成伏特加即為『教母』（GODMOTHER）
\* 將杏仁香甜酒換成蜂蜜香甜酒即為：『鏽丁』（RUSTY NAIL）。

## Notes 溫馨小提醒

冰是雞尾酒好喝的關鍵。有很多的雞尾酒所使用的冰塊要越大塊越好。大塊的冰融化較慢，比較不會稀釋雞尾酒。如果要做大塊的冰，可以把水加入比杯子小一點的容器，放在冷凍庫結冰後，在容器底部加熱水，即可把冰塊拿出來。如果要做不規則大塊的冰，在烤麵包模具裡加水，放在冷凍庫結冰後用冰錐敲碎。

## Historical Background 調酒小故事

就如同許多雞尾酒一樣，教父（**Godfather**）此款雞尾酒的名字的由來各有説法。**Disaronno** 杏仁甜酒品的製造商聲稱，教父雞尾酒是美國演員馬龍·白蘭度（**Marlon Brando**）最喜歡的雞尾酒。馬龍·白蘭度演過由馬里奧·普佐的小説「教父」（**Mario Puzo's The Godfather**）所改編的美國流行電影中教父一角，這部電影凸顯的特點是義大利黑手黨的故事。這個簡單的飲料在 **70** 年代開始流行，但沒有人真正知道它的起源。

## 4.6

# Sidecar 賽德卡

**Dialogue in the Bar** 吧台對話

**Jenny and customers are talking about the** 47 **variations on the Sidecar cocktails.**

珍妮和她的客人正在討論「賽德卡」的種類。

| | | |
|---|---|---|
| **Tiffany** | I had a Sidecar cocktail last night. I was very impressed. | 我昨天晚上喝一杯賽德卡。這款雞尾酒讓我印象非常深刻。 |
| **Paul** | Did you have it with whiskey? | 你喝的是威士忌做的嗎？ |
| **Tiffany** | Yes. It was made with Bourbon. I was told that brandy would work, too. | 是的。它是用波本威士忌。有人說也可以用白蘭地。 |
| **Jenny** (Bartender) | The Sidecar can be made in many variations. The Brandy Sidecar is great for starters. For the base spirit, I like to swap in whiskey, Añejo tequila, or any favorite aged rum. It gives a subtle variation on the theme. | 賽德卡可以有很多作法。對初試者來說，白蘭地賽德卡是不錯的選擇。就基酒來說，我喜歡用不同的威士忌、龍舌蘭酒或陳年蘭姆酒。不同的基酒喝起來會有微妙的變化。 |

| Paul | I had a Sidecar made with Añejo tequila and lime juice. It was not bad at all. | 我有喝過陳年龍舌蘭酒和萊姆汁調製的賽德卡。喝起來一點也不差。 |
| --- | --- | --- |
| Jenny | Lime juice and lemon juice are similar, but each actually reacts differently with different spirits. | 萊姆汁和檸檬汁是很相似的，但實際上放入不同的基酒會有不同的變化所以喝起來就很不一樣。 |
| Paul | I only like my Sidecar with Cointreau and lemon juice. When it comes to cocktails I love the classics. I prefer a Manhattan made with rye rather than bourbon, just as the original recipe calls for rye. I want a martini made with gin, not vodka. I don't really care for vodka at all, unless it's straight or on the rocks. That's just me. | 我只喜歡用君度橙酒和檸檬汁所調製的賽德卡。就雞尾酒來說，我是喜歡傳統的作法。我比較喜歡用裸麥酒調製的曼哈頓雞尾酒，而非用波本酒，原來的配方就是用裸麥酒做的。我也只喜歡用琴酒做的馬提尼而不是用伏特加。我不是很喜歡伏特加，除非是純喝或是加冰塊喝。我就是這樣啦。 |

**Unit 4**
**Whisky-based**

## Vocabulary 單字

swap   *vt.*   交換
subtle   *adj.*   微妙的
theme   *n.*   主題
react   *vt.*   有反應的
original   *adj.*   最初的

Cointreau is a French brand of triple sec, but stronger. It has an orange-flavored liqueur, and is made from bitter oranges. Cointreau has 40% alcohol. Average triple sec has 15% alcohol. If Cointreau cannot be found in local stores, DIY Cointreau is a solution. Use a fine grater and grate the outer peel off six oranges and one lime. Try to avoid getting the bitter white rind as much as possible. Mix 1 and 1/2 liters brandy with the citrus zest in a bottle and close the lid. Let it infuse for 4 weeks. Slightly rock the bottle daily to incorporate the flavors. After 4 weeks, strain the liquid then remove the citrus solids. Strain again through a coffee filter.  Heat one cup of water and 4 cups of sugar in a small saucepan over medium until sugar is dissolved. Remove from the heat and allow to cool. Add the simple syrup to the liquid and rebottle. Let sit for 4 weeks and gently rock the bottle once a day.

君度橙酒是法國品牌的柑橘香甜酒，但味道較強。這是一種柑橘香甜酒，材料是苦橙製成。君度橙酒有 40％的酒精。一般的柑橘香甜酒有 15％的酒精。如果在當地商店買不到君度橙酒，DIY 君度橙酒是一個解決方法。用細刨絲器來刨 6 個柳橙和一個萊姆的外皮。盡量避免刨到苦澀的白色果皮。把 1 和 1/2 公升白蘭地和刨好的水果外皮放在一個瓶子內並蓋上蓋子。讓其浸泡 4 週。每天輕微搖動瓶子讓味道融合。4 週後，過濾液體，然後取出水果外皮。再用咖啡過濾網再次過濾液體。在一個小鍋加熱一杯水和 4 杯糖直到糖溶解。從火上移開，並讓其冷卻。把糖漿加入過濾後的液體，重新裝瓶。每天輕輕搖晃瓶子一次，放置 4 週後就是自製的君度橙酒。

## Useful Sentences 好好用句型

It gives a subtle variation on the theme.
這樣的味道給整體帶來一種微妙的變化。

🚲 It just tastes slightly different.

這樣的味道略有不同。

🚲 It's a little different.

這是有點不同。

🚲 You can tell there is a little difference.

你可以知道就是有一點點不同。


It was not bad at all.
這是一點也不差。

🚲 It was good.

這是很好的。

🚲 It was decent.

這是不錯的。

🚲 It was nice.

這是很好的。

🚲 It was fairly good.

這是相當不錯的。

Unit 4
Whisky-based

# Mixology of the day 今日酒譜

## Whisky Sidecar
## 威士忌賽德卡

Glassware: Chilled cocktail cup（冰鎮雞尾酒杯）
Method: Shake（搖盪法）

### Ingredients 材料
2 oz. bourbon whiskey 波本威士忌
1 oz. triple sec 白橙皮酒
1/2 oz. fresh lemon juice 檸檬汁

### Instructions 作法
Pour the whiskey, triple sec and lemon juice into a cocktail shaker half-filled with ice cubes. Shake well. Strain into a chilled cocktail glass and serve.

將材料倒入雪克杯後加入半滿冰塊，搖勻搖盪後濾掉冰塊再倒入冰鎮雞尾酒杯。

## Notes 溫馨小提醒

要做好一杯威士忌賽德卡，需要比平時的搖盪更用力，搖盪也需要較久一點。這是唯一可以任小小碎冰能漂浮在雞尾酒上的作法。真正的威士忌賽德卡是不需要做裝飾但是可以用糖粘杯口。

## Historical Background 調酒小故事

威士忌賽德卡（The Sidecar）大約是在第一次世界大戰結束後所調製出的雞尾酒。至於是在哪一個城市第一個調出威士忌賽德卡則各說紛雲，有人說是倫敦，也有人說是巴黎。不論是在何地產生的，可以確定的是，這是在禁酒後期的美國和歐洲（post-Prohibition USA and Europe），威士忌賽德卡開始流行起來。

Unit 4
Whisky-based

# UNIT 5 Brandy-based 白蘭地

## 5.1 Metropolitan 大都會

### Dialogue in the Bar 吧台對話

**Conversations about experimenting with different bitters.** 49
有關嘗試不同苦精的對話。

| | | |
|---|---|---|
| **Ken** | I'm a big fan of brandy in cocktails. I especially like Metropolitans. I know the ingredients in a Metropolitan are very basic, such as brandy, vermouth, simple syrup, and bitters. | 我很喜歡有白蘭地的雞尾酒。我特別喜歡大都會雞尾酒。我知道大都會雞尾酒材料是非常基本，就是白蘭地、香艾酒、糖漿水和苦精。 |
| **John** (Bartender) | The Metropolitan is really all about the art of bitters. You can try the drink with a variety of bitters. Maybe skip the orange liqueur, but go with orange bitters instead of Angostura. There are many possibilities. | 大都會雞尾酒的真正藝術其實就是苦精。你可以用不同苦精來調調看。可以不要用橙酒，但是用橙味苦精來取代安格斯特拉苦精。有很多可能性。 |
| **Jenny** (Bartender) | Regardless, the brandy should be dominant. It's important to choose a quality brandy that holds up to that dominance. | 無論如何，白蘭地應該是主要的味道。重要的是，要選擇優質的白蘭地才可以讓雞尾酒顯示這樣的味道。 |

| | | |
|---|---|---|
| **John** | The vermouth softens it and even has enough sweetness that the simple syrup really isn't necessary. The bitters are the final measure that round out the drink. I used peach bitters, mostly because I thought this could use some fruit. | 香艾酒可以調和整體的味道，也有甜味，所以我覺得糖漿是沒有必要的。苦精是味道融合的主要功成。我用過水蜜桃苦精，主要是因為我覺得可以加入水果的味道。 |
| **Ken** | What are the proportions of the brandy to sweet vermouth? | 白蘭地和香艾酒的比例是多少？ |
| **Jenny** | Though the recipe says to use a ratio of 1 1/2 to 1 (brandy to sweet vermouth), some suggest two to one. If you're using Carpano particularly, a little less vermouth will make a sweeter, more robust brandy cocktail. But my advice is to experiment with different bitters. | 雖然配方說白蘭地和香艾酒的比例是 1 1/2 和 1，有些人建議二比一。如果你使用特別的 Carpano 香艾酒的話，試著加少一點點會讓味道更甜，這樣調出來會讓白蘭地雞尾酒更有味道。但是，我的建議還是用不同的苦精試試看。 |

**Unit 5**
Brandy-based

## Vocabulary　單字

variety　*n.*　多樣化

dominance　*n.*　優勢

particularly　*adv.*　特別

regardless　*adv.*　不管怎樣地

proportion　*n.*　比例

experiment　v.　進行實驗

# 調酒師的日誌 Bartender's Log Book 🔊

A Bitters is made with various herbs and fruit and it generally has bitter or bittersweet flavor.

Bitters do not always have to be used with alcohol. A dash of bitters in tonic water or club soda is good, too. Bitters can be used in regular cooking as well. Chefs like to add it in stew. It adds some depth and flavors to a soup. Angostura is probably the most recognizable bitters brand. It has the flavor of cardamom, nutmeg, and cinnamon and it can be used in many classic drinks. Adventurous bartenders always have different collections of bitters to experiment with in drinks. Orange Bitters has the special taste of cardamom. It is great for stronger spirits like scotch. Grapefruit and other citrus bitters are good with tequila drinks. Spicy Bitters are recommended for use with aged liquors. Fruit bitters are unusual. Cherry bitters or apple bitters are available in the market. Celery Bitters are a good choice for Bloody Mary.

苦精是用各種草藥和／或水果所做的，一般的苦精有苦味或苦苦甜甜的味道。苦精並不一定要用在雞尾酒上。苦精加通寧水或蘇打水也是很好喝的。苦精也可以用在一般的烹調。廚師喜歡在燉東西時加入苦精因為苦精會讓湯的味道增加一些層次感。安格斯特拉苦精可能是最知名的苦精品牌，這個苦精有荳蔻、肉荳蔻和肉桂的味道，所以可以在很多經典的雞尾酒。膽大的調酒師都會收藏不同的苦精用來調入雞尾酒。橙味苦精裡有辣荳蔻的味道，非常適合加入威士忌這種烈酒。葡萄柚苦精或其他柑橘類苦精很適合加入龍舌蘭酒雞尾酒。辣味苦精很適合加入有陳年酒的雞尾酒。水果苦精是很特別的。櫻桃苦味或蘋果苦精可以在市場上買得到。芹菜苦精，用在血腥瑪麗會是一個很不錯的選擇。

**Useful Sentences** 好好用句型

I'm a big fan of brandy.

我很喜歡白蘭地。

🚲 I love brandy.

　我喜歡白蘭地。

🚲 I am all about brandy.

　我就是喜歡白蘭地。

🚲 Brandy is the best.

　白蘭地是最棒的。


My advice is to experiment with different bitters.

我的建議是用不同的苦精調調看。

🚲 You should try to experiment with different bitters.

　你應該盡量用不同的苦精調調看。

🚲 Maybe try to experiment with different bitters.

　也許嘗試用不同的苦精調調看。

🚲 It's my recommendation to experiment with different bitters.

　我的建議是用不同的苦精調調看。

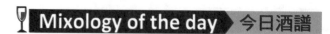

# Mixology of the day　今日酒譜

# Metropolitan
# 大都會雞尾酒

Glassware: Cocktail glass（雞尾酒杯）
Method: Shake and strain（搖盪法和過濾法）

**Ingredients 材料**
1.5 oz brandy 白蘭地
1 oz sweet vermouth 香艾酒
2 dashes bitters 苦精
1/2 simple syrup
Ice cubes 冰塊

**Instructions 作法**
Pour all the ingredients into a cocktail shaker filled with ice cubes.
Shake well and strain into a cocktail glass.
把所有的材料倒入滿冰塊的雪克杯。搖盪均勻後過濾到雞尾酒杯。

## Notes 溫馨小提醒

英文酒譜提到苦精，通常會用 "a dash of" 的用量，這是指約六分之一的茶匙。一茶匙的六分之一大約3-5滴左右，約為1ml。如果不能確定到底是多少，基本上是少量會比多量好。特別是琴酒若多加了苦精會有很不好的效果，但是在波本酒或黑麥酒裡多加了苦精則比較不會太糟糕。

## Historical Background 調酒小故事

大都會雞尾酒（the Metropolitan cocktail）酒譜最早出現在一本1884年經典調酒書「現代調酒師手冊」（Modern Bartender's Guide），作者是拜倫（O. H. Byron）。原始的酒譜是利用白蘭地和香艾酒，這也是當時普遍雞尾酒的基本材料，書裡的大都會雞尾酒用了很多的苦精，苦精所用的量高於同級的雞尾酒叫京華雞尾酒（Metropole）。書裡記載大都會雞尾酒起源當時的大都會酒店（Metropolitan Hotel），此款雞尾酒後來就以地緣而被命名。

Unit 5
Brandy-based

## 5.2
# Fort Washington Flip 華盛頓堡菲麗普

### 🍷 Dialogue in the Bar ▷ 吧台對話

**John and Jenny are talking about a new cocktail recipe.** 🔊51

約翰和珍妮正在討論一個新的酒譜。

| | | |
|---|---|---|
| **John**<br>(Bartender) | Compared with other classic cocktails, Fort Washington Flip is quite new. It was only recently created in 2007. | 和其他經典雞尾酒相比，華盛頓堡菲麗普是很新的一種雞尾酒。這是在最近 2007 年才創造出來的。 |
| **Jenny**<br>(Bartender) | Not many people have heard about the Fort Washington Flip in Taiwan. I heard about it last year at a party. | 在台灣沒有多少人聽說過華盛頓堡菲麗普。我是去年在一個派對聽說的。 |
| **John** | It uses Benedictine. It also has egg and maple syrup. The flavor combinations are quite unique. I was most impressed at how well the maple syrup and Benedictine notes played off of each other. | 這是有用班尼迪克丁。也有雞蛋和楓糖漿。這樣味道的組合是相當獨特的。我印象最深刻的是楓糖漿和班尼迪克丁的結合很對味。 |

| Jenny | It is definitely not a summer drink. | 這絕對不是夏天飲品。 |
|---|---|---|
| John | You are right. It's a winter drink. It's more like a Christmas holiday drink. | 你說得對。這是冬天的雞尾酒。比較像聖誕節時期的雞尾酒。 |
| Jenny | Does it use whole egg? | 是使用全蛋嗎？ |
| John | It does. You really need to vigorously shake the mixture so it will combine well. | 是的。要非常大力搖晃讓全蛋和其他材料完全結合。 |
| Jenny | I like the flavor of Applejack. This is a sweet drink. It is mixed with Applejack, Benedictine and maple syrup. It is a flip because it has a spirit, egg, sugar, spice, but no cream. | 我喜歡美國蘋果酒的味道。這是甜甜的雞尾酒。裡面有美國蘋果酒，班尼迪克丁和楓糖漿。這個是屬於「菲麗普」類型。因為有基酒、雞蛋、糖和香料，但沒有奶油。 |

**Unit 5**
Brandy-based

# ☿ Vocabulary ▶ 單字

recently    *adv.*    最近
maple    *n.*    楓樹
combination    *n.*    結合
definitely    *adv.*    明確地
vigorously    *adv.*    精神旺盛地
combine    v.    使結合

Applejack and Calvados are both apple brandy made from fermented cider. What's the difference between American Applejack and French Calvados? Applejack is made by the Laird family based in the United States and it is the No. 1 licensed distillery in the US. Calvados is a town from Normandy, France. It costs considerably more to produce apple brandy than grain-based spirits. In fact, Laird's Applejack is rarely 100 percent apple brandy anymore. On the label, the ingredients are listed as "Ingredients: 35% Apple Brandy, 65% Neutral Spirits". Calvados is made from 100 percent apple cider. Applejack is aged for a minimum of three years. Calvados is aged at least 6 years. Applejack producers use eating apples, resulting in a sweeter, less subtle spirit. Calvados use mix of sharp, bitter-sharp, bittersweet, and sweet apples. The difference between Calvados and applejack is like the difference between Coke and Pepsi. It's personal preference. Applejack is most popular used in the cocktail and is a lot cheaper than Calvados.

美國蘋果白蘭地和法國蘋果白蘭地都是用蘋果汁發酵製成的白蘭地。那美國蘋果白蘭地和法國蘋果白蘭地之間有什麼區別呢？美國蘋果白蘭地是由美國的萊爾德家族總部所製作的，這是在美國的第一個被許可的釀酒廠。法國蘋果白蘭地是在法國諾曼底的一個小鎮所釀造的。製造蘋果白蘭地比以穀物為主做的酒的成本高很多。事實上，萊爾德家族所做的美國蘋果白蘭地已經很少是100％的蘋果所做的。標籤上的成分是「成分：35％蘋果白蘭地、65％中性烈酒」。法國蘋果白蘭地則是由100％蘋果汁所做的。美國蘋果白蘭地的熟化至少三年。法國蘋果白蘭地熟化至少6年。美國蘋果白蘭地所用的蘋果是一般人在吃的蘋果，這樣比較甜，做出來是比較不烈的酒。法國蘋果白蘭地用的是口味重，苦澀和甜味的蘋果。美國蘋果白蘭地和法國蘋果白蘭地的區別就好像可口可樂和百事可樂之間的差異。這是純屬個人喜好。雞尾酒裡常用到美國蘋果白蘭地，美國蘋果白蘭地也比法國美國蘋果白蘭地便宜很多。

## Useful Sentences 好好用句型

It uses Benedictine.

這有用到班尼狄克丁藥草酒。

**It has Benedictine.**

這裡有用到班尼狄克丁藥草酒。

**Benedictine is one of the ingredients.**

班尼狄克丁藥草酒是成分之一。

I like the flavor of Applejack.

我喜歡美國白蘭地的味道。

**The flavor of Applejack is nice.**

美國白蘭地的味道的味道很不錯。

**I am fond of the flavor of Applejack.**

我喜歡美國白蘭地的味道。

**The flavor of Applejack is delightful.**

美國白蘭地的味道讓人喝起來很愉快。

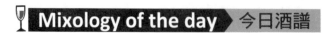

## Mixology of the day 今日酒譜

# Fort Washington Flip
# 華盛頓堡菲麗普

Glassware: Chilled cocktail glass（冰鎮雞尾酒杯）
Method: Dry shake and regular shake（乾式搖盪法和一般搖盪法）

**Ingredients 材料**
1 1/2oz apple brandy 蘋果白蘭地
3/4 oz Bénédictine 班尼狄克丁藥草酒
1/2 oz maple syrup 楓糖漿
1 egg 蛋
Fresh nutmeg for garnish 裝飾用荳蔻粉

**Instructions 作法**
Combine all the ingredients except nutmeg in a shaker and shake vigorously, without ice, for at least 10 seconds. Make sure the egg is thoroughly mixed in with the other ingredients. Add ice and shake again for at least 10 seconds; strain into a chilled cocktail glass and garnish with a grating of fresh nutmeg.
除了荳蔻粉外，將所有的材料放入雪克杯，不要加冰的劇烈搖盪，至少 10 秒。要確保整顆蛋有和所有材料徹底混合。加入冰塊後再至少搖盪 10 秒鐘，後過濾到冰鎮雞尾酒杯，在上面加上新鮮磨的荳蔻粉裝飾。

## Notes 溫馨小提醒

有加蛋的雞尾酒需要調酒師一些額外的精力才能把蛋白裡的蛋白質結構搖成泡沫，基本作法是要劇烈搖動雪克杯至少一分鐘才能完成此任務，有些雞尾酒的效果更需要蛋白做長達五分鐘的搖動。雖然這樣的搖法是很累人，但是蛋白泡沫如絲般光滑可以讓雞尾酒的層次喝起來更豐富也就值得了。

## Historical Background 調酒小故事

根據牛津英語詞典，翻動 "flip"（又稱菲麗普）雞尾酒這個名詞最早第一次出現在 1695 年，用來形容啤酒，蘭姆酒和糖的混合飲料放在很熱烙鐵鍋裡加熱，這樣的加熱法讓飲料產生了泡沫，這種發泡 frothing （或 flipping「翻動」）就是這個專有名詞的產生。隨著時間不同，酒譜裡後來加入了雞蛋和糖的比例也增加，也不用啤酒了，翻動雞尾酒變成是要趁熱喝的雞尾酒。

Unit 5
Brandy-based

169

## 5.3

# Brandy Old Fashioned 白蘭地古典雞尾酒

### 🍷 Dialogue in the Bar  吧台對話

**Mr. Smith and Mrs. Smith are talking about their experience with Brandy Old Fashioned in Wisconsin.**
史密斯先生和史密斯太太在聊有關他們在威斯康辛州喝白蘭地古典雞尾酒的經驗。

| | | |
|---|---|---|
| **Mr. Smith** | The Brandy Old Fashioned always reminds me of our days when we moved to Wisconsin. | 白蘭地古典雞尾酒會讓我想起我們搬到威斯康辛州的日子。 |
| **Mrs. Smith** | You are right. We first had one at a new friend's house. They said it was the state cocktail. | 你說得對。我們第一次喝到是在一個新朋友的家。他們說，這是這個州最具代表性的雞尾酒。 |
| **Mr. Smith** | We were told that the Old Fashioned is a cocktail that has been around since the 19th century. We did not know about it until I moved to Wisconsin. The Old Fashioned also encapsulates our experience in Wisconsin: it begins with a muddle and is sweet, bitter, and smooth all at the same time. | 他們跟我們說古典雞尾酒自 19 世紀就出現在威斯康辛州。我們沒有聽過直到我搬到了威斯康辛州。古典雞尾酒似乎也隱約代表我們當時在威斯康辛州的經驗：從搗杵到甜的、苦的、順口的，都在同一時間可以感受到。 |

| | | |
|---|---|---|
| **Mrs. Smith** | It was a new place for both of us. We eventually settled there and had children. | 那裡對我們倆來説都是個全新的環境。我們最終在那裡定居下來，並有了孩子。 |
| **John** (Bartender) | Nice story. There are a few ways to make an Old Fashioned. All of them begin with a sugar cube muddled with bitters and orange, followed by soda and a generous pour of booze. Whiskey is traditional but brandy is also popular. | 聽起來真是一個美好的故事。有幾種方法可以做古典雞尾酒。但都要用到方糖，苦精和柳橙搗杆在一起，其次是加蘇打水和很多的烈酒。傳統是用威士忌，但白蘭地酒也很受歡迎。 |
| **Mr. Smith** | Yes. The classic Old Fashioned cocktail with Brandy is smooth, buttery and satisfying, just like our memories of Wisconsin. | 是的。經典的白蘭地老式雞尾酒很順口也讓人感到很滿足，就像我們對威斯康辛州的記憶一樣。 |

**Unit 5** Brandy-based

## Vocabulary 單字

encapsulate　*vt.*　將……裝入膠囊
settled　*adj.*　感到舒適愜意
generous　*adj.*　慷慨的
booze　*n.*　含有酒精的飲料
buttery　*adj.*　像奶油的
satisfying　*adj.*　滿意的

A good bartender needs to know how to make a perfect Wisconsin-style Brandy Old Fashioned. It requires some muddling. First, chill an old fashioned glass. Add two dashes of Angostura bitters and a sugar cube. A sugar cube is preferable here because it's going to add some friction to the muddling. Next, take a thick-cut orange wedge and a maraschino cherry. If cherries are in season, try to make brandied cocktail cherries. A good quality cherry will make the drink so much better. Muddle the sugar, bitters, orange wedge and cherry into a thick paste. Try not to muddle the orange peel too much in order to avoid bitterness. After muddling, the ingredients should be thick and pasty. Add brandy or Cognac. Add crushed ice, and finish the drink sweet or sour. For a sweet taste, add a splash of Sprite or 7-Up. For a sour taste, a dose of sour mix.

一個好的調酒師需要知道如何做出一杯完美的威斯康辛白蘭地古典雞尾酒。這是需要用搗杵法。首先先冰鎮古典酒杯。加入安格斯特拉苦精和一個方糖。最好是用方糖，因為方糖會在搗杵過程產生摩擦添加味道。用厚切的橙片，酒漬櫻桃。如果是櫻桃季節，盡量自己做酒釀雞尾酒櫻桃。良好的櫻桃品質會讓飲料好喝多。把糖、苦精、橙片和櫻桃搗杵成稠膏狀。盡量不要搗杵橘皮太用力避免搗出苦味。搗杵之後的材料應該是濃濃的糊狀。之後加入白蘭地或干邑白蘭地。加入碎冰。此款雞尾酒可以喝甜或者是酸的。如果要喝甜的，加入一點雪碧或七喜。如果要酸味的，加入酸味調料。

## Useful Sentences 好好用句型

Nice story.

很美好的故事。

🍒 Interesting story.

很有趣的故事。

🍒 What a good story.

真是很棒的故事。

🍒 Very delightful to hear that.

非常令人愉快的聽到這樣的故事。

🍒 What a charming story.

真是一個溫馨的故事。

We did not know about it.

我們不知道有這種。

🍒 We have never heard of it before.

我們從來沒有聽說過。

🍒 We had no idea about it.

我們不知道這種。

🍒 We had no clue about it.

我們根本不知道有這種。

## Mixology of the day　今日酒譜

# Easy Brandy Old Fashioned
# 白蘭地古典雞尾酒

Glassware: Old fashioned glass（古典酒杯）
Method: Muddle（搗杵法）

**Ingredients 材料**
3 oz. brandy 白蘭地
2 dashes Angostura bitters 安格斯特拉苦精
1 sugar cube 方糖
7-Up or Sprite 七喜或雪碧
1 orange slice 柳橙片

**Instructions 作法**
Muddle the sugar with the bitters and the orange slice in the bottom of an Old fashioned glass. Add the brandy and some ice cubes. Stir gently to combine then pour in some 7-Up or Sprite.

在古典酒杯底加入糖與苦精和柳橙片攪杵後，加入白蘭地和一些冰塊。輕輕攪拌結合材料，再加入些許的七喜或雪碧。

## Notes 溫馨小提醒

搗杵法是要釋放新鮮材料的味道，讓其更加的融合在酒精裡。但是務必不要搗杵過度，如薄荷和九層塔這種材料過度搗杵會有苦味，這當然會影響成品的整體味道。材質比較軟的材料在搗杵時要輕輕，用搗棒攪和材料來回幾次。材質比較硬的材料如迷迭香，檸檬則可以比較用力搗杵。

## Historical Background 調酒小故事

在 **1919 – 1933** 年美國的禁酒時代（**Prohibition-era**）當時真正的挑戰是酒的取得。如果有的是好酒，當然是很昂貴的。比較容易取得的酒，絕大部分是品質較低劣的酒。調酒師或家庭用途通常手上不會有什麼好酒，也就絞盡腦汁要調出好喝的酒。也就在這個時期，果汁和各種糖漿真正開始出現在雞尾酒配方。

## 5.4

### Brandy Sidecar 白蘭地側車

### 🍷 Dialogue in the Bar ▸ 吧台對話

**Talking about different Sidecar inspired drinks.** ⑤⑤
談論不同側車雞尾酒。

| | | |
|---|---|---|
| **John**<br>(Bartender) | I think the Brandy Sidecar is a good cocktail, but many people don't like it. | 我覺得白蘭地側車是很不錯的雞尾酒，但很多人不喜歡。 |
| **Jenny**<br>(Bartender) | The Sidecar is on my list. It's refreshing and delightful. The mix of brandy, triple-sec, and lemon juice is irresistible. | 側車是有被列在我的個人酒單上的。這是一個很令人感到清爽和愉快的雞尾酒。白蘭地、橙味利口酒和檸檬汁的組合令人無法抗拒。 |
| **John** | The Sidecar is my absolute favorite cocktail. In fact, it's the drink I always order first at a bar. | 側車是我絕對最喜愛的雞尾酒。事實上，我去酒吧一定會先點這個。 |
| **Jenny** | Do you know what Sidecar means? | 你知道側車的意思嗎？ |

| | | |
|---|---|---|
| **John** | Sidecar is a term that bartenders use for the leftover liquor they pour into shot glasses, which is more likely where the cocktail got its name. | 知道啊，側車是調酒師為倒入烈酒杯後所剩的烈酒，這非常可能是這個雞尾酒名字的來源。 |
| **Jenny** | The Brandy Sidecar has influenced many other cocktails and includes the Boston Sidecar, Pisco Sidecar or Rum Sidecar. The Chelsea Sidecar is a delicious cocktail that has gin, triple sec and lemon juice. It is a clear drink with a strong citrus flavor and it is also called a White Lady. | 白蘭地側車影響了許多其他的雞尾酒，其中包括波士頓側車、皮斯科側車或蘭姆酒側車。切爾西側車是一種很美味的雞尾酒，裡面有琴酒、橙味利口酒和檸檬汁。這看起來透明但有強烈的柑橘味雞尾酒，也被稱為白色女士。 |
| **John** | I know another one. The Balalaika is also a Sidecar inspired drink. It is a simple, intoxicating yet fruity vodka drink. It only has three ingredients to make this drink - vodka, Cointreau and lemon juice. | 我知道的還有一個。巴拉萊卡的靈感也是來自側車。這是一個簡單但令人陶醉也有水果味的伏特加雞尾酒。裡面只有三個成分，就是伏特加、君度酒和檸檬汁。 |

**Unit 5**
Brandy-based

### 🍸 Vocabulary 單字

| | | | |
|---|---|---|---|
| irresistible | *adj.* | 不可抵抗的 | |
| term | *n.* | 名詞 | |
| influenced | *vt.* | 影響 | |

| | | | |
|---|---|---|---|
| absolute | *adj.* | 絕對的 | |
| leftover | *n.* | 剩下的東西、剩菜 | |
| include | v. | 包括 | |

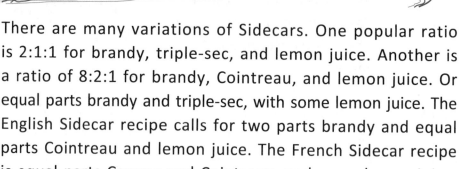

There are many variations of Sidecars. One popular ratio is 2:1:1 for brandy, triple-sec, and lemon juice. Another is a ratio of 8:2:1 for brandy, Cointreau, and lemon juice. Or equal parts brandy and triple-sec, with some lemon juice. The English Sidecar recipe calls for two parts brandy and equal parts Cointreau and lemon juice. The French Sidecar recipe is equal parts Cognac and Cointreau, and some lemon juice. Most importantly, a good bartender should know which recipe to use depending on the quality of the ingredients. Use equal parts brandy and Cointreau, if both are cheap quality. Use less Cointreau, if it is a top-quality because the flavor is more intense. For a French version, use good quality Cognac instead of brandy. There are two options for garnishes. One is rimming the glass with sugar. Or just garnish with a twist of orange, or frame the orange peel to make it look more spectacular.

白蘭地側車是可以做許多變化。一般作法的比例是２：１：１的白蘭地、橙味利口酒和檸檬汁。另一種是是８：２：１的白蘭地、君度酒和檸檬汁。也有等比例作法的白蘭地和橙味利口酒再加少許檸檬汁。英式的白蘭地側車配方是同等比例的白蘭地和君度酒，再加少許檸檬汁。法式的白蘭地側車配方是用同等比例的干邑白蘭地和君度酒，再加少許檸檬汁。最重要的是，一個好的調酒師應該知道比例是取決於所用材料的品質的好壞。如果白蘭地和君度酒都是比較劣等的，那就用同等份來調。 如果是高檔的君度酒，味道會比較強烈，所以要加比較少量。對於法式的白蘭地側車，應該用高檔的干邑白蘭地取代一般白蘭地。對於裝飾有兩種選擇。一種是用糖沾杯口。或者只是用橙片裝飾，也可以在橙皮上點燃火，這樣看起來會很壯觀。

## Useful Sentences 好好用句型

Many people don't like it.

很多人不喜歡這個。

🍒 Many people dislike it.

很多人不喜歡這個。

🍒 Many people don't care much about it.

很多人不那麼在意這個。

🍒 Many people find it distasteful.

很多人覺得這個沒有好味道。

🍒 Many people disapprove it.

很多人否定這個。

In fact...

事實上

🍒 Actually...

其實

🍒 In reality...

在現實中

🍒 As a matter of fact...

事實上

🍒 To tell the truth...

就實話實說

## Mixology of the day 今日酒譜

## Brandy Sidecar
## 白蘭地側車

Glassware: Chilled cocktail glass（冰鎮雞尾酒杯）
Method: Shake and strain（搖盪法和過濾）

### Ingredients 材料
Ice cubes 冰塊
1/2 oz freshly squeezed lemon juice 鮮榨檸檬汁
1 oz triple sec 橙味利口酒
1.5 oz brandy 白蘭地
1 lemon twist 螺旋形檸檬皮

### Instructions 作法
Fill a cocktail shaker 3/4 full with ice cubes. Pour in lemon juice, triple sec, and brandy. Cover and shake vigorously for about 30 seconds until the outside of the shaker becomes cold and frosty. Strain into a chilled cocktail glass and garnish with a lemon twist. If desired, rim a chilled cocktail glass with sugar.

在雪克杯裡裝滿 3/4 冰塊。倒入檸檬汁、橙味利口酒和白蘭地。蓋上蓋子，劇烈搖晃約 30 秒，直到雪克杯外是冰冷也有霜。過濾到冰鎮雞尾酒杯，用螺旋形檸檬皮裝飾。也可以在冰鎮雞尾酒杯的杯邊沾糖。

## Notes 溫馨小提醒

冰鎮雞尾酒杯前要先用水沖一下杯子，不要擦乾。然後就放置在冰櫃內，約 10 至 15 分鐘的玻璃表層會結霜。先用水沖杯子會讓杯子更迅速結霜。如果時間不夠，五分鐘內要冰鎮的話，在杯子內加入水和冰塊，放到冰庫，約五分鐘就會有冰鎮的杯子。

## Historical Background 調酒小故事

根據，大衛 . 安伯力（David Embury）在 1948 年出版的「混合飲料的藝術」（The Fine Art of Mixing Drinks）裡有提到側車雞尾酒是在第一次世界大戰期間在巴黎小酒館調製出來的，當時有一個人把側車摩托車騎入他最喜歡的酒吧裡。至於是哪一個酒吧？普遍認為是哈里的紐約酒吧（Harry's New York Bar）。

### 5.5

# Weng Weng 心醉神迷

### 🍷 Dialogue in the Bar   吧台對話

**Andrew is asking John if he can make him a special** 🔘 **Filipino cocktail which is called Weng Weng.**

安德魯正在問約翰是否能幫他調製一杯名為 "**Weng Weng**" 的特別的菲律賓雞尾酒。

| | | |
|---|---|---|
| **Andrew** | The first time I tried a Weng Weng was on a business trip to the Philippines. Weng Weng is a popular but strong drink from the Philippines. It's such a tropical drink. | 我第一次喝到心醉神迷是在菲律賓出差時。心醉神迷在菲律賓很流行，這是濃度高的雞尾酒，也是非常熱帶型的飲料。 |
| **John**<br>(Bartender) | It is a strong but nice and smooth drink. It is made by adding various alcohols such as rum, bourbon, vodka, scotch, Tequila, brandy, orange juice, pineapple juice and a splash of Grenadine. | 這是一個強烈的飲料，喝起來很棒也很順口。這是有混合很多不同的基酒，有波旁威士忌、伏特加、威士忌、龍舌蘭酒、白蘭地、橙汁、鳳梨汁和一點的紅石榴糖漿。 |

| Andrew | I had it at a party with many Filipinos. We also had some Filipino barbecue on sticks. It goes together really well. | 我在一個有許多菲律賓人的慶祝會裡有喝過這種雞尾酒。那時我們也有吃一種菲律賓燒烤，和心醉神迷很配。 |
| --- | --- | --- |
| John | Its sweet taste makes you forget how strong this drink is! | 這種雞尾酒的甜味會讓你忘了這是很強的雞尾酒！ |
| Andrew | That's true. I had two Weng Wengs at that time. It tasted great, but the walk back to my hotel room, two blocks away, was difficult though. | 這是真的。我那時喝了兩杯的心醉神迷。味道真的很好，但之後要走路回到我住的飯店時還有點困難，也才兩條街遠而已。 |
| John | Weng Weng is very appealing. The drink appears orange in color. It is a treat to the taste buds, but is very strong, so it should be consumed accordingly. | 心醉神迷是非常有吸引力。這個雞尾酒看起來是柳橙色。對味蕾是一種享受，但因為是用烈酒調的，所以喝的時候要酌量。 |

**Unit 5**
Brandy-based

## Vocabulary　單字

business　*n.*　商業
various　*adj.*　不同的
Filipino　*n.*　菲律賓人
appealing　*adj.*　動人的
taste bud　*n.*　味蕾
accordingly　*adj.*　相應地

The Weng Weng Cocktail normally has about six kinds of alcohol, rum, gin, vodka, tequila, brandy, and whiskey. The liquors are mixed with orange juice, pineapple juice and a dash of Grenadine syrup. Although freshly made juice is always the first choice, ripe and tasty fresh fruits are not always easy to find. Canned juice is sometimes a better choice than freshly made juice. Many canned juices have the citrusy taste of ripe and flavorful oranges. They contain 100% of the daily vitamin C value per serving. Canned juice doesn't require refrigeration until after it is opened. Canned juice is easy to use, versatile, and fresh-tasting. Read the label carefully. The term fruit "juice" is a broad term. It can mean anything from 100% fruit content to less than 1% fruit content with a lot of added sugar. Juices which are all fruit will spoil sooner than juices with added sugar and preservatives.

心醉神迷裡通常有大約六種酒精包括有蘭姆酒、琴酒、伏特加、龍舌蘭酒、白蘭地以及威士忌。這些烈酒混合後有加入柳橙汁，鳳梨汁和一點紅石榴糖漿。雖然新鮮的果汁始終是第一選擇，成熟和可口的新鮮水果並不一定容易找到。罐裝果汁有時是會比新鮮果汁較好的選擇。很多罐裝果汁是從成熟和可口的柳橙所做的。這樣的柳橙汁裡含有100%的每日維生素 C。罐裝果汁在打開前是不需要冷藏。罐裝果汁也容易取得及多樣化，也有新鮮味道。但是要小心閱讀標籤。標籤上所謂的"果汁"是很廣義的術語。這個術語的範圍可以從100%的水果到加很多糖卻小於1%的水果含量。比起添加了糖和防腐劑的果汁來說，如果全是水果做的果汁會比較容易壞掉。

## 🍶 **Useful Sentences** 好好用句型

It tasted great.

味道很不錯。

🚲 It was delicious.

很美味。

🚲 It was tasty.

很美味。

🚲 It was great.

很棒。

It should be consumed accordingly.

喝的時候要適量。

🚲 You should be careful when you drink it.

喝的時候要小心不要喝太多。

🚲 It should be consumed appropriately.

喝的時候要適量。

🚲 If you are not careful, you will pay the consequences.

如果不小心，結果你就會知道。

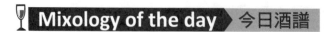

## Mixology of the day 今日酒譜

# Weng Weng
# 心醉神迷

Glassware: Hurricane glass（颶風杯）
Method: Build（直接注入法）

**Ingredients 材料**
3/4 oz. bourbon 波本酒
3/4 oz. vodka 伏特加
3/4 oz. tequila 龍舌蘭
3/4 oz. Scotch 蘇格蘭威士忌
3/4 oz. brandy 白蘭地
3/4 oz. rum 蘭姆酒
2 oz. orange Juice 柳橙汁
2 oz. pineapple Juice 鳳梨汁
1 dash grenadine 紅石榴糖漿
ice cube 冰塊
One slice of orange 柳橙片

**Instructions 作法**
In a hurricane glass full half with ice cubes. Build all the alcohols. Add a dash of Grenadine. Add orange and pineapple juice. Garnish with one slice of orange.
在颶風杯加入半杯冰塊，注入所有的酒精後加入紅石榴糖漿再加入柳橙汁和鳳梨汁。用柳橙片裝飾。

## Notes 溫馨小提醒

「心醉神迷」（Weng Weng）的酒譜裡有用不同的方法。有些是 "mix and stir"，有些是 "shaken thoroughly"，有些則是 "build"，無論哪種方法，「心醉神迷」的特點是至少有五種酒精的混合，也是冰飲的雞尾酒，而其熱帶水果的裝飾也是特點。

## Historical Background 調酒小故事

「心醉神迷」（Weng Weng）是菲律賓的「國飲」，此款雞尾就來源說法有很多種。有人說是一名調酒師創造的，他的暱稱是 Weng Weng，也就這樣命名此款雞尾酒。另一種說法是 Weng Weng 也是菲律賓俚語裡用來形容喝醉的人 "completely intoxicated"。也有人說此款酒的發明是紀念七十年代的電影演員叫埃內斯托·德拉克魯茲（Ernesto de la Cruz），他的藝名就叫 Weng Weng，他當時演過菲律賓版本的詹姆斯·邦德。

## 5.6
# Pisco Sour 皮斯可酸酒

### Dialogue in the Bar 吧台對話

**John and Jenny are talking about the ingredients and** (59)
**glassware to make a Pisco Sour after the rush hour.**

約翰和珍妮在過了店裡尖峰時刻之後，正在聊做皮斯可酸酒的材料及杯子。

| Jenny | There are many interesting cocktails made with Pisco. | 有許多有趣的雞尾酒是用皮斯科做的。 |
| John | Pisco has high alcohol content but it tastes very smooth and many people enjoy it straight. | 皮斯科具有較高的酒精含量，喝起來很順口，所以很多人喜歡直接喝。 |
| Jenny | Pisco has been known to surprise first-timers with its potency, especially when blended into a cocktail. Pisco sours are notoriously strong. | 對很多第一次喝皮斯科的人來説，會感到後勁很強，尤其是加在雞尾酒裡，皮斯可酸酒是出了名的烈。 |
| John | It is very exotic. This cocktail has sweet and sour flavors. | 這酒是非常奇特的。這款雞尾酒有酸和甜的味道在裡面。 |
| Jenny | Do you use fine sugar or simple syrup? | 你用精細糖或是糖漿？ |

188

| John | I use Simple syrup (one part sugar, one part water). I just think it is the easiest. | 我是用糖漿（糖和水一比一的比例）。我覺得這是最簡單的。 |
| Jenny | What kind of glass do you use? An old fashioned, highball glass or Champagne flute? | 你用什麼樣的杯子？古典酒杯，高球玻璃或笛型香檳杯？ |
| John | I use an old fashioned glass. | 我用的是古典酒杯。 |
| Jenny | That's classic. I like to use a Champagne flute because it looks very inviting. | 這是經典的喝法。我喜歡用笛型香檳杯，因為看起來非常誘人。 |
| John | Angostura bitters is another key ingredient. The combination of Angostura bitters is perfect. I like to add a drop on the top. | 安格斯特拉苦精是另一個關鍵材料。安格斯特拉苦精的結合是很完美的。我喜歡在上面滴上一滴苦精。 |
| Jenny | I agree. Angostura bitters really beautifully combine all the ingredients together. I add a dash and I like to use a straw to swirl the bitters into a simple design, so it looks fancy. | 我同意。安格斯特拉苦精和所有成分真的是完美的結合在一起。我都會在上面加一點，然後用吸管攪一下苦精，這樣看起來會花俏一點。 |

**Unit 5**
**Brandy-based**

## 🍸 Vocabulary ▶ 單字

notoriously *adv.* 惡名昭彰地
flute *n.* 笛形物
beautifully *adv.* 美麗地

exotic *adj.* 奇特的
inviting *adj.* 吸引人的；誘人的
straw *n.* 吸管

Pisco is a style of brandy from Peru and Chile. It is made by the distilling fermented grape juice. Pisco is made from only certain varieties of grapes, grown in particular regions of Peru and Chile. The grapes are brought by the Spanish conquistadores to South America in 1500. The Spanish wanted to make wine for their own consumption and export. Pisco from Peru is never diluted. Pisco from Chile is sometimes mixed with distilled water. Pisco puro and Pisco acholado are the Piscos most often used to make Pisco Sours. Pisco is the Peruvian's national spirit. June 4th is a national holiday called the Peruvian Pisco. The Peruvian government does not allow the mass production of Pisco. Peruvian Pisco must be produced according to traditional, small-batch methods. Chilenian Pisco is more of mass production with industrial methods. Even though Pisco is named after Peruvian town, both Peru and Chile claim the Pisco Sour as their national drink. France is the main international buyer of Chilean Pisco in 2012. The U.S. is Peru's main Pisco exports.

皮斯可（**Pisco**）是來自秘魯和智利的白蘭地。這是由葡萄汁發酵蒸餾製成。用來做皮斯可的葡萄只限於生長在秘魯和智利的特定區域的特定品種。這類型的葡萄是在 1500 年西班牙的征服者到南美時所帶來的，當時西班牙想做葡萄酒主要是供自己國人的飲用和出口。秘魯的皮斯可是沒有做稀釋的。智利的皮斯可有時會與蒸餾水混合。**Pisco Puro** 和 **Pisco Acholado** 這兩種皮斯可是最常用來調製皮斯可酸酒（**Pisco Sour**）。皮斯可是秘魯的國酒。每年 6 月 4 日是秘魯一個全國性的節慶日稱為秘魯皮斯可（**Peruvian Pisco**）。秘魯政府不允許大規模生產皮斯可。秘魯皮斯可必須按照傳統小批量的方法來製造。智利皮斯可則有比較大規模的工業生產方法。儘管皮斯可這個名字是來自秘魯的小鎮，秘魯和智利都聲稱酸味皮斯可是他們的國飲。在 2012 年法國是智利皮斯可的主要國際買家，秘魯的皮斯可主要出口到美國。

## Useful Sentences 好好用句型

It is very exotic.

這是非常奇特的。

🍒 It's very unusual.

　　這是非常不尋常的。

🍒 It's very different.

　　這是非常不同的。

🍒 It's very particular.

　　這是非常特別的。

It looks fancy.

看起來很花俏。

🍒 It looks very special.

　　看起來很特別。

🍒 It looks elegant.

　　看起來優雅。

🍒 It is unusual.

　　這是很不尋常的。

## Mixology of the day 今日酒譜

# Pisco Sour
# 皮斯可酸酒

Glassware: Old fashioned glass（古典酒杯）
Method: Shake and strain（搖盪和過濾法）

**Ingredients 材料**
2 oz Pisco brandy 皮斯可白蘭地
1 oz lemon juice 檸檬汁
0.5 oz simple syrup 糖漿
1 egg white 蛋白
3 drop of Angostura bitters 安格斯特拉苦精
1 lemon wheel 檸檬片

**Instructions 作法**
Add all the ingredients to the bar shaker and fill with ice. Shake vigorously about 15 times.
Strain into a chilled old fashioned glass. Garnish with Angostura bitters and a lemon wheel.

把皮斯可、檸檬汁和冰塊加入雪克杯。在一個碗裡打入蛋白和糖，快速攪動讓糖溶解後加到雪克杯，劇烈搖盪雪克杯約 15 次。過濾到冰鎮古典酒杯。加入安格斯特拉苦精及檸檬圈作為裝飾。

## Notes 溫馨小提醒

萊姆汁可以用來代替檸檬汁。糖可以加多加少依個人喜好，如果沒有精細糖，可以用簡單糖漿（simple syrup）替代。如果酒譜的材料有精細糖（superfine sugar），不要用一般細糖代替。一般細糖可以放入果汁機裡攪拌一到兩分鐘即可成為精細糖。

## Historical Background 調酒小故事

智利和秘魯這兩個國家長久以來雙方都宣稱他們是皮斯可酸酒的原產地。大部分資料顯示皮斯可是在 1920 年由維克多·莫里斯（Victor Morris）在一個智利的利馬（Lima, Chile）的酒吧最先調製的。智利一直聲稱皮斯可酸酒（the Pisco Sour）是在智利發明的，很多廣告也都說莫里斯酒吧（the Morris Bar）就是發明皮斯可酸酒的地方。但有人在一本 1903 年秘魯所印的食譜裡就有皮斯可酸酒這個飲料。在 2013 年，歐洲聯盟在公開認定秘魯是皮斯可酒的原產地後，智利舉國對此消息感到悲傷。

# UNIT 6 Tequila-based 龍舌蘭

## 6.1 Margarita 瑪格麗特

### 🍸 Dialogue in the Bar ▷ 吧台對話

**John and Jenny are having a discussion about** 🔊 **how to make the best Tequila-Margarita.**

約翰和珍妮在談論如何做出最好的以龍舌蘭作為基酒的瑪格麗特雞尾酒。

| | | |
|---|---|---|
| **John**<br>(Bartender) | The Margarita is quite popular in Taiwan. | 瑪格麗特在台灣很流行。 |
| **Jenny**<br>(Bartender) | It is also one of the most popular cocktails in North America. It's sweet and sour. It is a must summer cocktail. It is very refreshing. | 這個雞尾酒在北美也是最流行的一種。這是酸酸甜甜。這是夏季雞尾酒，喝起來非常清爽。 |
| **John** | Margarita can be made in so many ways. You can serve this cocktail on the rocks, or frozen. You can put salt, sugar or nothing on the rim of the glass. The possibilities are endless. | 做瑪格麗特可以有很多方式。調好後可以倒在冰塊上飲用，或是做成冰沙。你也可以有鹽口，糖口或在杯口都不加東西。變化的可能性是無窮無盡的。 |

| Jenny | You are right. The level of difficulty is low and the ingredients are few, but it is still important to know a few details in order to make the best Margarita. | 你説得對。做好瑪格麗特的難度不高，材料也只有一點點但是還是需要知道一些細節才能做出最好的瑪格麗特。 |
| --- | --- | --- |
| John | I agree. The single most important ingredient is fresh lime juice. For parties, juice the limes ahead and fill a squeeze bottle to keep at the ready. Never use store bought bottled lime juice. | 我同意。此款雞尾酒最重要的成分是新鮮的萊姆汁。如果是在開趴時，可以把萊姆汁先榨好放入可以擠出的瓶子，這樣隨時可以用。絕對不要買瓶裝的萊姆汁。 |
| Jenny | For Margaritas, use only Blanco (a.k.a. silver or white) tequilas, which have a peppery, vegetable kick that won't get buried when mixed. Save your aged reposado tequilas for sipping. Salt brings out the flavor in everything, but too much can be overwhelming. So we only salt halfway around the rim and are careful not to get any in the drink. | 就瑪格麗特來説，應該只用布蘭科龍舌蘭酒（又名銀色或白色），這種酒有一個胡椒和蔬菜味，調酒後還是可以喝得出來。如果你有陳年的龍舌蘭酒，那就留著做品嚐會比較好。鹽會把一切的味道帶出來，但也不能太多。因此，鹽杯我們只會沾半邊，而且要小心不要讓鹽掉入雞尾酒裡。 |

**Unit 6**
Tequila-based

## ▼ Vocabulary ▶ 單字

endless *adj.* 無盡的

overwhelming *adj.* 勢不可擋的

detail *n.* 細節

halfway *adj.* 中途的

Many Margarita recipes use Triple Sec, Cointreau or simple syrup or agave syrup for the sweetness. Agave syrup has its complementary flavors and shared origin with tequila. Agave is the plant that tequila is made from. The nectar made from the plant is known in Mexico as "honey water." Agave syrup is mostly made from the Blue Agaves that grow in the volcanic soils of Southern Mexico. Agaves are large, spikey plants that are similar to Aloe Vera. Over 200 species of Agave have been identified. The Blue Agave is used for producing nectar. It is also the same plant that's used to make tequila. Different brands of agave syrup have different levels of richness and flavor. Flavored nectars are available and can put a whole new twist on your cocktails. Agave Nectar is at least 30% sweeter than sugar, but has less calories and has higher nutritional benefits. Despite having less calories and higher nutritional benefits, Agave syrup is highly processed, so it is basically like high-fructose corn syrup.

許多瑪格麗特酒譜是用橙味利口酒、君度酒或是用糖漿水或龍舌蘭糖漿來調甜度。龍舌蘭糖漿和龍舌蘭酒具有互補的味道，也來自相同的產地。龍舌蘭植物是用來做龍舌蘭酒。這個植物所製成的甜蜜（nectar）被稱為墨西哥的「蜂蜜水」。龍舌蘭糖漿大多來由生長在墨西哥南部火山土壤的藍龍舌蘭（Blue Agave）所做的。龍舌蘭植物長的很大，這是一種類似於蘆薈的有刺植物。龍舌蘭有超過 200 種被鑑定的品種。藍色龍舌蘭是用來生產甜蜜，和用來製作龍舌蘭酒是同一植物。不同品牌的龍舌蘭糖漿會有不同程度的口感和味道。有加香料的甜蜜在市面上可以買得到，這類型的香料的甜蜜會讓調製出的雞尾酒有全新不同的味道。龍舌蘭甜蜜比蔗糖甜度至少高 30%，也有較少的熱量但有較高的營養益處。儘管有較少的熱量和高營養的好處，龍舌蘭糖漿高度加工的過程讓此糖漿基本上就是類似果糖玉米糖漿。

# 🥤 **Useful Sentences** ▶ 好好用句型

It is very refreshing.

這是讓人感到很清爽。

🍒 It's very energizing.

　　這是讓人感到精神都來了。

🍒 It's very different.

　　這是非常不同的。

🍒 It is very unique.

　　這是非常獨特的。

It can be overwhelming.

會讓人感到太有壓迫感。

🍒 It can be just too much.

　　會讓人感到承受不了。

🍒 It can be staggering.

　　會讓人感到太驚人的。

## Mixology of the day ▶ 今日酒譜

# Margarita
# 瑪格麗特雞尾酒

Glassware: Chilled margarita glass（冰鎮瑪格麗特杯）
Method: Shake（搖盪法）

**Ingredients 材料**
1 1/2 oz tequila 龍舌蘭酒
1 oz triple sec 橙味利口酒
0.5 oz fresh lime juice 萊姆汁
Lime wedge for garnish 裝飾用萊姆片
Rim the glass with salt or sugar 用鹽或糖沾杯口

**Instructions 作法**
Fill a cocktail shaker half with ice. Pour the ingredients into shaker. Shake well.
If desired, rim the glass with salt or sugar. Pour contents, with ice, into the glass.
Garnish with the lime wedge.
在雪克杯裡倒入一半量的冰塊，把龍舌蘭酒，橙味利口酒和萊姆汁倒入雪克杯，搖盪均勻。
可以在杯口沾鹽或糖。把雪克杯內的材料倒入杯子，用萊姆片裝飾。

## Notes 溫馨小提醒

市面上有很多百分之百的龍舌蘭酒，也有很多非百分之百的龍舌蘭酒，調製瑪格麗特可以用百分之百龍舌蘭做的 Blanco 或 Reposado Tequilas。Añejo Tequilas 比較高檔但是很值得。試試看不同的龍舌蘭酒，也可以稍微調整熟悉的味道。用在瑪格麗特雞尾酒的萊姆需要選成熟、薄皮的。根據萊姆的澀味和甜味，可以調整要加入的糖分，在成品完成後，應該試試看味道做調整。

## Historical Background 調酒小故事

如果要稱為龍舌蘭酒，至少要由 **51**％的龍舌蘭（**agave**）所做，這是一種沙漠植物。龍舌蘭酒實際上有一些健康的好處，龍舌蘭植物常見的實用的方式是龍舌蘭花蜜，這是可以替代傳統的砂糖。也可生吃，煮熟或乾燥，這三種形式的食用法都有提供幾個關鍵營養成分包括有鐵質、鈣質和鋅。龍舌蘭酒裡看起來有點神秘的蟲其實是一種來自梅斯卡爾植物的 gusano（Mezcal gusano），在做酒的植物上來說，梅斯卡爾和龍舌蘭是同種類，但是梅斯卡爾是比較赤品的。把蟲放在龍舌蘭酒裡只是一種營銷策略，對酒的品質沒有多大作用，gusano 是住在梅斯卡爾植物上的蛾的幼蟲。

# UNIT 6 Tequila-based 龍舌蘭

## 6.2
## Rosemary Bloody Mary 迷迭香血腥瑪麗

### 🍷 Dialogue in the Bar ▷ 吧台對話

**Talking about rosemary in the Rosemary Bloody Mary.** 🔢63

在談論迷迭香血腥瑪麗裡的迷迭香材料。

| | | |
|---|---|---|
| **Tania** | That looks so scrumptious! What is it? | 這看起來好好喝！這是什麼？ |
| **Tony** | That's Rosemary Bloody Mary with tequila in it. | 這是迷迭香血腥瑪麗，有龍舌蘭酒在裡面。 |
| **Tania** | I definitely love rosemary. | 我非常喜歡迷迭香。 |
| **Tony** | Yes. This is something different. The addition of rosemary is so pretty and perfect. | 是的。這喝起來很不一樣。加入迷迭香看起來不只漂亮也是很完美的搭配。 |
| **Tania** | I will have to try this one. It looks amazing! I can just imagine how the herbal flavor goes with the tomatoey taste. | 我要來試試看。看起來太棒了！我可以想像的草藥味和番茄味道的融合。 |

| | | |
|---|---|---|
| **Jenny**<br>(Bartender) | Some of the ingredients seem odd, but the combination is wonderful. Fresh rosemary is great! | 有一些成分似乎很奇怪，但其實調起來是很好的。新鮮的迷迭香真的很棒！ |
| **Tania** | Does it have Worcestershire sauce in it? | 裡面有加伍斯特醬嗎？ |
| **Jenny** | Yes, it does. I also use Bloody Mary mix. | 有的。我也有加血腥瑪麗混合液。 |
| **Tony** | There is another drink called Bloody Maria. It is my favorite cocktail. It also uses tequila. You can use regular Bloody Mary recipe, but substitute vodka with tequila and the liquor substitution make a noticeable difference in the flavor. The tequila in the background stands out. I love everything spicy. When I have Bloody Maria, I like the garnish with jalapeno stuffed green olives. It is so delicious. | 還有一種雞尾酒叫血腥瑪麗亞。這是我最喜愛的雞尾酒，裡面有加龍舌蘭酒。妳可以用一般的血腥瑪麗配方，但是用龍舌蘭酒替代伏特加，風味會很明顯的不同，妳會喝出龍舌蘭酒的不同味道。我喜歡辛辣的味道。我在喝血腥瑪麗亞時，我喜歡用包有墨西哥辣椒的綠橄欖來當裝飾，真的很棒。 |

**Unit 6**
**Tequila-based**

## Vocabulary 單字

| | | | | | |
|---|---|---|---|---|---|
| scrumptious | *adj.* | 極好的 | herbal | *adj.* | 草本的 |
| substitute | *vt.* | 用……代替 | noticeable | *adj.* | 顯而易見的 |
| spicy | *adj.* | 辣味 | delicious | *adj.* | 美味的 |

Bottled Bloody Mary mix is available in regular liquor store. DIY Bloody Mary mix is quiet easy. Especially when tomatoes are in season, there is always extra to make tomato juice. The recipe is 3 cups tomato juice, 3 tablespoons lemon juice, 3 tablespoons lime juice, 1 tablespoon horseradish, 1 tablespoon Worcestershire Sauce, 3/4 teaspoon hot sauce, 3/4 teaspoon salt, 1/2 teaspoon freshly ground black pepper. For the mix, place all of the ingredients in a nonreactive 1-quart container and whisk until well combined. Or use a blender to mix well. Cover and refrigerate until the flavors meld and the mix is chilled, at least 2 hours or preferably overnight. It's best to make the mix the day before so the flavors can mix well. Store the mix in a lid-tight bottle in a refrigerator for a week for freeze for up a month.

瓶裝血腥瑪麗調和液在一般酒類專賣店可以買的到。DIY 血腥瑪麗調和液其實很容易做。特別當番茄是旺季時，總會有多餘的番茄可以做番茄汁。配方可以用 3 杯番茄汁、3 湯匙檸檬汁、3 湯匙檸檬汁、1 湯匙辣根、1 湯匙伍斯特醬、3/4 茶匙辣椒醬、3/4 茶匙鹽和 1/2 茶匙現磨黑胡椒。把所有的材料放入 1 夸脫容器，攪拌直到完全混合。或者用攪拌機拌勻。蓋好蓋子放入冰箱冷藏，直到口味融合，至少 2 小時後，或者放過夜會更好。最好要做血腥瑪麗的前一天把調和液做好，這樣味道才會均勻。把調和液放在蓋好的密封瓶，可以在冰箱冷藏一週，或在冷凍庫可以放長達一個月。

## Useful Sentences 好好用句型

I love everything spicy.

辛辣的東西我都喜歡。

🚲 Everything that is spicy I love it.

一切辛辣的味道我都喜歡。

🚲 If it is spicy, I love it.

如果是辣的，我都會喜歡。

🚲 I love it when it tastes hot.

如果吃起來是辣的，我就會喜歡。

This is something different.

這是不一樣的。

🚲 This is not what you think it is.

這不是你所想的。

🚲 This is different.

這是不同的。

🚲 This is not usual.

這是不常見的。

## Mixology of the day 今日酒譜

# Rosemary Bloody Mary
# 迷迭香血腥瑪麗

Glassware: Highball glass（高球杯）
Method: Stir（攪拌法）

**Ingredients 材料**
Bloody Mary mix 血腥瑪麗調和液
Fresh rosemary 新鮮迷迭香
1/2 lime 萊姆
1 oz tequila 龍舌蘭
0.5 tsp. Worcestershire sauce 英國伍斯特醬
Ice 冰

**Instructions 作法**
Fill the highball glass about halfway with the Bloody Mary mix (or half glass of Bloody Mary). Add 1 ounce tequila. Squeeze the juice of half a lime into the drink. Add 1/2 a teaspoon Worcestershire sauce. Add few ice and stir all ingredients together. Garnish with a slice of lime.

在海波杯裡加入半杯的血腥瑪麗調和液（或是半杯調製好的血腥瑪莉）。加入 **1** 盎司龍舌蘭酒。擠入半個萊姆汁。加入 **1/2** 茶匙的伍斯特醬。加入少量冰塊，攪拌所有配料使其混合在一起。用一片萊姆裝飾。

## Notes 溫馨小提醒

迷迭香血腥瑪麗最有趣的部分是裝飾，把迷迭香切的細細碎碎後和海鹽混合可以做杯口的鹽杯材料，鹽和迷迭香味道的結合是非常美味和芳香的。另外再加上一小片萊姆，插上一串的迷迭香和一串的橄欖，才會是一杯讓人印象深刻的迷迭香血腥瑪麗。

## Historical Background 調酒小故事

屬於龍舌蘭種類的植物有三百多種，其中有兩百多種被認定。龍舌蘭酒是其中一種龍舌蘭植物叫 blue agave 所做的，這樣的龍舌蘭是生長在墨西哥的哈利斯科州（Jalisco, Mexican）的瓜達拉哈拉（Guadalajara）外的乾旱低地和多雨高地處，墨西哥法律規定，龍舌蘭酒只能在墨西哥的四個州製造。最基本品質的龍舌蘭酒必須是百分之百用龍舌蘭所做，沒有任何添加劑。絕對不要買沒有標有"100% agave"的龍舌蘭酒。

## 6.3

# Paloma 帕洛瑪

### 🍷 Dialogue in the Bar ▶ 吧台對話

**Lauren, Andy and Jenny are talking about** 🔘65 **the different tastes of Tequila.**

勞倫，安迪和珍妮在談論不同味道的龍舌蘭酒。

| | | |
|---|---|---|
| **Lauren** | I love tequila. I recently tried a Paloma cocktail that has tequila in it. It is a refreshing Mexican cocktail with grapefruit and tequila! I loved it. The blend of grapefruit, lime, and sugar blended perfectly with the tequila. | 我很喜歡龍舌蘭酒。我最近試過帕洛瑪雞尾酒，裏面有龍舌蘭酒。這是一個令人耳目一新的墨西哥雞尾酒，裡面有加葡萄柚和龍舌蘭酒！我很喜歡。葡萄柚、萊姆和糖的混合和龍舌蘭酒非常的對味。 |
| **Andy** | What does the tequila taste like? | 龍舌蘭酒的味道是怎麼樣？ |
| **Lauren** | It is acquired taste. It has a lot of kick and bite, but I find that most tequilas have a slightly sweet taste at the end. It just tastes like tequila. | 這是一種喝習慣才會喜歡的味道。味道很刺激，但我發現大多數龍舌蘭酒都略帶甜味。就是龍舌蘭酒的味道。 |

| | | |
|---|---|---|
| **Jenny**<br>(Bartender) | It has an oak taste due to the fact that if you are drinking reposado or Anejo tequila, it gets aged in oak barrels before being bottled. It's quite delicious! If you are not used to drinking hard liquor straight, a cocktail is a good way to try it. | 如果你喝 Reposado 或 Anejo 龍舌蘭酒，喝起來有橡木的味道，因為在製酒過程裝瓶之前，是在橡木桶中發酵。真的相當不錯！如果你不習慣直接喝烈酒，雞尾酒是一種很好的方式來喝烈酒。 |
| **Lauren** | Definitely. The Paloma cocktail is a fruity cocktail. I had it with a sugar rimmed glass and it is just unforgettable. | 當然。帕洛瑪雞尾酒是一種果味雞尾酒。我有喝過的是在杯口有製作糖圈的，味道真的是太令人難忘了。 |
| **Jenny** | The Paloma cocktail has tequila, club soda, grapefruit juice and lime juice. It can be served with either a salt rimmed glass or a sugar rimmed glass. | 帕洛瑪雞尾酒有龍舌蘭酒、蘇打水、葡萄柚汁和萊姆汁。是可以倒入有製作鹽圈或是糖圈的杯中以供飲用。 |

**Unit 6**
Tequila-based

## Vocabulary　單字

blende　*vt.*　使混和
acquire　*vt.*　取得，獲得
slightly　*adj.*　稍微地
straight　*adj.*　挺直的
unforgettable　*adj.*　忘不了的
either　*adj.*　兩者之中

Grapefruit is sour and tangy with some sweetness. Many cocktail recipes use grapefruit as an ingredient such as a Sex on the Beach, Salty Dog, Hurricane, Hemingway Special, Paloma, etc. Though freshly squeezed grapefruit is always recommended, sometimes busy bartenders just don't have enough time to do that. It could be that it's not possible to get good tasty fresh grapefruit. It is good to know what to look for when buying bottled or canned grapefruit. There are pasteurized and non-pasteurized grapefruit juices. Non-pasteurized juices taste fresher. The process of pasteurization kills microorganisms in the juice that could spoil it, so the shelf life is longer.  Always read the label carefully. Is it 100% grapefruit juice or just juice blend? The juice blends are often a mix of grape, apple, and grapefruit juices which is not as good as 100% grapefruit juice, and it has 50% more sugar. Other blends can be 100% grapefruit juice from concentrate, white grape juice from concentrate, and carrot juice.

葡萄柚吃起來酸酸的，但也有甜味。許多雞尾酒配方會用葡萄柚，例如性慾海灘、鹹狗、颶風、特調海明威或帕洛瑪等。雖然鮮榨的葡萄柚會是最好的，但是調酒師有時太忙就是沒有足夠的時間來做鮮榨葡萄柚汁。也可能葡萄柚不一定會很好。所以，調酒師應該知道要如何買瓶裝或罐裝葡萄柚汁。非高溫殺菌的葡萄柚汁喝起來比較新鮮。高溫殺菌的過程會破壞微生物，這也讓果汁可以放得比較久。務必仔細閱讀標籤。是否是 100%葡萄柚汁或只是混合果汁？混合果汁往往會有葡萄，蘋果和葡萄柚汁混合在其中，也會有高於 50%以上的甜度。有些品牌可能是 100%葡萄柚汁濃縮，加上白葡萄汁和胡蘿蔔汁。

## 🔊 **Useful Sentences** ▶ 好好用句型

I love it.

我很喜歡。

🚲 I like it.

　　我喜歡。

🚲 I am fond of it.

　　我很喜歡。

🚲 I am crazy about it.

　　我很瘋這個。

🚲 I can't get enough of it.

　　再多都沒關係。


It is just unforgettable.

真是令人難忘的。

🚲 It's remarkable.

　　真的很特別。

🚲 It's extraordinary.

　　非常的不一樣。

🚲 It's outstanding.

　　很優秀。

🚲 It's terrific.

　　很棒。

## Mixology of the day 今日酒譜

# Paloma
# 帕洛瑪

Glassware: Cocktail glass（雞尾酒杯）
Method: Stir（攪拌法）

## Ingredients 材料
1.5 oz tequila 龍舌蘭酒
1.5 oz club soda 蘇打水
1.5 oz fresh grapefruit juice 新鮮葡萄柚汁
Grapefruit wedge 葡萄柚角

## Instructions 作法
Sprinkle sugar on a small plate. Cut grapefruit in half, rubbing outer edge of cocktail glass on grapefruit to wet and dip rim of glass in sugar. Pour tequila, club soda, grapefruit juice, and ice in the glass and stir. Garnish with a wedge of grapefruit.

在盤子上灑上糖。把葡萄柚切一半，沿著雞尾酒杯杯口畫一圈，使其濕潤，以沾糖製作糖口。將龍舌蘭酒、蘇打水、葡萄柚汁和冰倒入雞尾酒杯並攪拌。用葡萄柚裝飾即可。

## Notes 溫馨小提醒

如果在家宴客時，若有要提供鹽杯的雞尾酒，可以事前將杯口用鹽沾好後，放入冰櫃可以保持鹽杯的原狀。另外一種作法是每一個酒杯只把鹽沾一半的杯口，這樣的準備不只看起來特別，客人也有選擇是否要使用鹽杯。

## Historical Background 調酒小故事

龍舌蘭酒埃拉杜拉（Tequila Herradura）（正式名稱是 Grupo Industrial Herradura），這是位在 Amatitán, Jalisco, Mexico 的龍舌蘭酒公司。在 1870 年由費利克斯·洛佩斯（Félix López）正式成立，也運行了超過 125 年。現在這家公司是由美國飲料製造商布朗 - 福曼（US beverage maker Brown-Forman）所擁有，但是他們的龍舌蘭酒是由在墨西哥的子公司在相同的地方和設施所製造的。Herradura 公司所生產的龍舌蘭酒是 100％龍舌蘭所做，其作法和上世紀傳統的作法是一模一樣。

# Tequila Sunrise 龍舌蘭日出

## Dialogue in the Bar 吧台對話

**Talking about the red effect in a Tequila Sunrise.** 🔊
在討論龍舌蘭日出裡的紅色日出效果。

| | | |
|---|---|---|
| **Ben** | By the looks of the cocktail, the Tequila Sunrise has a perfect name. | 就雞尾酒的外觀看來，龍舌蘭日出這個名字很完美。 |
| **Jenny**<br>(Bartender) | It is. The building and floating methods for a Tequila Sunrise are not too difficult, but they are artistic. | 是的。龍舌蘭日出的直接注入法和漂浮法不是太困難，但很有藝術。 |
| **Ben** | Is it always served in a long glass? I think that's what I always see. | 此款酒都是用長杯裝的嗎？我好像看到的都是這樣。 |
| **Jenny** | Yes. The Tequila Sunrise is considered a long drink and is usually served in a Collins or highball glass. | 是的。龍舌蘭日出被認為是一種長飲型雞尾酒，通常可以用可林杯或高球杯。 |

| | | |
|---|---|---|
| **Ben** | What's the red stuff on the top? | 上面的紅色是什麼材料呢？ |
| **Jenny** | That's grenadine. We float the grenadine on top. The drink is mixed by pouring in Tequila, then the juice, and lastly, the syrup. The signature look of the drink depends on adding the syrup without mixing it with the other ingredients. A spoon may be used to guide the syrup down the glass wall to the bottom of the glass with minimal mixing. | 那是紅石榴糖漿。我們會把紅石榴糖漿漂浮在上面。此款雞尾酒是通常是倒入龍舌蘭酒，然後果汁，最後再注入糖漿。此款雞尾酒的特色是把注入糖漿但讓其不與其它成分混合。可以用湯匙讓糖漿注入到玻璃底部也能避免最少程度的混合。 |
| **John** (Bartender) | Have you heard of the Tequila Sunset? Grenadine is substituted with blackberry brandy, or dark rum. | 你有沒有聽説過龍舌蘭日落呢？這不用紅石榴糖漿而是用黑莓白蘭地，或黑蘭姆酒。 |

**Unit 6**
Tequila-based

# Ⓨ Vocabulary 單字

artistic　*adj.*　藝術的
perfect　*adj.*　完美
considered　*adj.*　經過深思熟慮的
stuff　*n.*　東西
minimal　*adj.*　最少的
blackberry　*n.*　黑莓

# 調酒師的日誌 Bartender's Log Book

Grenadine is mostly used to color a drink. If a Tequila Sunrise is made right, a sunrise phenomenon can be seen in the drink. Because of grenadine's specific gravity, it will gradually settle in the bottom of the glass beneath the glowing orange juice. The trick to making a Tequila Sunrise work is all in the pouring. Pour the ingredients slowly, and never over ice, or you will lose the effect. Therefore, chill the tequila first. If you decide to shake, omit the grenadine from the shaker and add it later. White tequila is always used. There is also a Tequila Sunset. The ingredients are tequila, blackberry brandy, honey and orange juice. To make a Tequila Sunset cocktail, pour the tequila, orange juice and honey into a shaker with ice and shake. Pour into a cocktail glass and top it off gently with blackberry brandy. The brandy will also eventually settle in the bottom of the glass creating a laying effect.

紅石榴糖漿主要是在雞尾酒裡當顏色的作用。如果龍舌蘭日出雞尾酒有做好,在雞尾酒裡是可以看出一個朝陽的現象。因為紅石榴糖漿的特別比重所以會逐步沉澱在杯子底部。因此,做龍舌蘭日出的訣竅在於如何倒入材料。首先要把材料慢慢倒入,也不能倒在冰塊上,這樣就做不出日出的效果。一定要先冰鎮龍舌蘭酒,如果要搖盪材料,先不要加紅石榴糖漿,要搖盪後再添加紅石榴糖漿。一定要用白龍舌蘭酒。還有一種叫龍舌蘭日落。材料是龍舌蘭酒、黑莓白蘭地、蜂蜜和柳橙汁。要做龍舌蘭日落雞尾酒時,首先倒入龍舌蘭酒、橙汁和蜂蜜加冰塊放入雪克杯搖盪後倒入雞尾酒杯,然後慢慢在上面倒入黑莓白蘭地。黑莓白蘭地最終會沉澱在杯子底部製造出層次的效果。

## 🎥 **Useful Sentences** ▷ 好好用句型

Grenadine is substituted with blackberry brandy.

黑莓白蘭地取代紅石榴糖漿。

🚲 Instead of grenadine, blackberry brandy is used.

　黑莓白蘭地替代紅石榴糖漿。

🚲 As an alternative, blackberry brandy is used not grenadine.

　作為替代材料，黑莓白蘭地用來替代紅石榴糖漿。

🚲 As a replacement for grenadine, blackberry brandy is used.

　作為替代紅石榴糖漿，用的是黑莓白蘭地。

🚲 In place of grenadine, blackberry brandy can be used.

　代替石榴紅石榴糖漿的材料可以用黑莓白蘭地。


Have you heard of Tequila Sunset?

你聽說過龍舌蘭日落雞尾酒嗎？

🚲 Do you know about Tequila Sunset?

　你知道龍舌蘭酒日落雞尾酒嗎？

🚲 Are you aware of Tequila Sunset?

　你知道龍舌蘭酒日落雞尾酒嗎？

🚲 Have you heard about Tequila Sunset?

　你有沒有聽說過龍舌蘭日落雞尾酒嗎？


〈heard of〉〈aware of 〉〈about〉因為有介系詞所以後面一定加名詞

## Mixology of the day 今日酒譜

# Tequila Sunrise
# 龍舌蘭日出

Glassware: Chilled highball glass（冰鎮高球杯）
Method: Build（直接注入法）

**Ingredients 材料**
1.5 oz. chilled Tequila 冰過的龍舌蘭酒
4 oz. fresh orange juice 新鮮的柳橙汁
1 dash of Grenadine 紅石榴糖漿
1 slice of orange 柳橙片

**Instructions 作法**
Add the Tequila and then the orange juice to a chilled highball glass. Add the Grenadine on top and garnish with an orange slice.
把龍舌蘭酒和柳橙汁先後直接注入冰鎮過的高球杯。在上面加上紅石榴糖漿，用柳橙片裝飾。

## Notes 溫馨小提醒

當龍舌蘭酒開封後，就會受到空氣的氧化，就像一般的酒一樣。氧化會讓龍舌蘭的味道在幾個星期到一個月內慢慢淡化，酒精也會慢慢蒸發。開封後的龍舌蘭酒不會無限期的維持在一樣的狀態，所以必須在 1-2 個月之內盡快飲用。

## Historical Background 調酒小故事

原始酒譜的龍舌蘭日出（Tequila Sunrise）包含有龍舌蘭酒，奶油黑醋栗，青檸汁和蘇打水，是由金恩.蘇羅特（Gene Sulit）在 1930 年或 1940 年所調製出的，當時她是亞利桑那比爾特莫爾飯店（Arizona Biltmore Hotel）的調酒師。鮑比.拉佐夫和比利·賴斯（Bobby Lazoff and Billy Rice）在 1970 年代所調製的是後來比較廣受歡迎的「龍舌蘭日出」酒譜，他們酒譜的材料是龍舌蘭酒，橙汁和紅石榴糖漿。在 1973 年，美國老鷹樂團（the Eagles）錄製了一首歌就叫龍舌蘭日出（Tequila Sunrise），當時這首歌和這款雞尾酒紅遍全美國。

**Unit 6**
Tequila-based

## 6.5

## Bitter Salty Perro 苦鹹狗

### 🍷 Dialogue in the Bar ▷ 吧台對話

**Paul and Ken are talking about a new drink.** 🔘69
保羅和肯恩在談論一種新的雞尾酒。

| | | |
|---|---|---|
| **Paul** | I am tired of Margaritas. Is there any good cocktail with grapefruit? | 我喝膩了瑪格麗特。有什麼有加葡萄柚的雞尾酒呢？ |
| **Ken** | I just had a Bitter Salty Perro last night. It is a twist on a drink called Salty Dog. "Perro" means dog in Spanish. | 我昨晚喝了一杯叫苦鹹狗。這是鹹狗的改編版。"Perro" 在西班牙語是指狗的意思。 |
| **Paul** | Isn't Salty Dog made with gin and grapefruit juice and serve with a salted rim? | 鹹狗不就是用琴酒和葡萄柚汁倒入鹽杯喝的嗎？ |

| **Ken** | Bitter Salty Perro is Tequila-based. It also has freshly squeezed pink grapefruit juice, tonic water and a healthy dose of bitters. I made it at home last night because I had all the ingredients on hand. It was good. It's bitter and lip-puckering, but also seriously refreshing. It is just perfect for a summer night. | 苦鹹狗的基酒是龍舌蘭酒。這個用的是新鮮榨的紅葡萄柚汁，通寧水加上一點苦精。我昨晚有在家裡做，因為我手上剛好有所有的材料。很好喝。是有點苦，會讓人緊抿嘴唇但也很有新鮮感。此款雞尾酒很適合夏日夜晚。 |
|---|---|---|
| **Paul** | You actually squeezed pink grapefruit? | 你真的是用新鮮現榨的紅葡萄柚汁嗎？ |
| **Ken** | Yes. It is a must. Grapefruit juice and tequila go really well together. At first, I was worried the drink would be too bitter, but grapefruits are actually sweeter than limes. Tonic water also has a lot more sugar, so it all goes well together. A dash of Angostura bitters is brilliant to blend everything together. | 是的。這是必須要新鮮的。紅葡萄柚汁和龍舌蘭酒搭配的很好。起初，我很擔心會過於苦澀，但葡萄柚實際上比萊姆還甜。通寧水裡也有很多糖份，所以加在一起很不錯。再加上幾滴的安格斯特拉苦精真的很對味。 |

**Unit 6**
**Tequila-based**

## Vocabulary 單字

| mean | v. | 表示……之意 | serve | v. | 供應 |
|---|---|---|---|---|---|
| healthy | n. | 健康 | freshly | adv. | 新鮮地 |
| puckering | v. | 使起皺 | brilliant | adj. | 聰明的 |

219

Tequila and Mezcal are related in nature. They are produced in different states of Mexico. By Mexican law, Tequila can only be made with one variety of agave: the Blue Agave. Mezcal, however, can be made with upwards of 30 varieties of agave, but five different varieties are commonly used. A single Mezcal may contain a blend of agaves. Is there a worm in the bottle? No. It is not a worm at all. It's a larva. There are two types of larvae in Mezcal bottles: gusano rojo (red) and gusano de oro (white or gold). The red larva lives in the root and heart of the agave plant. The white larva lives on the leaves. The red version is more prized as a Mezcal additive. In fact, the worm is not an ancient tradition. It only started in 1950. It was discovered by accident that adding larvae to bottles looks intriguing. Customers liked it so much that sales went up. Not all Mezcal has a worm in the bottle. Premium brands on the market today don't have larvae at all.

龍舌蘭酒和梅斯卡爾酒彼此很類似。他們都產自墨西哥的不同州。墨西哥法律規定，龍舌蘭酒只能由一種龍舌蘭品種所製成。然而，梅斯卡爾酒可以用 30 個不同龍舌蘭的品種所做，但最常見的是五個不同品種所做。一瓶梅斯卡爾酒可能包含不同的龍舌蘭植物。酒瓶裡有蠕蟲嗎？不是的，這一點也不是蠕蟲，那是一種幼蟲。在梅斯卡爾酒瓶裡可以看到兩種類型的幼蟲：gusano rojo（紅色）和 gusano de oro（白色或金色）。紅色的幼蟲是住在龍舌蘭植物的根和鱗莖部分。白色的幼蟲是住在葉片上。紅色的的幼蟲對梅斯卡爾酒來說是比較珍貴的添加劑。事實上，酒瓶裡裝幼蟲並不是一種舊傳統。這是可以追溯到 1950 年左右，酒商意外發現，幼蟲加入酒瓶內看起來很有趣，也會幫助銷售量。並非所有的梅斯卡爾酒在瓶內都會有幼蟲。目前市場上比較好的梅斯卡爾酒裡是沒有幼蟲的。

## Useful Sentences 好好用句型

I am tired of Margaritas.

我喝瑪格麗特喝的很煩了。

🍒 I am bored with Margaritas.

我已經受夠了瑪格麗特。

🍒 I am not interested in Margaritas.

我對瑪格麗特不感興趣。

🍒 I have had enough of Margaritas.

我喝夠了瑪格麗特。

It is a must.

這是必須的。

🍒 You have to.

你必須要這樣做。

🍒 It is necessary.

有必要這樣做。

🍒 It is essential.

這是必不可少的。

## Mixology of the day 今日酒譜

# Bitter Salty Perro
# 苦鹹狗

Glassware: Old fashioned glass（古典酒杯）
Method: Shake and strain（搖盪和過濾法）

**Ingredients 材料**
2 oz. fresh-squeezed grapefruit juice 鮮榨葡萄柚汁
1 oz. 100% agave blanco Tequila 100％龍舌蘭龍舌蘭布蘭科
2 dashes Angostura bitters 安格斯特拉苦精
Tonic water to top (about 2 oz.) 通寧水用來加滿的量
Salted rim 鹽杯

**Instructions 作法**
Rim an old fashioned glass with salt then fill it with ice. Combine grapefruit juice, tequila and bitters in a cocktail shaker with ice. Shake and strain into the rocks glass. Top with tonic and serve.
在古典酒杯的杯沿沾鹽，然後加滿冰塊。把葡萄柚汁，龍舌蘭酒，苦精和冰塊加入雪克杯。搖盪後過濾到古典酒杯。加入通寧水加到滿。

## Notes 溫馨小提醒

有些人認為布蘭科龍舌蘭酒（blanco Tequila）是唯一「真正的」龍舌蘭酒，但是因為價格比 Reposados 和 Anejos Tequila 較貴，所以在雞尾酒裡常常是用 Reposados 和 Anejos Tequila。真正的瑪格麗特（Margarita）應該用的是布蘭科龍舌蘭酒。無論如何，至少買龍舌蘭酒一定要買標有 100% 藍色龍舌蘭（100% blue agave）。

## Historical Background 調酒小故事

梅斯卡爾酒（Mezcal）和龍舌蘭酒（Tequila）的歷史根源遠比在歐洲人到達美洲之前還要久。龍舌蘭（Agave）已被種植了幾個世紀，當時是用來做香料和甜味劑，也有被發酵成輕度酒精飲料類似龍舌蘭酒（pulque），其歷史可追溯到至少 2000 年前。當西班牙人到達美洲後，他們帶來了蒸餾的知識；他們發現龍舌蘭的汁是很容易萃取的。於是產生了現代的龍舌蘭酒。第一個梅斯卡爾酒是出現在 1500 年左右，後來這個酒在接下來的幾個世紀傳遍整個墨西哥，也出口到西班牙。

Unit 6
Tequila-based

### 6.6
## Tequila Sour 龍舌蘭酸酒

🍷 **Dialogue in the Bar** 吧台對話

Jane is asking about superfine sugar in a cocktail. 🎧
簡恩在問有關雞尾酒裡用的超細糖。

| | | |
|---|---|---|
| **Jane** | I've recently run across three cocktail recipes calling for superfine sugar. One is the Tequila Sour. Is it really important to use superfine sugar? | 我最近無意中看到三個雞尾酒酒譜裡説要用超細糖。一個是龍舌蘭酒酸酒。使用超細糖是非常重要的嗎？ |
| **Jenny** (Bartender) | The answer is, for the most part, yes. If a recipe calls for superfine sugar, there's generally a reason. | 答案是，在大多數情況下，是的。如果食譜要求超細糖，通常是有原因的。 |
| **John** (Bartender) | The most common reason is that it's going to melt faster and incorporate itself into the mixture more quickly and smoothly, since it's finer than the regular granulated sugar. | 最常見的原因是，這種糖會融化的比較快，在酒裡混合更迅速更順暢，因為這種糖比普通砂糖還要細。 |

| **Jenny** | That's correct. If you go ahead with regular sugar, it might not dissolve completely. It would probably be the proper sweetness, but the texture would be off. | 這是正確的。如果你只用一般的糖，可能無法完全溶解。這樣調出來的甜度可能是對的，但質感喝起來就不對。 |
|---|---|---|
| **Jane** | What should you do if you don't have superfine sugar at home? | 如果在家裡沒有超細糖，那你會怎麼做呢？ |
| **John** | To make superfine sugar at home, simply run one cup plus two teaspoons of white sugar in the food processor for 30 seconds. This gives you one cup of superfine sugar. | 在家裡可以簡單地作超細糖，把一杯又多兩茶匙的白糖放入食物調理機裡打約 30 秒後就是超細糖。 |

## Vocabulary 單字

generally    *adv.*    一般地
incorporate    *vt.*    把⋯⋯合併
quickly    *adv.*    迅速地
dissolve    v.    融化
teaspoon    *n.*    茶匙
processor    *n.*    調理機

**Unit 6**
Tequila-based

Syrup is usually just sugar and water. There is also flavored syrup or syrup with herbs. Different syrups added to a Sour can turn the Sour into something totally different. Try the chamomile syrup. Combine water and sugar in a saucepan over high heat. Stir to dissolve the sugar and bring to a boil. Immediately remove from heat and add the chamomile tea bags. Steep for 30 minutes then remove the tea bags. Cool and refrigerate. Hot pepper Sour is for people who love spicy taste. Fiery hot pepper syrup is good in the tequila cocktail. To make a hot pepper syrup, add 1 cup water and 1 cup sugar to a saucepan over medium-high heat then add 4 roughly chopped hot peppers and simmer for 10 to 15 minutes. Puree until smooth and fine-strain into a storage container. Let cool completely and store in the refrigerator for up to 2 to 3 weeks. Strawberry-Balsamic Tequila Sour is also another variation. To make balsamic syrup, combine 2/3 cup balsamic vinegar and 2 tablespoons sugar. Bring to a simmer and simmer gently until reduced by 1/3. Allow to cool before using. Balsamic syrup can be stored in the refrigerator for a very long time.

糖漿通常只是糖和水。也可以買到有調味糖漿或草藥糖漿。不同的糖漿加入酸味雞尾酒可以讓雞尾酒喝起來很特別。試試看洋甘菊糖漿。把水和糖在鍋裡用高火加熱。攪拌讓其溶解和煮滾。立即關火，加入甘菊茶包。浸泡 30 分鐘，然後取出茶葉。涼爽和冷藏。辣椒酸酒是給喜愛辛辣味的人。火熱的辣椒糖漿也很適合放入龍舌蘭雞尾酒。辣椒糖漿的作法是把 1 杯水和 1 杯糖放入鍋中，用中上火加熱後再加入 4 個切碎的辣椒，煮約 10～15 分鐘後放入調理機裡打爛後過濾到存儲容器。讓其完全冷卻，可以存放在冰箱裡長達 2～3 週。草莓巴薩米可醋龍舌蘭酸酒也是另一種口味的變化。巴薩米可醋糖漿的作法是把 2/3 杯巴薩米可醋和 2 湯匙糖放入鍋內煮到沸騰。煮到液體減少約 1/3。使用前先冷卻。香醋糖漿水可以存儲在冰箱中很長的一段時間。

## 🔊 Useful Sentences ▷ 好好用句型

I've recently run across three cocktail recipes.

我最近發現三個雞尾酒食譜。

🍒 I recently <u>found</u> three cocktail recipes by chance.

我最近無意中發現三個雞尾酒食譜。

🍒 I recently <u>stumbled upon</u> three cocktail recipes.

我最近無意中發現三個雞尾酒食譜。

🍒 I recently <u>came across</u> three cocktail recipes.

我最近無意中發現三個雞尾酒食譜。

這些片語（標示底線的部分）都有「在不刻意的情況下找到或遇到」的意思。

If a recipe calls for superfine sugar, there's generally a reason.

如果食譜說要用精細糖，通常是有其理由的。

🍒 If the recipe asks for superfine sugar, there's generally a reason.

如果食譜說要用精細糖，通常是有其理由的。

🍒 If the recipe requires superfine sugar, there's generally a reason.

如果食譜規定要用精細糖，通常是有其理由的。

🍒 If the recipe needs superfine sugar, there's generally a reason.

如果食譜需要用精細糖，通常是有理由的。

🍒 If the recipe says to use superfine sugar, there's generally a reason.

如果食譜說要用精細糖，通常是有理由的。

〈calls for〉、〈asks for〉的介系詞後面可以接「想要得到的事或人」。

例如：

• He is asking for Mr. Johnson.

• She is calling for Phillips.

Unit 6
Tequila-based

## Mixology of the day 今日酒譜

# Tequila Sour
# 龍舌蘭酸酒

Glassware: Sour glass（酸酒杯）
Method: Shake（搖盪法）

### Ingredients 材料
2-3 ounces tequila 龍舌蘭
2 tablespoons lemon juice 檸檬汁
1/2-1 teaspoon superfine sugar 精細糖
3 or 4 ice cubes 冰塊
1 orange slice 柳橙片

### Instructions 作法
Combine the tequila, lemon juice, and superfine sugar with ice into a cocktail shaker and shake vigorously. Strain into a sour glass. Garnish with one orange slice and serve.

把龍舌蘭酒，檸檬汁和精細糖以及冰塊一起放入雪克杯後和劇烈搖盪後過濾到酸酒杯。用柳橙片裝飾即可。

## Notes 溫馨小提醒

水果片是最簡單的雞尾酒裝飾方式，如果是整片的水果片就叫 "wheel"，橘子有大有小，如果是大的雞尾酒杯，就應該用大的柳橙片，但是如果視覺上不平衡，則可以彈性的把柳橙片切一半。

## Historical Background 調酒小故事

數字顯示墨西哥龍舌蘭酒在未來將會征服中國市場。在 2013 年，墨西哥龍舌蘭酒酒商出口到全世界總共超過 1.5 億公升（150 million litres）龍舌蘭酒，那是當時歷史上龍舌蘭酒出口最高的量。在 2013 年墨西哥出口到中國只有 70,000 瓶的 100% 龍舌蘭酒。在中國大陸市場的需求下，墨西哥總統在 2014 年預測，光在 2019 年龍舌蘭酒出口到中國就會有一千萬公升（10 million litres）。

# PART 2

## Liqueur
# 利口酒

## UNIT 7 Liqueur-based 利口酒

### 7.1
## Jägermeister 野格酒

🍷 **Dialogue in the Bar** 吧台對話

**A conversation about different Jägermeister mixed drinks.** 🎧73

關於調製不同野格酒雞尾酒的對話。

| | | |
|---|---|---|
| **Mark** | I really enjoy Jägermeister. It is a potent, bittersweet herbal liqueur. I had the greatest memories with Jägermeister when I first visited Germany. I think the best way to enjoy Jägermeister is an ice cold shot. | 我真的很喜歡野格酒。這是後勁很強，苦甜參半的草藥酒。我第一次訪問德國時，就對野格酒留下美好的回憶。我覺得品嚐野格酒最好的方式是加冰塊直接喝。 |
| **John**<br>(Bartender) | This is very classic; simply pour ice cold Jägermeister in a shot glass. Yes. It is that easy. | 這是非常經典的；只需把冰野格酒倒入小酒杯。沒錯，就是這麼容易。 |
| **Jenny**<br>(Bartender) | That's the most common way to drink Jägermeister. But there are other great drink recipes with Jägermeister. Have you tried a Jägermeister Rudi? It is just 1 part Jägermeister and 1 part bitter beer. | 那是喝野格酒最常見的方式。但也有其他很不錯的野格酒雞尾酒酒譜。你是否喝過「野格酒魯迪」？那只用一比一的野格酒和苦啤酒調製。 |

| | | |
|---|---|---|
| **Mark** | I haven't tried that, but it sounds interesting. It does not sound bad at all. | 我還沒有試過，但聽起來很有意思。聽起來不錯。 |
| **John** | I like the Jägermeister Ginger. It's similar to a Moscow mule but with the added flavor of Jägermeister, this is a refreshing summertime drink. It has Jägermeister, lime, Ginger Beer and uses a cucumber to garnish it. | 我很喜歡「野格酒生薑」。這和「莫斯科騾子」很類似，但野格酒的風味更好，這是清涼的夏季飲料，酒譜是野格酒、萊姆、薑汁啤酒，再用小黃瓜裝飾。 |
| **Jenny** | Another easy one is a Jägermeister and tonic water. No gin. Combine all the ingredients in a tall glass with ice, stir well, and garnish with an orange slice. | 另一個簡單的作法是野格酒加通寧水，不是加琴酒。把所有材料加入有冰塊的杯子中，攪拌均勻後，用柳橙片裝飾。 |

# 🍸 Vocabulary ▶ 單字

potent　*adj.*　強有力的
bittersweet　*adj.*　又苦又甜
summertime　*n.*　夏季
cucumber　*n.*　小黃瓜
combine　v.　結合
slice　*n.*　切片

Unit 7
Liqueurs

For a busy bartender, there are several perfect easy cocktail recipes for Jägermeister drinks. "The Jägermeister after Dark" is 1/2 part dark chocolate liqueur and 1 part Jägermeister. Pour in the chocolate liqueur and then top with Jägermeister. "The Jäger Energy Drink" is 1 1/2 part Jägermeister, 1 can energy drink, some ice cubes and a slice of lime. Pour the energy drink in a glass and then top it off with 1.5 oz. of Jägermeister and finish with a slice of lime. The Redhead is 1/3 part Jägermeister, 1/3 part peach schnapps, 1/3 part cranberry juice. Combine all ingredients in a shaker with ice, shake well and strain into a shot glass. The Jägermeister Float is 1 1/2 parts Jägermeister, 3 parts root beer and vanilla ice cream. Pour the Jägermeister in a large glass, add two scoops vanilla ice cream, and then add root beer.

對於繁忙的調酒師來說，手邊有幾個完美卻簡單的野格酒雞尾酒酒譜是不錯的。〈黑暗後的野格〉是 1/2 份黑巧克力利口酒和 1 份野格酒。把巧克力利口酒倒入杯內，然後把野格酒倒在上面。〈野格能量飲料〉是用 1 和 1/2 份的野格酒、1 罐能量飲料、冰塊和萊姆片。把能量飲料倒入酒杯，加入 1.5 盎司野格酒，在加入冰塊和萊姆片就完成。〈紅頭〉是 1/3 的野格酒、1/3 桃杜松子酒和 1/3 蔓越莓果汁。將所有材料放入搖杯，和冰塊均勻搖晃，過濾到酒杯。〈漂浮野格酒〉是 1 份半野格酒、3 份沙士和香草冰淇淋。把野格酒倒入大杯子，加入兩勺香草冰淇淋，然後加沙士。

NOTE: "1 part" is a full jigger. "2 1/2 parts" is two and a half jiggers. "1/2 part" is one half of the jigger full.

解釋：「份」指的是量酒器的容量，用量酒器來做比例。「1 份」是一個滿量酒器，「2 又 1/2 份」是二又二分之一個量酒器，「1/2 份」是半杯量酒器。

## 🔊▶ **Useful Sentences**　好好用句型

This is very classic.

這是非常經典的。

🚲 **That is pretty standard.**

　　這是非常標準的。

🚲 **It's a model of its kind.**

　　這是這個類型中的典範。

It does not sound bad at all.

這聽起來並不壞。

🚲 **It sounds pretty good.**

　　這聽起來很不錯。

🚲 **It's a good idea.**

　　這是一個好主意。

🚲 **It's not a bad idea.**

　　這不是一個壞主意。

## Mixology of the day 今日酒譜

# Jäger Bomb
# 野格炸彈

Glassware: Shot glass and highball glass（烈酒杯和高球杯）
Method: Build（直接注入法）

### Ingredients 材料
1 1/2 oz Jägermeister 野格酒
1/2 can Red Bull energy drink 紅牛能量飲料

### Instructions 作法
Fill a shot glass with Jägermeister. Fill a highball glass with Red Bull. Drop the shot glass into the taller glass and drink immediately.

在烈酒杯裡裝滿野格酒，在高球杯倒入半罐的紅牛，把裝滿野格酒的烈酒杯直接放入有紅牛的高球杯，一次暢飲。

## Notes 溫馨小提醒

野格炸彈很特別的是同時用了兩種杯子，小的烈酒杯直接放入高球杯中，因為這個作法太特別了，如果讀者很難想像的話，可以上網搜尋照片，就能知道是怎樣的調製的方式。不過現在市面上也可以買到特製的野格炸彈杯（Jäger Bomb Cup）。

## Historical Background 調酒小故事

野格酒是一種德國原產的藥酒。由 56 種不同的草藥、花和植物的根，以及來自世界不同的水果所做的，其中有錫蘭的肉桂樹皮、澳大利亞的苦橙皮、東印度的檀香，以及亞洲的薑。德國在 1934 年就有野格（Jägermeister）這個名詞，當時是用來形容獵場看守人。直到 1935 年，德國才有了真正野格酒的專有名詞。野格酒的發明者柯特・買斯特（Curt Mast）是一名狂熱的獵人。在德文裡，Jäger 意味著獵人，Meister 是指大師，所以 Jägermeister 這個字直接翻譯的意思就是「狩獵高手」。

Unit 7
Liqueurs

237

## 7.2

## Amaretto 杏仁香甜酒

### Dialogue in the Bar 吧台對話

**Talking about different recipes for Amaretto sour.** (75)
談論不同杏仁酸酒的酒譜。

| | | |
|---|---|---|
| **John**<br>(Bartender) | As a bartender I am frequently looking for different recipes to test out. | 身為一個調酒師，我常常會找不同的酒譜來試試看。 |
| **Andy** | A friend gave me a new recipe for the Amaretto sour last week, and I love it. | 一個朋友上星期給我杏仁酸酒的新酒譜，我很喜歡。 |
| **Jenny**<br>(Bartender) | I love the amaretto flavor too. What's so special about the new Amaretto sour? | 我也很喜歡杏仁的味道。新口味的杏仁酸酒有什麼特別之處？ |

| | | |
|---|---|---|
| **Andy** | It's the frothy egg white. I froth egg white with my battery operated frother. Then squeeze one lemon, mix in the amaretto and bourbon. It's a good and quick homemade amaretto sour! The recipe calls for simple syrup but I omitted it because amaretto is already sweet enough. The drink is awesome! | 祕訣就在蛋白霜上。我用電動打蛋器把蛋清打發泡，然後加入檸檬汁、杏仁香甜酒和波旁威士忌。就是一杯簡單又好喝的自製杏仁酸酒！酒譜是説要用糖漿，但我沒有加，因為杏仁已經夠甜了。這款雞尾酒真的很好喝！ |
| **John** | Amaretto is sweet. It is okay to omit the sugar syrup completely. When I make Amaretto Sour, I don't add sugar unless someone asks for it. | 杏仁酒是甜的。所以不加糖漿無所謂。當我做杏仁酸酒時，我是不加冰糖的，除非有客人指明要更甜的味道。 |
| **Jenny** | One of my favorite recipes is called a Blood Rum Sour. It brings amaretto and dark rum together. I also add a dash of angostura bitters. It's quite good. | 我最喜歡的一個酒譜是「血腥蘭姆酸酒」。此款雞尾酒融合了杏仁香甜酒和黑蘭姆酒。我也會加幾滴的安格斯特拉苦精。味道很不錯。 |

**Unit 7**
Liqueurs

## ⍙ Vocabulary 單字

battery　*n.*　電池
omit　*vt.*　遺漏
unless　prep.　除……外

operate　*vi.*　運作
add　*vt.*　添加

The original Amaretto Sour recipe was equal parts amaretto and lemon juice over ice. Mix liquids together and pour over ice into an old fashioned glass. Garnish with a maraschino cherry or an orange slice. Amaretto is also popular in different cooking recipes. Add Amaretto to the popular Italian cake Tiramisu. Add Amaretto in chicken. Add some amaretto to pancake batter for a richer flavor. Amaretto is often added to almondine sauce for fish and vegetables. Amaretto is also delicious in coffee, hot cocoa and black tea. Amaretto can be added to cheesecake or pound cake. Or, just drizzle warmed amaretto over a bowl of ice cream and enjoy. For a Coffee Amaretto, put 1.5 ounces amaretto into a coffee mug and fill it up with coffee. Top it with a little whipped cream. For a Tea Amaretto, add amaretto into a cup of hot tea, but do not stir it. Top with chilled whipped cream and serve. This is a perfect tea for a cold, dreary day!

原始的杏仁酸酒配方是用一比一的杏仁酒和檸檬汁加入冰塊。把所有的材料混合在一起後，倒入有冰塊的古典酒杯。用酒櫻桃或柳橙片裝飾。杏仁香甜酒也可以加在不同的烹飪食譜。可以把杏仁酒添加到受歡迎的義大利蛋糕提拉米蘇。煮雞肉時也可以加入杏仁香甜酒。把杏仁香甜酒加入美式煎餅麵糊會讓味道更豐富。用杏仁香甜酒做魚和蔬菜的醬料也很不錯。杏仁香甜酒加入咖啡、熱巧克力和紅茶都很美味。杏仁香甜酒也可以加入乳酪蛋糕或磅重蛋糕。或者，只是把溫熱的杏仁香甜酒加在冰淇淋上面也很棒。「咖啡杏仁」是把 1.5 盎司的杏仁香甜酒倒入一般咖啡杯後，在填滿咖啡，上面加少許奶油。「杏仁茶」是把杏仁酒倒入熱茶裡，但不要攪拌它，上面加入奶油就可以飲用了。這樣的喝法很適合在寒冷沉悶的天氣裡喝！

## 📷 Useful Sentences 好好用句型

What's so special about the new Amaretto sour?

新口味的杏仁酸酒有什麼特別之處？

🍒 **What makes the new Amaretto sour so special?**

是什麼讓新口味的杏仁酸酒如此特別？

🍒 **Why is the new Amaretto Sour so different?**

為什麼新口味的杏仁酸酒會如此不同？

The drink was awesome!

此款雞尾酒是真的很棒！

🍒 **What a wonderful drink!**

多麼棒的雞尾酒！

🍒 **That is an amazing drink.**

這是一個很棒的雞尾酒。

🍒 **I love that drink.**

我喜歡這樣的雞尾酒。

Unit 7
Liqueurs

## Mixology of the day 今日酒譜

# Amaretto Sour
# 杏仁香甜酸酒

Glassware: Old fashioned glass（古典酒杯）
Method: Dry shake and regular shake（乾式搖盪法和一般搖盪法）

**Ingredients 材料**
1.5 oz. amaretto 杏仁香甜酒
0.75 oz. bourbon 波本酒
1 oz. lemon juice 檸檬汁
1 tsp. simple syrup 糖漿
0.5 oz. egg white 蛋白

**Instructions 作法**
Vigorously dry shake all ingredients to combine, then shake well with cracked ice. Strain over fresh ice in an old fashioned glass. Garnish with an orange slice and a cherry.
大力搖盪讓所有材料融合，加碎冰後，再搖盪均勻。接著，過濾到有加冰塊的古典酒杯中。用柳橙片和櫻桃裝飾。

## Notes 溫馨小提醒

杏仁香甜酒可以用 Lazzaroni Amaretto 的品牌，也可以用 DiSaronno 的品牌。在製作杏仁香甜酸酒（Amaretto Sour）時，如果沒有糖漿的話，可以用柳橙汁代替，柳橙汁會讓此款雞尾酒多一點澀味而有層次感。

## Historical Background 調酒小故事

根據官方資料，義大利在 1525 年就有杏仁香甜酒。百年來義大利人在烹調時就會用杏仁香甜酒當食材，尤其會加在甜食和咖啡裡增加風味。但是讓人驚訝的是，這樣的義大利傳統一直到 1960 年代才傳入北美洲。據說自 1525 年杏仁香甜酒發明以來，配方就保持不變。現在的杏仁香甜酒含有精心打造的高品質天然成分，由無水酒精、焦糖和 17 種挑選過的水果和藥材所做成。

## 7.3
## Bailey's Irish Cream 愛爾蘭香甜奶酒

### 🍷 **Dialogue in the Bar** ▶ 吧台對話

**A discussion about Irish Cream mixed drinks.** 🎧
關於愛爾蘭香甜奶酒雞尾酒的討論。

| | | |
|---|---|---|
| **Wendy** | The first time I had Irish Cream was with coffee on a cold night. The Irish Cream with coffee was just unforgettable. | 我第一次喝愛爾蘭香甜奶酒加咖啡是在一個寒冷的夜晚。愛爾蘭香甜奶酒加咖啡真是令人難忘。 |
| **Irene** | Doesn't that have alcohol? | 那不是有酒精在裡面嗎？ |
| **Wendy** | Yes. It is a mixture of whiskey, cream, and sugar. It mostly uses Irish whiskey as its base. Bailey's Irish cream is the most popular brand on the market. | 是的。是威士忌、奶油和糖的甜酒。主要是用愛爾蘭威士忌做的。百利愛爾蘭香甜奶酒是市面上是最流行的品牌。 |
| **Irene** | My friend gave me a bottle last Christmas. I have not opened it yet. It is displayed nicely in my living room. | 我的朋友去年聖誕節送我一瓶。我還沒打開來呢。這瓶酒就漂亮地陳列在我的客廳裡。 |

| | | |
|---|---|---|
| **John**<br>(Bartender) | You can add it in your coffee. Or even drizzle it on top of ice cream. Most Irish cream smells of hazelnuts or sweet almonds, and it is very sweet to taste; so it goes good with coffee or cream. There is another less-alcoholic version called Baileys Glide, which is sold prepackaged in small bottles. | 你可以加在咖啡裡。或是加一點在冰淇淋上。大部分的愛爾蘭奶酒聞起來有榛果或甜杏仁的香味，這是非常甜的味道，所以和咖啡或奶油很配。還有另一種低酒精版的稱為〈百利滑翔〉，通常是小瓶販售。 |
| **Irene** | Any suggestions for an Irish cream cocktail? | 你有任何建議愛爾蘭奶酒的酒譜嗎？ |
| **John** | The Mudslide is similar to the White Russian. The difference between the two is that The Mudslide uses Irish cream liqueur instead of cream. Mix 1 ounce vodka, 1 ounce coffee liqueur and 1 ounce Irish cream into a cocktail shaker filled with ice. Shake well. Strain into an old-fashioned glass filled with ice. | 「土石流」雞尾酒和「白俄羅斯」雞尾酒很像。兩者之間的區別是，「土石流」加的是愛爾蘭奶油酒。把 1 盎司伏特加、1 盎司咖啡利口酒和 1 盎司愛爾蘭奶酒放入搖杯，加滿冰塊，均勻搖晃後，在過濾到裝滿冰塊的古典酒杯中。 |

**Unit 7**
Liqueurs

# 🍸 Vocabulary  單字

| | | | |
|---|---|---|---|
| display | *vt.* 陳列 | nicely | *adj.* 令人滿意地 |
| drizzle | *vi.* 下毛毛雨 | hazelnut | *n.* 榛果 |
| prepackage | *vt.* 先包裝好的 | suggestion | *n.* 建議 |

245

DIY Irish Cream at home? No problem! And it is not hard at all. In a small saucepan, set over medium low heat, warm 1/4 cup heavy cream with 2 tablespoons chocolate syrup, 1 1/2 teaspoons instant coffee granules and 1/4 teaspoon salt. Whisk until the coffee granules and salt have dissolved and the consistency is smooth. Add the coffee and cream mixture, 3/4 cup heavy cream, one can of sweetened condensed milk and 1 teaspoon vanilla extract in a blender. Blend until very smooth. With the blender running, slowly pour in the whiskey. It is very important to make sure it does not curdle. Add the alcohol slowly and make sure to use heavy cream. Add the alcohol at the very end, with the blender going, at a very slow speed to avoid possible curdling. Transfer to a bottle and refrigerate until cold. Right before serving, give it a good stir. Irish Cream is perfect for adding to coffee, drizzling on ice cream, or using as an ingredient in dessert recipes such as Irish cream cupcakes, Irish cream chocolate pie, Irish cream Tiramisu, Irish cream pudding, and Irish cream cheesecake.

自己在家做愛爾蘭奶酒？沒問題！其實一點都不難。在一個小鍋裡加入 1/4 杯鮮奶油和 2 湯匙巧克力糖漿、1 又 1/2 茶匙的速溶咖啡和 1/4 茶匙的鹽，用中火加溫。輕輕攪拌直到咖啡顆粒和鹽溶解後，倒入自動攪拌機裡，在加入 3/4 杯鮮奶油、一個罐頭的煉乳和 1 茶匙香草精。讓攪拌機攪拌。隨著攪拌機的攪拌，慢慢倒入威士忌。這個步驟非常重要，要確保混合物不會凝固。添加酒精時要很緩慢，而且一定要使用鮮奶油。重點是要在最後才加酒精，得在攪拌器運行時才非常緩慢地加入酒精，以避免液體有可能會凝結。接著把液體倒入瓶子後，放入冰箱冷藏直到冷凍。在喝之前要先好好的攪拌一下。愛爾蘭奶酒和咖啡是完美的結合，淋在冰淇淋上也很不錯，或是也可以加入點心的材料中，如愛爾蘭奶油蛋糕、愛爾蘭奶油巧克力派、愛爾蘭奶油提拉米蘇、愛爾蘭奶油布丁及愛爾蘭奶油乳酪蛋糕。

## 🍵 Useful Sentences 好好用句型

You can add it in your coffee.

你可以加在咖啡裡。

🍒 Add that in your coffee.

加一點在你的咖啡裡。

🍒 Put that in your coffee.

加在你的咖啡裡。


Any suggestion for Irish cream cocktail?

有任何愛爾蘭奶酒雞尾酒酒譜的建議嗎？

🍒 Any idea for Irish cream cocktail?

有任何愛爾蘭奶酒雞尾酒酒譜的想法嗎？

🍒 Do you have recipe for Irish cream cocktail?

你有愛爾蘭奶酒雞尾酒酒譜嗎？

🍒 Do you know anything about Irish cream cocktail?

你知道有什麼愛爾蘭奶酒調的雞尾酒嗎？

**Unit 7**
Liqueurs

## **Mixology of the day** 今日酒譜

# Irish Coffee
# 愛爾蘭咖啡

Glassware: Irish coffee glass（愛爾蘭咖啡杯）
Method: Stir（攪拌法）

### Ingredients 材料
2 oz. Baileys Irish cream 愛爾蘭香甜奶酒
6 oz. hot coffee 熱咖啡
1 oz. Irish whiskey 愛爾蘭威士忌
1 dollop whipped cream (optional) 鮮奶油（可不加）

### Instructions 作法
Combine all the ingredients in a tall Irish coffee glass and stir softly. Then top with whipped cream.
將所有材料加入愛爾蘭咖啡杯中並輕輕攪拌。再加上鮮奶油即成。

## 🍸 Notes ▶ 溫馨小提醒

像愛爾蘭香甜奶酒這種有加奶油的利口酒，通常在瓶子上會有保存說明。未開封的愛爾蘭香甜奶酒可以存放 2 年，一旦開封後有六個月的保質期，但是一定要冷藏才能保持最好的味道。愛爾蘭香甜奶酒也可以用在烘焙上，如乳酪蛋糕、冰淇淋、蛋糕和鬆餅。

## Historical Background ▶ 調酒小故事

愛爾蘭香甜奶酒（Baileys Irish Cream）是愛爾蘭的 Gilbeys 公司所製造的。1974 年，該公司的愛爾蘭香甜奶酒正式上市。百利愛爾蘭奶酒 Baileys 這個名字完全是虛構的，百利愛爾蘭奶酒產於都柏林。百利愛爾蘭奶酒只用來自愛爾蘭的牛所生產的牛奶。這個品牌一年使用 72,600,000 加侖的牛奶。根據 Gilbeys 公司統計，愛爾蘭香甜奶酒受到大眾喜愛的程度是在世界各地，平均每一分鐘就會被喝掉 2,300 杯。

## 7.4
# Kahlua 卡魯哇咖啡香甜酒

### 🍷 **Dialogue in the Bar** ▶ 吧台對話

**Talking about the homemade version of Kahlua.** (79)

談論卡魯哇咖啡香甜酒的自製版。

| | | |
|---|---|---|
| **Vincent** | My friend visited Mexico last month and he brought me a bottle of Kahlua. I am researching online about how to use Kahlua. | 我的朋友在上個月去墨西哥玩，他送我一瓶卡魯哇咖啡香甜酒。我就在網路上研究如何使用卡魯哇咖啡香甜酒。 |
| **Jenny** (Bartender) | Kahlua is a rich, dark and smooth coffee based liqueur from Mexico. Although it is a liqueur, it is extremely versatile. It can be enjoyed in a variety of ways. | 卡魯哇是來自墨西哥香濃的咖啡甜酒。雖然這是利口酒，但是可以有很多用途。可以用各種方式享受這種酒。 |
| **Vincent** | On the bottle, rum is listed in the ingredients. | 標簽上說蘭姆酒是其中一項材料。 |

| | | |
|---|---|---|
| **Jenny** | Kahlua is a coffee-flavored rum-based liqueur. It also contains sugar, corn syrup and vanilla bean. Kahlua is used to make cocktails and as a topping or ingredient in several desserts, including ice cream, cakes, and cheesecakes. | 卡魯哇就是以咖啡味為主的甜酒。這種酒裡還含有糖、玉米糖漿和香草豆莢。卡魯哇可以用來調製幾款雞尾酒，也可用在甜點裡，包括冰淇淋、蛋糕和乳酪蛋糕。 |
| **John**<br>(Bartender) | Kahlua is just the most famous one of the types of liqueur. It is rum-based but people also make it with vodka. It is easy to make at home. Mix 4 cups of water, 8 cups sugar and 1 1/2 cups coffee crystals. Heat and stir until dissolved. Cool to room temperature. Add 4 1/2 cups 100 proof vodka. Stir to combine. Pour mixture into two bottles. Cut two vanilla beans into thirds and drop a bean into each bottle. After 2-3 weeks, strain, remove the beans, and rebottle. That's my homemade version of Kahlua. | 卡魯哇是這種類型的甜酒中最有名的品牌。這是以蘭姆酒為主的利口酒，但也可以用伏特加酒來做。這種酒在家裡很容易做。把 4 杯水、8 杯糖、1 又 1/2 杯咖啡粉加熱並攪拌至溶解。在室溫冷卻後，加入 4 杯 又 1/2 杯 的 伏特加。攪拌混合。將其倒入兩個瓶子中。把兩條香草豆莢各切成三份並分別放入每個瓶子中。2-3 週後，過濾混合物，把香草豆莢拿掉，再倒入兩個瓶子中。這就是我的自製版卡魯哇咖啡香甜酒。 |

**Unit 7** Liqueurs

## 🍸 Vocabulary 單字

| | | | | | |
|---|---|---|---|---|---|
| version | *n.* | 版本 | research | v. | 研究 |
| extremely | *adv.* | 極端地 | versatile | *adj.* | 多變化的 |
| contain | v. | 容納 | vanilla | *n.* | 香草 |

To make a "Kahlua on the Rocks" just simply add a couple of shots of Kahlua to a rocks glass filled with ice. However, it is easy to make delicious Kahlua cocktails. The Kahlua Black Russian is two parts vodka and one part Kahlua. Kahlua White Russians are made the same way as the white Russian; only take out the milk or cream. Mudslide is two parts vodka, two parts cream or milk, one part Kahlua and one part Irish cream liqueur. Coffee Martini is two parts vodka, one part Kahlua, and one part chocolate liqueur. Add the ingredients to a shaker with ice. Shake until cold and strain into a martini glass. Kahlua with Hot Chocolate is regular hot chocolate with one shot of Kahlua. Kahlua with Coffee is eight ounce cup of coffee and a shot of Kahlua. No need to add sugar since the Kahlua is sweetened, but add milk or cream, if desire.

「加冰的卡魯哇」是簡單的把 2 盎司的卡魯哇咖啡香甜酒倒在冰塊上飲用。然而，好喝的卡魯哇雞尾酒很容易做。「卡魯哇黑俄羅斯」是把兩份伏特加加入一份卡魯哇中。「卡魯哇白俄羅斯」和「白俄羅斯」的作法是相同的，只是不需要用牛奶或奶油。「土石流」是兩份伏特加、兩份的奶油或牛奶、一份卡魯哇和一份愛爾蘭奶油利口酒。「咖啡馬提尼」是兩份伏特加、一份甘露和一份巧克力利口酒，把材料放入有冰塊的搖杯，搖晃直到冰涼後過濾到馬提尼酒杯。「卡魯哇熱巧克力」是用一般的熱巧克力在加上一點卡魯哇。「卡魯哇咖啡」是 8 盎司的咖啡加卡魯哇，不需要加糖，因為卡魯哇很甜了，如果喜歡的話是可以加入牛奶或鮮奶油。

## Useful Sentences　好好用句型

I am researching online about how to use Kahlua.

我在網路上研究如何使用卡魯哇咖啡香甜酒。

&#x26B7; I am looking at different websites about how to use Kahlua.

我在看不同的網站有關如何使用卡魯哇咖啡香甜酒。

&#x26B7; I am checking online about Kahlua.

我在網路上查看有關卡魯哇咖啡香甜酒。


It is extremely versatile.

非常靈活的。

&#x26B7; It can be used in many ways.

可以用在許多不同的方式。

&#x26B7; There are different ways to use it.

有很多不同的方式可以用。

## ♼ Mixology of the day ▶ 今日酒譜

# B-52
## 轟炸機

Glassware: Shot glass（一口杯）
Method: Float（漂浮法）

### Ingredients 材料
1/3 shot Kahlua 卡魯哇咖啡香甜酒
1/3 shot Baileys Irish Cream 愛爾蘭香甜奶油酒
1/3 shot Grand Marnier 香橙干邑甜酒

### Instructions 作法
Begin with Kahlua, next add Irish cream and finish with Grand Marnier. Carefully pour each ingredient on the back of a bar spoon so that each liqueur end up creating a separate layer.

首先先倒卡魯哇咖啡香甜酒，然後加愛爾蘭香甜奶油酒，最後加香橙干邑甜酒。每一個材料都要很小心地、慢慢地倒在酒吧匙的背面，這樣就會做出一層層的雞尾酒。

## Notes 溫馨小提醒

B-52 轟炸機是很小的一杯，但在調製的時候要很小心，不然無法清楚調出三種顏色的分層。先加咖啡酒，在用低管慢慢加入奶酒，最後是伏特加。滴酒時要很緩慢，不要讓酒產生混濁。喝時可以點火且一口飲盡。

## Historical Background 調酒小故事

B-52 轟炸機（The B-52 shot）的命名是來自越戰時所使用的戰機。B-52 轟炸機雞尾酒有幾種可信的起源故事。其中一個説法是此款雞尾酒是在 1977 年，由加拿大有名的班夫溫泉酒店（Banff Springs Hotel）所調配出來的。當時的調酒師，也是酒店負責人 Peter Fich 擁有多家餐廳，其中一家是位在加拿大卡爾加里的小桶牛排餐廳（Keg Steakhouse in Calgary），很多人認為這是 B-52 轟炸機的起源地。

# UNIT 7 Liqueur-based 利口酒

## 7.5 Midori 蜜瓜香甜酒

### Dialogue in the Bar 吧台對話

**Talking about different ways to make Midori mixed drinks.** 181
談到不同蜜瓜香甜酒雞尾酒的作法。

| | | |
|---|---|---|
| **Kelly** | When I first had Midori, I loved it right away. The color and the taste are just amazing. I don't remember the name of the cocktail I had, but I was told Midori was used. | 當我第一次喝到蜜瓜香甜酒，我馬上就愛上它了。顏色和味道都太特別了。我不記得當時喝的雞尾酒的名字，但我被告知它有使用蜜瓜香甜酒。 |
| **Ken** | You probably will like a Midori Sour. | 你應該會喜歡甜瓜香甜酸酒。 |
| **Kelly** | What's in it? | 裡面有什麼材料？ |
| **Ken** | It has Midori, sweet and sour mix, and Sprite soda. It's very easy to make. | 有蜜瓜香甜酒、酸甜混合液和雪碧。很容易做的。 |
| **Kelly** | What's the sweet and sour mix? | 什麼是酸甜混合液？ |

| Ken | It's a mixture that is yellow-green in color and is used in many cocktails. It is made from approximately equal parts lemon and/or lime juice and simple syrup, which is shaken vigorously with ice. I have all the ingredients. We can make it right now. | 這是一種混合物，是黃綠色的，可以加在許多雞尾酒裡。通常是由一比一的檸檬和／或萊姆汁和糖漿調配，加冰劇烈搖晃後做成的酸甜混合液。我有所有的材料。我們現在就可以來做。 |
| Kelly | Great. Let's try it. | 好啊。我們試試吧。 |
| Ken | After Midori Sour, we can make Japanese Slipper. It is also easy to make. I also have all the ingredients including Midori, Triple Sec and lemon juice. I even have maraschino cherries that we can use for garnish. | 做完甜瓜香甜酸酒後，我們可以做「日本拖鞋」。這也很容易做。我也有所有的材料，包括蜜瓜香甜酒、橘子利口酒和檸檬汁。我還有酒漬櫻桃，可以用來當裝飾。 |
| Kelly | Sure. This is the Midori night. | 當然。今晚是蜜瓜香甜酒之夜。 |

# Ⓨ Vocabulary 單字

remember   v.   記得
probably   *adv.*   很可能
approximately   *adv.*   大概
equal   *adj.*   相等的
vigorously   *adv.*   有力地
even   *adj.*   對等的

Unit 7
Liqueurs

Melon liqueur is a useful mixer for cocktails, but the price of melon liqueur can range from low to very high. Vok Melon from Australia is made with lots of melon and other sweet fruits. It is a low budget alternative to other high priced green liqueurs. It is cheaper than Midori but it tastes just as good. It goes well with either pineapple juice or lemonade. DeKuyper Melon is a fruit liqueur from the United States and has an alcohol percentage of 23%. Bols Melon is a light green liqueur with the fresh taste and mild aroma of honeydew melon. Leroux Melon has the sweet, juicy flavor of honeydew and other melons. Midori Melon is a vibrant green, honeydew flavored liqueur. Many believe Midori is the best melon liqueur on the market and that there are no substitutes whatsoever. It is worth the extra money.

蜜瓜香甜酒是一個很好用雞尾酒材料，不過蜜瓜香甜酒的價格範圍可低也可高。**Vok Melon** 是來自澳大利亞的蜜瓜香甜酒，這是用大量的甜瓜和其他甜味水果所做的。和其他高價位的綠色香甜酒來說，此款酒是比較平價的。**Vok Melon** 比日本的蜜瓜香甜酒還便宜，但味道不相上下。此款香甜酒和鳳梨汁或檸檬水的味道都很配。**DeKuyper** 甜瓜是美國的水果利口酒，含有23％的酒精。**Bols Melon** 是一種淺綠色的酒，有新鮮的味道和甜瓜的香氣。**Leroux Melon** 有哈蜜瓜的瓜果甜味與多汁的好味道。**Midori Melon** 是一款充滿活力綠色的甜酒，有哈蜜瓜味。許多人認為 **Midori Melon** 是目前市面上最好的蜜瓜利口酒，沒有任何替代品，額外所付的錢是值得的。

## Useful Sentences 好好用句型

I loved it right away.

我馬上就愛上它了。

🍒 I felt in love with it immediately.

我馬上就愛上它了。

🍒 It became my favorite instantly.

這個馬上就成為我的最愛。

🍒 At the very moment I had it, I loved it.

我在喝的時候就愛上它了。


We can make it right now.

我們現在就可以做。

🍒 Let's make it now.

我們現在就來做吧。

🍒 Let's do it.

我們開始做吧。

🍒 Let's get to it now.

我們開始做吧。

## **Mixology of the day** 今日酒譜

# My Sweet Midori
# 我親愛的 Midori

Glassware: Old fashioned glass（古典酒杯）
Method: Build and stir（注入法和攪拌法）

### Ingredients 材料
1 oz Midori 蜜瓜香甜酒
2 oz ginger ale 薑汁汽水
2 wedges of lime 萊姆角
1 lime wedge for garnish 裝飾用萊姆角

### Instructions 作法
Fill the old fashioned glass with ice, pour in Midori, squeeze in 1-2 wedges of lime, add 2 parts ginger ale and stir gently. Garnish with one lime wedge.

在古典酒杯裡加滿冰塊，倒入蜜瓜香甜酒，擠入 2 個萊姆角的汁，加薑汁汽水後輕輕攪拌。用一個萊姆角裝飾。

## Notes　溫馨小提醒

蜜瓜香甜酒可以直接喝，水果酒是利口酒的一種，可以當開胃酒純喝，或是加點柳橙汁或雪碧口感都不錯。蜜瓜香甜酒酒精濃度大約是在 18-25% 的範圍內。

## Historical Background　調酒小故事

蜜瓜香甜酒（Midori）是一種亮綠色、甜甜的、有哈蜜瓜味的利口酒，這是三得利公司（Suntory）所推行的。此款酒在日本、墨西哥和法國都有製造，但是直到 1987 前都只有在日本國內製造。蜜瓜香甜酒通常含有 20-21% 的酒精。Midori 這個詞在日文裡就是「綠色」的意思。法國製造的蜜瓜香甜酒比日本製造的還要甜。

## **7.6**

# **Drambuie** 蜂蜜香甜酒

### **Dialogue in the Bar** 吧台對話

Denny, Jenny, Mary and John are talking about 🔘
their favorite Drambuie cocktails.

丹尼、珍妮、瑪莉及約翰正在談論他們最喜歡的有含蜂蜜香甜酒的調酒。

| **Denny** | Drambuie on ice has always been my drink. | 蜂蜜香甜酒加冰塊一直是我最喜歡的雞尾酒。 |
| --- | --- | --- |
| **Jenny** (Bartender) | It is fantastic over ice because Drambuie is smooth with a lovely balance of sweet and spice. | 蜂蜜香甜酒加冰塊是很不錯的,因為蜂蜜香甜酒有甜味也有香料,喝起來很順口。 |
| **Mary** | I have loved the taste of Drambuie for years. It's good on ice in the summer and raw in the winter. Once at a party, I had Drambuie with Praline Pecan ice cream. It was very good. | 我喜歡蜂蜜香甜酒這樣的味道已經有很多年了。在夏天可以加冰塊喝,在冬天就直接喝。有一次在一個聚會上,我喝到了蜂蜜香甜酒加山核桃果仁冰淇淋。口感非常不錯。 |

| | | |
|---|---|---|
| **Jenny** | Drambuie can be used in many dishes. I had it in a Pumpkin Chiffon Pie. It tasted so good. | 蜂蜜香甜酒可以加在許多菜餚裡。我有吃過南瓜餡餅，裡面就有加蜂蜜香甜酒。味道真的很棒。 |
| **Denny** | What's your favorite cocktail with Drambuie? | 妳最喜愛的蜂蜜香甜酒雞尾酒是哪一款？ |
| **Jenny** | The Bonnie Prince Charlie is a classic. This cocktail combines Drambuie with bubbles. The lemon peel will help the sparkling wine keep bubbling and bubbling. If you aren't careful as you add the lemon peel, you might have an unexpected sparkling volcano. | 「邦尼查理王子」是很經典的。此款雞尾酒結合蜂蜜香甜酒加氣泡。檸檬皮可以保持酒裡的氣泡。如果你沒有小心地添加檸檬皮，你可能會引起意想不到的火山爆發。 |
| **John** (Bartender) | My favorite is the Scotch Ice Coffee. I use high-quality, freshly-made coffee and pairing it with Drambuie, and a dash of Angostura bitters. I add all the ingredients in a cocktail shaker with ice. Shake well and you have a nice Scotch Ice Coffee. | 我最喜歡的是「蘇格蘭冰咖啡」。我用高品質、新鮮的咖啡搭配蜂蜜香甜酒和一點的安格斯特拉苦精。我把所有的材料加入有冰塊的搖杯中，均勻搖晃後，就會有很好喝的蘇格蘭冰咖啡。 |

**Unit 7**
Liqueurs

## Ｙ Vocabulary  單字

lovely    *adj.*   動人的
pecan    *n.*   胡桃
sparkling    *adj.*   有汽泡的

balance    *n.*   平衡
bubbles    *n.*   氣泡
unexpected    *adj.*   想不到的

Drambuie is Scotch-based honey liqueur. Drambuie is easy to find in stores but it's pricy. For a professional bartender, Drambuie in the collection is a must. DIY Drambuie and experiment with different ingredients can have a surprising result. Drambuie is a blend of aged Scotch, heather honey and herbs. Use a mortar to break up 1 teaspoon whole fennel seeds. Combine 1/3 cup honey, 1/2 cup water, fennel, and 1 tablespoon rosemary leaves in a pot over medium heat, stirring frequently about 5 minutes until it is syrup consistence. Let mixture cool. Scrape off any white foam. Once the syrup has cooled, pour the liquid (with the fennel and rosemary still in it) into a sealable glass jar. Add 3/4 cup Scotch, seal it, and shake it. Steep for 3 days at room temperature, and strain it. Liqueur can be stored in the refrigerator for up to 6 months. For a different result, play around with what type and how much Scotch and honey to use. Also, you can replace fennel and rosemary with flavors like citrus, chamomile, or lavender for different results.

蜂蜜香甜酒是以蘇格蘭酒為主所做的蜂蜜酒。蜂蜜香甜酒很容易在商店找到，但是價格昂貴。對於專業的調酒師來說，一定要有蜂蜜香甜酒。自己做蜂蜜香甜酒，並用不同的材料實驗不同的口味，說不定會有很令人驚喜的結果。蜂蜜香甜酒是融合蘇格蘭酒、石楠蜂蜜和草藥所做的。把 1 茶匙的茴香種子整個磨碎。在鍋裡放入 1/3 杯蜂蜜、半杯水、茴香和 1 湯匙迷迭香的葉子，用中火加熱慢慢攪拌約 5 分鐘，直到呈現糖漿狀後。讓混合物冷卻。刮去白色泡沫。一旦糖漿冷卻後，把液體（茴香、迷迭香仍在裡面）倒入可密封的玻璃罐中。加入 3/4 杯蘇格蘭威士忌，密封並搖晃。讓其在室溫下浸泡 3 天並過濾。這樣的利口酒可以存儲在冰箱中長達 6 個月。如果要有不同的口味，可以試試看不同類型的蘇格蘭酒和不同種類的蜂蜜。也可以用柑橘、甘菊、薰衣草來替代茴香和迷迭香。

## Useful Sentences 好好用句型

Drambuie on ice has always been my drink.
蜂蜜香甜酒加冰塊一直是我最喜歡的飲料。

🚲 Drambuie on ice is my favorite.
　　蜂蜜香甜酒加冰塊是我的最愛。

🚲 I love Drambuie on ice the most.
　　我最喜歡蜂蜜香甜酒加冰塊。

🚲 Nothing is better than Drambuie on ice.
　　沒有什麼比蜂蜜香甜酒加冰塊更好喝的。

It is fantastic.
這是夢幻般的。

🚲 It's wonderful.
　　這是很棒的。

🚲 It's excellent.
　　這是非常好的。

🚲 I love it.
　　我很喜歡。

🚲 It's superb.
　　這是極好的。

Unit 7
Liqueurs

## Mixology of the day 今日酒譜

# Rusty Nail
# 鏽丁

Glassware: Old fashioned glass（古典酒杯）
Method: Stir（攪拌法）

### Ingredients 材料
1.5 oz Scotch 蘇格蘭威士忌
0.75 oz Drambuie 蜂蜜香甜酒
Ice 冰塊

### Instructions 作法
Combine the Scotch and Drambuie in an old fashioned glass, add lots of ice, and stir. Another way of Rusty Nail is to dash in some Angostura bitters. Stir until well-chilled, and then strain into an old fashioned glass with ice. Garnish with a lemon peel.

把蘇格蘭威士忌和蜂蜜香甜酒加入古典酒杯中，再加入很多的冰塊，攪拌融合。「鏽丁」的另一種作法是加入一些安格斯特拉苦精，一直攪拌至充分地冰涼為止，再過濾到放有冰塊的古典酒杯裡。用小片檸檬皮裝飾。

## Notes　溫馨小提醒

有些「鏽丁」酒譜是用一比一的比例去調。但是有些人會認為太甜，所以蜂蜜香甜酒可以先加酒譜所說一半的量，再視個人口味做添加。「鏽丁」的傳統作法是用蘇格蘭威士忌（Blended Scotch）去調配，但還是用高檔的比較好。如 Johnny Walker Black（約翰走路黑牌），Dewar's 12（帝王 12 年）都可以。

## Historical Background　調酒小故事

蜂蜜香甜酒（Drambuie）起源於距今兩百多年前的 1746 年 7 月。當時的查爾斯王子愛德華·斯圖爾特（Prince Charles Edward Stuart），因為在卡洛登戰役中（Battle of Culloden）戰敗而逃亡。當時的國王派兵要逮捕他，有一個部族的頭目約翰·麥金農（John MacKinnon）幫助查爾斯王子脫逃到斯凱島（The Isle of Skye）。為了感謝頭目勇敢的幫助，查爾斯王子就給了約翰·麥金農他私人利口酒的秘方當作禮物，這就是蜂蜜香甜酒，也讓這個部族的人受益了好幾代。

# 英語學習 —職場系列—

定價：NT$349元/HK$109元
規格：320頁/17＊23cm

定價：NT$360元/HK$113元
規格：328頁/17＊23cm

定價：NT$349元/HK$109元
規格：304頁/17＊23cm

定價：NT$360元/HK$113元
規格：320頁/17＊23cm

定價：NT$369元/HK$115元
規格：312頁/17＊23cm/MP3

定價：NT$369元/HK$115元
規格：320頁/17＊23cm

定價：NT$360元/HK$113元
規格：288頁/17＊23cm/MP3

定價：NT$329元/HK$103元
規格：304頁/17＊23cm

定價：NT$369元/HK$115元
規格：328頁/17＊23cm/MP3

# 英語學習 —生活・文法・考用—

定價：NT$369元/K$115元
規格：320頁/17＊23cm/MP3

定價：NT$380元/HK$119元
規格：320頁/17＊23cm/MP3

定價：NT$349元/HK$109元
規格：352頁/17＊23cm

定價：NT$380元/HK$119元
規格：288頁/17＊23cm/MP3

定價：NT$329元/HK$103元
規格：352頁/17＊23cm

定價：NT$349元/HK$109元
規格：304頁/17＊23cm

定價：NT$380元/HK$119元
規格：352頁/17＊23cm

定價：NT$369元/HK$115元
規格：304頁/17＊23cm/MP3

定價：NT$380元/HK$119元
規格：304頁/17＊23cm/MP3

Leader 025

# Bartender 的英文手札
*Raise Your Glass! Bartending in English*

作　　者　林昭菁
封面構成　高鍾琪
內頁構成　華漢電腦排版有限公司

發 行 人　周瑞德
企劃編輯　陳欣慧
校　　對　陳韋佑、饒美君、魏于婷
印　　製　大亞彩色印刷製版股份有限公司
初　　版　2015 年 8 月
定　　價　新台幣 450 元
出　　版　力得文化
電　　話　(02) 2351-2007
傳　　真　(02) 2351-0887
地　　址　100 台北市中正區福州街 1 號 10 樓之 2
E - m a i l　best.books.service@gmail.com

港澳地區總經銷　泛華發行代理有限公司
地　　　　址　香港新界將軍澳工業邨駿昌街 7 號 2 樓
電　　　　話　(852) 2798-2323
傳　　　　真　(852) 2796-5471

國家圖書館出版品預行編目(CIP)資料

Bartender 的英文手札 / 林昭菁著. -- 初版. --
臺北市：力得文化, 2015.08
　　面 ； 公分. -- (Leader ; 25)
ISBN 978-986-91914-3-2(平裝附光碟片)

1.英語 2.調酒 3.會話

805.188　　　　　　　　　104013137